Also by Lisa Renee Jones

Revealing
Us

Revealing Us

Lisa Renee Jones

Gallery Books

New York London Toronto Sydney New Delhi

G

Gallery Books
A Division of Simon & Schuster, Inc.
1230 Avenue of the Americas
New York, NY 10020

Copyright © 2013 by Julie Patra Publishing, Inc.

All rights reserved, including the right to reproduce this book or portions thereof in any form whatsoever. For information address Gallery Books Subsidiary Rights Department, 1230 Avenue of the Americas, New York, NY 10020.

First Gallery Books trade paperback edition September 2013

GALLERY BOOKS and colophon are registered trademarks of Simon & Schuster, Inc.

For information about special discounts for bulk purchases, please contact Simon & Schuster Special Sales at 1-866-506-1949 or business@simonandschuster.com.

The Simon & Schuster Speakers Bureau can bring authors to your live event. For more information or to book an event contact the Simon & Schuster Speakers Bureau at 1-866-248-3049 or visit our website at www.simonspeakers.com.

Designed by Ruth Lee-Mui

Manufactured in the United States of America

3   5   7   9   10   8   6   4

Library of Congress Cataloging-in-Publication Data
Jones, Lisa Renee.
Revealing us / Lisa Renee Jones.—First Gallery Books trade paperback edition.
    pages   cm
    1. Secrets—Fiction. I. Title.
    PS3610.O627R48   2013
    813'.6—dc23
    2013019277

ISBN 978-1-4767-2722-6
ISBN 978-1-4767-2724-0 (ebook)

To Diego,
I knew it was love when we met in a bookstore.

Acknowledgments

I want to thank my Underground Angels, who were excited about my books enough to shout about them from rooftops. Your love for this series and your efforts to support it are appreciated so much. Special thanks to Brandy, Laura, Rae, Zita, and Mandy. You ladies are wonderful. I want to thank Alyssa and Aemelia for working with me on my crazy deadlines.

Thanks to everyone at Simon and Schuster who work on the series, especially my editor, Micki Nuding.

Thanks to Louise Fury for her support, dedication, and hard work.

And thanks to Diego for finding the journal in the storage unit that inspired the series and then deciding I had to write something sexy involving a storage unit and a journal (as long as someone else dies!).

Revealing Us

Wednesday, July 11, 2012

It is midnight, and I'm sitting on a hotel balcony in Maui. The sound of the ocean crashing against the shore is like a drug, calming the disarray inside me a little. It's hard to believe that I am now a world traveler and art expert, rather than a bar waitress struggling to make ends meet. Me. Rebecca Mason. A world traveler. It's as hard to believe as most of what has happened to me this past year.

My new man is only a few feet away, naked and gorgeous beneath the sheets of our hotel bed, sated from a night of dinner, drinks, and passionate sex. Sex. I have to call it that. I cannot call it lovemaking, though he does. I wish that I could. Oh, how I wish that I could.

Why am I not in bed, pressed to all that sinewy muscle, basking in his male sensuality? I should be, but the cell phone in my lap is the reason why I'm not. "He" left me a message to call him. He, who I simply can't forget, who I cannot stop craving: his touch, his kiss, the wicked lash of a flogger against my skin that is both pleasure and pain.

I'm fighting the urge to dial his number, telling myself not to do it. My new man deserves better—just as I deserved better than what my Master ever offered me. To call him back is to disrespect the new person in my life, and myself. If only he hadn't sounded desperate to talk to me . . . which is insane. The man I knew was never desperate.

The past few weeks have been a wonderful ride of passion and exploration, both in the bedroom and around the world. I should be reveling in these things and the man making them possible. He is handsome and successful, and sexy in all possible ways, though it isn't his money that attracts me. It's his passion for how he makes that money, how he lives his life, how he makes love to me. He is supremely confident, apologizes for nothing, and embraces who he is, and yet . . . he is not the one I once called "Master," nor would I ever consider him such. I don't understand why I am not in love with him. I don't understand why, even if he asked (and he wouldn't), I would never consider submitting to him.

If I'm honest with myself, I think the reason I can't fully fall into my new potential love is simple. "He" is still my Master in my heart and soul, even in my mind.

But he doesn't love me. He doesn't even believe in love. He's told this to me too many times to ignore.

I told him good-bye, and I will not call him. I know if I do, it will be my undoing, and I'll once again be caught up in his spell. I will once again be . . . lost.

One

~~~

No talking. No in between. All or nothing, Sara. I'm offering that to you, and you have to decide if you really want it. There's a reservation in your name with American Airlines. I'll be on the plane. I hope you will be, too.

Chris had issued that ultimatum and deadline and left me sitting on my missing best friend's bed, staring at the empty doorway where he'd stood moments before. Emotions explode inside me and twist me into knots. He sought me out, found me here. After our devastating fight last night, he still wants me to go to Paris with him. He wants to find "us" again. But how can he expect me to pick up and leave at a moment's notice? I can't just leave—but . . . *He's leaving.* I can barely breathe at the idea of losing him and, deep down, I know if I let him leave, I *will* lose him. We have to talk. We have to work through what happened last night before we leave for Paris.

With a jerky movement I reach for my phone, punching

the button to auto-dial Chris. My heart hammers in my chest as I wait for him to answer.

Ring. Ring. Ring. Ring.

Then his voice, deep and raspy in that sexy way, fills the line. It's his voice mail. My fingers tunnel through my long brown hair and helplessness rolls through me. *No. No. No.* This is not happening. It *can't* happen. It's too much, after nearly being killed by Ava last night. How can Chris not *know* this is too much right now? I want to scream at the phone.

I dial again, hear the unbearable ringing tone over and over, and I get his voice mail again. Damn! I'll have to go try to catch him at home before he leaves for the airport.

I jump to my feet and rush for the door, my hand shaking as I flip the lock closed. I pray that Ella will return safely from her trip to Europe. I'm unable to help comparing her silence to Rebecca's. I shiver as I step into the dark corridor outside Ella's apartment, wishing I was in Chris's arms. Wishing I could forget the hell of Ava killing Rebecca and then trying to kill me.

Once I'm in the parking lot, I glance at the apartment building and my gut twists into knots. "Ella's okay," I promise myself as I unlock my silver Ford Focus and slide inside. And it's clear to me that I have two reasons to go to Paris: Chris and Ella. And they are good ones.

The drive to the apartment I share with Chris is less than fifteen minutes but feels like an eternity. By the time I pull into the drive in front of the fancy high-rise I am one big ball of tension. I hand my keys to the attendant, a new guy I don't know. "Hold my car here, please." The very act suggests I'm thinking of going to the airport.

Even if I do, I tell myself, it doesn't mean I'm getting on the plane. Not yet. Not like this. I'll convince Chris to delay the trip.

I barely see the lobby as I rush through it and step into the elevator. The doors close and I am suddenly, ridiculously nervous about seeing him. It's insane. This is *Chris*. I have no reason to be nervous with him. I love him. I love him as I have never loved another human being. Yet the ride to the twentieth floor is excruciating, and I wish I had asked the attendant if Chris was in the building.

"Please be here," I whisper as I near my destination. "Please be here."

The elevator dings and the doors slide open. For a moment, I just stare into the open space of the entrance to our apartment. *Our* apartment. But will it still be our apartment if I don't go with him to Paris? Just last week he'd pulled away from me, shut me out over the loss of Dylan, a child stolen by cancer, instead of letting me help him through the pain. He'd made me feel that my "home" with him had been stripped away. He's sworn that will never happen again, that I would never feel that lost again in the future—but the future is now, and I do.

Lost without *him*.

"Chris," I call out, stepping into the foyer, only to be answered by silence. Two steps inside the apartment, and I am as hollow inside as I have ever been. He isn't here. He's gone.

I slowly turn to face the sunken living room and floor-to-ceiling windows, where the early dawn is beginning to creep over the city. Memories flood my mind, so many memories of Chris and me in this room, in this apartment. I can smell him, almost taste him. Feel him. I *need* to feel him.

Flipping on a dim light, my gaze catches on something clinging to the window. A taped note, and my chest tightens as I realize it's in the exact spot Chris had once fucked me, and made me feel heat and passion and yes, the fear of falling. And fall I had. For him.

I walk down the steps, past the furniture, and tug the note from the window.

Sara—

Our flight is at nine. You need to be there an hour early to ensure you get through security, and international luggage has a strict cutoff time. It's a long flight. Dress comfortably. Jacob will be downstairs to drive you at seven to allow for traffic. IF you decide to come.

Chris

No "I love you." No "please come."

But then, there wouldn't be. This is Chris, and while I don't know all of his secrets, I do know him. I know this is one of his tests. I know he needs this to be my decision, not influenced by his words. That's why he's not here.

Realization hits me hard: I *know* this. I know what he is thinking. *I know him.* The words are comforting. In the ways that matter, *I know him.*

I turn and look at the clock near the kitchen entry to my left and I swallow hard. It's almost six now. I have an hour to decide if I'm leaving the country with Chris, and to pack.

I sink to the floor, leaning against the very window I'd

leaned on that first night he'd brought me here. I'm exhausted, and I feel just as naked and exposed as I had then.

One hour. I have one hour to make it to the airport if I decide to go. My jeans are dirty from rolling around on the ground while a crazy woman tried to kill me, and my hair feels like a long, dark drape that's as heavy as my thoughts. I need a shower. I need sleep.

I need to make a decision about what I'm going to do, right now.

Dressed in a soft black velvet sweat suit with a bag over my shoulder, I stare at the gate labeled "DFW/Dallas" and "Paris." My heart is in my throat.

I'm here. I have a bag on my shoulder. I have a boarding pass. I draw in a labored breath and I think I might be on the verge of hyperventilating, something I've done only twice before in my life. Once when I was told a heart attack had killed my mother, and once when I was in Rebecca's storage unit and the lights went out. Why I'm doing it now, I don't know. I just feel so damn out of control.

My name is called over the intercom. I have to board.

Somehow, I step forward and raise my hand to let the attendant know I'm here. I hand her my ticket without really seeing her, and my voice is raspy when I reply to questions that I don't remember two seconds later. I need to get this weird breathing in check before I pass out; I'm definitely hyperventilating. I hate that I'm this weak. When will I finally not be this weak?

My knees wobble as I lift my Louis Vuitton carry-on bag,

which Chris bought me when we'd traveled to Napa to meet his godparents, over my shoulder.

I've made it to the boarding ramp. I round the corner, and my heart skips a beat. Chris is standing at the door of the plane waiting for me, and he looks deliciously male and so perfectly *him* in his jeans, navy T-shirt, and biker boots. With one-day stubble and his longish blond hair a wonderful finger-rumpled mess, he is rugged perfection. And everything else fades away but him, and everything in my world is right.

I start running toward him and he meets me halfway, pulling me into his warm, strong arms. His addictive rich, earthy scent invades my senses and I am alive, breathing freely, my feet on solid ground, with no doubt left in me. I belong with Chris.

I wrap my arms around him and press into his hard body. His mouth comes down over mine and the taste of him, spicy and male, overwhelms me in all the right ways.

I am home. I'm home because I'm with him. And I kiss him as if I will never kiss him again, as if I'm dying of thirst and he is all that can quench me. And I believe he is. He has always been the answer to the question of what was missing from my life, even before I met him.

He tears his mouth from mine and I want to pull him back, to taste him just a little longer. I'm breathing hard again, but from emotion and need, and passion.

He brushes my silky, freshly washed hair from my face and stares down at me with earnest green eyes. "Tell me you're here because you want to be, not because I forced you."

"You aren't leaving without me," I promise him, and I hope

he hears everything that means. I haven't said that he isn't leaving. I've said he isn't doing it without me.

Instant understanding fills his face, seeping into the depths of his probing stare. "I didn't want to force you," he says, his voice gravelly, tormented. This man lives in a tormented state I burn to make go away. He hesitates. "I just needed—"

"I know what you needed," I whisper, my fingers curling on his jaw. I understand what I should have before now. "You needed to know that I love you enough to do this for you. You needed to know that, before you let me discover whatever you think I'm going to discover in Paris."

"Mr. Merit, we need you to board now," a stewardess calls from the doorway.

Neither of us looks at her. We watch each other and I see the emotions playing on Chris's face, the emotion he lets only me see. And that means everything to me. He wants *me* to see what he's never shown anyone else.

"Last chance to back out," he says softly, and there is a raw, hesitant quality to his voice, a dash of what I think is fear in his eyes. Fear that I will back out?

Yes, I think so, but there is more there, too. He is also afraid I *won't* back out, afraid of what he hasn't revealed yet. And it's hard not to fear this right along with him, when I've seen some pretty dark sides to Chris. What awaits us in Paris? What is it that he thinks will rock me when I discover it?

"Mr. Merit—"

"I know," he says sharply, without looking away from me. "It's time. Sara—"

"Whatever it is," I say, "I can handle it. *We* can handle it." I think of him fighting for my honor with my ex and my father. Chris is giving me what I want by opening the closed doors of his life, his emotions, and I won't make him sorry. I'll fight for him and us.

I lace my fingers with his. "Let's go to Paris."

On the plane, my hope of some privacy is quickly dashed when we stop at the first row and I discover an elderly woman in a bright purple shirt occupying the aisle seat next to us. She gives me a smile that is as boldly friendly as her tropical shirt, a smile I manage to return, considering I'm a load of emotional baggage, not to mention an uneasy flier.

Chris motions me forward and I sit by the window, while he fits my bag into the overhead bin. I'm spellbound by this man who has become my world. My gaze traces the handsome lines of his face, the broadness of his shoulders, the flex of muscle beneath his snug T-shirt. And just thinking about how deliciously powerful he looks when he's wearing nothing but the vivid dragon tattoo of reds, yellows, and blues exposed beneath his right sleeve, sends heat dashing through my body. I love that tattoo, and the link it holds to the past I'm now going to fully discover. I love *him*.

After closing the overhead compartment, Chris murmurs something I can't hear to our elderly companion, who smiles in reply. I smile watching them interact until I catch a moment of bleakness in Chris's eyes, reminding me of the pain he hides beneath all his sexy charm. My decision to travel to Paris with him was absolutely the right one. Somehow, some way, I'm going to make that pain go away.

As Chris settles into the seat between me and our companion, I glance at the Band-Aid on his forehead and then at the bandage covering his arm. I knew he'd cut his head last night, but not his arm.

My stomach flutters at how easily he could have died, crashing his bike on the lawn to try to save my life. "How are you?" I ask, gently covering the bandage with my hand.

"The head was more minor than I thought. The arm was a surprise, but a few stitches and it's fine." His hand covers mine—big and warm, and wonderful. "And the answer to your question is, I'm perfect. You're here."

"Chris." His name comes out as a silky rasp of pent-up emotion. There is so much unspoken between us, so much tension created from the fight we had before I'd left for Mark's house, and he'd followed. "I—" Laughter from the row behind us cuts off my words, reminding me of our lack of privacy. "We need to—"

He leans in and kisses me, a soft caress of lips against lips. "Talk. I know. And we will. When we get home, we'll figure it all out."

"Home?"

"Baby, I've told you." He laces our fingers together. "What's mine is yours. We have a home in Paris."

Of course he has a home in Paris. I just hadn't given it any thought until now. My gaze drops to where our fingers are twined and I wonder: Will his house there feel like home to me, as well?

Chris touches my chin and I look at him. "We'll figure everything out when we get there," he repeats.

LISA RENEE JONES

I search his face, looking for the confidence in his vow that a man who is always in control would have, and I don't find what I seek. The shadows in his eyes tell a story of doubt. Chris isn't certain we'll figure things out—and because he's not certain, neither am I.

But he wants us to, and so do I. His words have to be enough for now, but we both know it's not enough for the future. Not anymore.

Friday, July 13, 2012

I called him.

I shouldn't have called him, but I did, and just hearing him say "Rebecca" in that rich, velvety voice was nearly my undoing. I'm supposed to leave for Australia tomorrow, and I'm not sure I can do it. I'm not sure it's fair to my new man—not when I now know that I'm still in love with my Master.

And tonight he was different. He was more than a Master. Tonight he was a man who seemed to recognize me as a woman, not just his submissive. I heard vulnerability in his voice. I heard raw need, and even a plea. Could I dare believe he is a man who is ready to discover that love exists?

Now I am swimming in a sea of his promises that everything will change if I go home. He called San Francisco, and his house, my home. He wants me to move back in with him, to get rid of my apartment and the backup plan it had been. There will be no contract between us. There will be just us.

I want us. I need us. So why does this deep foreboding claw at me, the same feeling I got when I was having those horrible nightmares of my mother? What is there to fear about my decision to go to him, but heartache? And it's worth a little heartache to reveal the real us I've always believed we can be. . . .

Two

I blink awake, the haze of sleep clinging to my mind, seeing Chris lying in front of me, his lashes lowered in slumber. The sound of an odd announcement begins to permeate my fog, and I remember I'm in a private section of the international flight we'd boarded in Dallas many hours ago. One of the flight attendants is speaking in French over the intercom, and the only word I understand is "Paris."

I focus on Chris, his sensual mouth relaxed, his hair a rumpled, adorable mess. My lips curve at the thought of how he'd react to being thought of as adorable, and my fingers go to his cheek, trailing softly over his strong jaw. He is so beautiful, not classically like Mark, but raw and masculine, so completely male. Not that I'm sure I think Mark is handsome anymore. I'm not sure what I think of Mark anymore at all.

Chris's lashes lift and those brilliant green eyes of his find mine. "Hey, baby." He grabs my hand from where it's trailing over his lips and kisses my palm. The touch tingles up my arm and over my chest, and settles low in my belly.

"Hey," I say. "I think we're about to land in Paris." The flight attendant starts speaking in English, confirming what I'd surmised. "The prior announcement was in French, and as you know, I don't speak French."

"We'll fix that," he promises me as we raise our seat backs.

I give a delicate snort. "Don't get your hopes up. The foreign language part of my brain doesn't work." I swipe at my hair, certain I look like a complete mess. If not for the fact that Chris has seen me sick and throwing up and still loves me, I might feel insecure. Then again, I'm probably too tired to be insecure right now.

"You'll be surprised how easily you'll pick it up from being around it," he promises. "Why don't I give you a small lesson while we descend? I know that's the part of flying you hate the most. It'll keep your mind off the landing."

I shake my head. "I'm too tired to get scared of crashing, and too tired to handle a French lesson."

"Je t'aime."

"I love you, too," I say, having watched enough television to know what he'd said. But that's the extent of my French.

His lips curve in that sexy way they always curve. "Montrez-moi quand nous serons rentrés."

The way the words roll off his tongue sends a shiver of pure female appreciation down my spine. I've officially found a reason to like the French language. "I have no idea what you just said, but it was sexy as hell coming from you."

Chris leans in close and nuzzles my neck. "To which I

repeat," he murmurs, "montrez-moi quand nous serons rentrés. Show me you love me when we get home."

And just like that, I'm not nearly as tired as before, but eagerly looking forward to this new home. What could possibly go wrong here in Paris? There is art and culture and history. There are new adventures. There is living life. And I'm with Chris.

When we step off the plane, I will myself to be excited about being in Paris, the city of lights and romance, but I fail. That bone-weary feeling has returned like a steam engine, and even Chris admits he needs rest. I *can* truly say that I'm looking forward to sleeping in a real bed with Chris very soon.

We clear the ramp from the plane, stepping into the airport, which looks pretty much like any other airport. Signs in English and French point us in the right direction. Back in the States the signs would be in English and Spanish, so it feels familiar and that's comforting. I also hope it means I won't be completely disabled by my lack of French.

Then we step onto a moving sidewalk that takes us through a strange, winding underground tunnel. Beside it is an odd, awkward stairwell that juts up and down in an uneven line, and I can't imagine anyone using it. Why does it jut up and down? I find it illogical and disconcerting, and my comfort level plummets again.

Suddenly our bags are on the belt by our feet, and Chris pulls me close, his hard body absorbing mine. I don't look at him. I don't want him to see how out of sorts I am. Besides, he is warm and wonderful, and I wrap my arms around him, inhaling his familiar scent, reminding myself he is why I'm here. That's what matters.

"Hey," he says softly, leaning back and sliding a finger under my chin, not allowing me to escape his inspection.

When my eyes meet his, I find them filled with concern. It never ceases to amaze and please me that he can be so gentle and sensitive, and also be the man who finds pain to be pleasure.

I raise to my toes and touch my lips to his for an instant. "I'm just tired." My fingers replace my mouth on his, tracing the sensual curve of his lips.

He captures my hand and holds it. "You know I'm not buying that, right?"

I manage a weary smile. "I'm just ready to be alone with you." And oh, how true this is.

He runs his hand down the back of my hair, his touch protective, possessive, and I have the sense he feels a need to hold on to me, like I could change my mind and leave at any moment. He murmurs, "That makes two of us, baby."

I'd promise him I'm not going anywhere, but I'm not sure words matter at this point. Actions do. Me being here. Me weathering the storm he believes is coming, without abandoning ship.

Once we're inside the main area on the opposite side of the tunnel, we're greeted with restaurants and stores to our left and a huge security line that winds seemingly forever. "I am so incredibly glad that's not for us," I gush with relief.

"Actually, it is," Chris replies grimly. "That's to clear our passports and enter the airport."

I stop dead in my tracks and turn to him. "No. Please tell me we don't have to stand in that line when I'm this tired."

He shifts the bags on his shoulders. "It won't take as long as it looks like it will."

"Says the receptionist in the packed doctor's office," I reply, and sigh. "I have to go to the bathroom before I stand in that line."

He leans in and kisses my forehead. "Sounds like a good plan. I'll go, too."

We part ways at the restrooms, which say "toilette." *Toilette* sounds so crass to me, and as I walk into the crowded facility I wonder if *bathroom* seems the same to the French. There's a line of at least five women ahead of me and only two sinks and two stalls. No hope of a speedy departure.

A woman gives me an up-and-down look as she passes, her gaze lingering on my face, and I wonder if I look more American than I realize. Not that I know what an American looks like. I look like them. I think. My phone beeps and I pull it from my purse to find a message from my cell provider, basically telling me I'll spend a small fortune to use my phone if I don't adjust my plan. One of many things I have to deal with, I suspect.

I glance up as the line moves. Another woman stares at me and I wonder if, when I brushed my teeth and applied lipstick on the plane, I created a mess. Do I have lipstick smeared on my face? I scan for a mirror, but there isn't one. What? No mirrors? No American woman would stand for such a thing. Women around the world can't be so different, can they?

"Is there a mirror somewhere?" I ask the general population

of the room, and get blank stares. "English?" I get more blank stares and two shakes of the head. Great.

Certain I'm a mess, I sigh, wishing my cosmetics were in my purse with a mirror, rather than in the bag Chris has with him. I glance at the time on my phone, and try to set my world clock without success. It's early morning here, and I think San Francisco is six or eight hours different. Or is it nine? Regardless, if I go to sleep anytime soon, I'll never adjust to the time change.

When I finally exit the bathroom I do so with hurried steps, and run smack into a hard body. With a gasp, I look up as strong hands right me before I fall. "I'm sorry," I say, blinking as a big man with rumpled dark hair and handsome thirty-something features comes into view. "I didn't mean . . ." I hesitate. Does he even speak English?

He says something in French, and then says, "Pardon" before he departs.

An uncomfortable shiver races down my spine and the unexplainable need to follow him has me whirling around, only to find Chris there.

His brows dip. "Something wrong?"

Yes. No. Yes. "I just bumped into a man, and—"

Chris curses and grabs my purse, and I look down to realize it's unzipped. I'm certain it was zipped before. "Oh no," I say, and shove it open to find that my wallet is missing. "No. No no no no. This can't be happening. He took my wallet, Chris!"

"What about your passport?" he asks calmly, setting our bags down between us.

My eyes go wide and I quickly dig for it. Feeling sick, I shake my head. "It's gone. What does this mean?"

"It's okay, baby. I forgot to give you your plastic card; I still have it. That'll get us past the entry in France with some extra effort. And you can use it at the consulate to get a new booklet."

I draw a deep breath and let it out. The way he says "us" is calming. I'm not alone. He is with me every step of the way, not just here and now. I know this, and I want to believe it won't change. It's one of the many things about him, and us, that delivered me to the airport today. "Thank God you have my card."

Chris reaches over the bags and caresses my cheek. "I should have warned you how bad the pickpockets are here."

"Pickpockets," I repeat. "Here in the airport, or everywhere?"

"Any tourist area." He hikes the bags back on his shoulder.

Welcome to the land of romance, I think, but then romance has never been an easy ride for me. "I have to call all my credit card companies, and I have no affordable cell service."

"You can use mine when we get to the other side of security."

I nod and zip my purse, then slide it cross-body and hold it with my hand. My world is spinning out of control and I am thankful Chris is a rock, or else I might just plain panic. It's not that I want to dart back across the border, though I'm actually not sure I've technically passed it yet. I couldn't go back to the States right now if I wanted to; a stranger has stolen that freedom from me. And I'm worried about my personal information in an unknown person's hands, too.

I comfort myself with the fact that they don't have my Paris address, though; I don't even have that yet.

Then I look up at Chris, feel that familiar punch of intimacy between us, and correct that statement. Yes, I do know my address. It's with Chris.

Three

After an hour of being drilled by the border police, Chris and I have our bags on a cart and we're ready to leave the airport. We halt at the sliding doors under a "taxi" sign.

"I'll go find us a private car and driver," Chris informs me. "You stay with the bags."

I purse my lips. "Yes, Master."

He arches a brow. "Why is it that I can only get you to say that sarcastically?"

"Because according to you," I remind him, "you don't want me to call you Master."

"Are you saying you would if I wanted you to?"

"Absolutely not."

Chris laughs, a sexy rumble and it is a soothing balm on my nerve endings. "On a totally different subject," he says, pulling me close, a light in his eyes I see too rarely, "the area we're

23

headed to is the Times Square of Paris. You're going to love it." He leans down and kisses me. "I'll be right back."

I stare after him, watching his sexy swagger and warming to the idea that I am here. And I know that no matter how much he fears the ultimate outcome of my being here, he's also excited to show me Paris. I'm excited to see it with him, too.

I wait eagerly for his return, ready to share my excitement with him, disappointed when it becomes apparent that he's going to be a few minutes. With a sigh, I snag my cell phone to set up an international plan. I'm almost done when Chris rushes back inside with a man I assume is the driver. Just watching the way Chris moves, all lean muscle and power, my heart skips a beat. I doubt if I'll ever stop reacting to the first moment I see him, and I smile.

"Ready?" he asks as I try to finish up with the cell company. The driver takes over our baggage cart and we follow him outside. I end my call and wait for Chris by the car door while he helps the driver fit our bags inside the trunk.

When Chris joins me and holds the door open for me, I hug him, then tilt my chin up to meet his eyes. "I just want you to know that I understand why you needed to do this the way you did it, but I would have come anyway. I'm glad I'm here with you." I kiss him, planning on a quick brush of my mouth over his, and, to my shock, considering how private a person he is, Chris slides his hand beneath my hair, around my neck, and slants his mouth over mine. I moan as his tongue caresses mine, stroking deeply into my mouth.

"I'm glad you're here, too," he assures me, pulling his mouth from mine and setting me away from him, as if he has to do it right now or he won't be able to. As if he might take me right here. And only he could make this once-conservative school-teacher wish that were possible.

I wet my lips and his hot gaze follows, and just that easily I'm tingling all over, hot inside and out. Someone shouts out something in French and Chris's head jerks toward the speaker, mine following.

I see the driver's head above the roof of the car, as if he'd gotten inside and popped out to get our attention. Chris answers him in French and then shifts his attention back to me. His lips quirk and his eyes dance with amusement. "He wants to know if we're ready."

We both start laughing. "We are definitely ready," I say and duck inside the car.

Forty-five minutes later, I've canceled my credit cards and our driver has navigated us through morning traffic to Avenue des Champs-Élysées, a famous street lined with imposing old white buildings filled with stores and cafés. When we drive past the Arc de Triomphe, I take photos with my cell phone. Its spectacular carvings are illuminated, aglow against the darkness of Paris's shorter winter days. And while I'd swear I'm not a structure kind of person, much preferring paintings to steel towers, I gape as the Eiffel Tower comes into view, twinkling with lights in the inky gray sky. There was a time when I thought I'd never see . . . well, much of anything.

We turn down a narrow side street lined with brownstone buildings and I frown at all the tiny cars lining the sidewalks. I cringe at how unsafe they look.

"Please tell me you don't drive one of those," I say.

"No," Chris assures me with a bark of that rich laughter I adore so much. "My Harley is as close to that small as I'll ever get."

A sudden flashback of him showing up, after weeks of shutting me out of his life, and ordering me onto the back of his Harley, in a skirt of all things, is an unwelcome memory I shove away. I won't let myself worry about him doing that to me again. Especially not today.

I'm alive, which is a gift I value more than ever before.

I'm with Chris.

I'm in Paris, which I'm experiencing because of Chris, when everyone else in my life has always kept me in a box.

I lean over and kiss his cheek.

"What's that for?" he asks, his strong arm wrapping around my waist.

I can think of a million ways to answer, and a million things I want to say to him. I simply say, "For being you."

The tenderness in his face melts the last remnants of my bad memory. "If this is the reaction I get to a little sightseeing, I can't wait to see how you react when you see the art galleries. You're going to go nuts, baby." His cell phone rings, and with the obvious reluctance I love, he lets go of me.

"It's Blake," he announces after glancing at the caller ID.

The name is like a cold splash of water on the warm, wonderful adventure we're sharing. Since Blake has been investigating both Rebecca's and Ella's disappearances, I'm not sure if I should expect good or bad news.

"Easy, baby," Chris murmurs, running his hand up and down my arm as if he feels my sudden chill. "Everything's okay."

But I don't know that. Who would have imagined that the missing Rebecca was dead, murdered by someone we all knew? How can I ever assume anything to be okay after that?

Chris's hand settles on my leg as he answers his call, and his protectiveness raises a lump in my throat. I'm supposed to be here for him, yet he's still acting like my Prince Charming.

And he is my Prince Charming. My dark, damaged Prince Charming. My idea of perfect. Now I just have to make *him* believe that.

"Tell me you have good news on Ella," Chris says, listening before he glances at me, his sensual mouth thinning. "Nothing good or bad," he tells me.

Nodding, my gaze drifts blindly to the window. There was no news on Rebecca for months, either, and her ending was murder. The only ending Ella is supposed to have is a "happily ever after" with a new husband.

An idea hits me, and my lips part at the obvious part I've missed. A wedding—Ella had a wedding! There would be proof at the courthouse. Has Blake thought of this?

I touch Chris's arm to get his attention before he hangs up.

"Check your messages," he tells me before I can ask my question. "See if you have one you missed." His tone is nonchalant, but the subtle tension in him creates tension in me.

I frown, reaching for my phone, unable to read his expression in the flickering shadows of the dark car. Glancing through my calls, I note an unfamiliar San Francisco number in my history. "Actually, yes. I didn't get an alert, so I didn't see it." I start to hit the playback button, but hesitate, hoping to listen in on Chris's call and figure out what is going on.

"She'll do it right away," Chris assures Blake. "And yes, I'll let you know." He ends the call. "The lead detective on Rebecca's case wants to ask you a few more questions."

I have no idea what I expected him to say, but certainly not this. I shake my head in instant rejection and start to put my phone away. "I can't think about that right now. I'll call him tomorrow, after I rest."

"Apparently it's urgent. The detective stopped by our place and talked to Jacob. Jacob tried to call us, but kept getting a fast busy signal on our phones. He and Blake have been trying to reach us for hours."

I wet my suddenly parched lips. "What could be this urgent? They interviewed me less than a day ago."

"This isn't unusual; they'll want to deal with Ava as quickly as possible. And the charges against her won't be just about Rebecca. They'll charge her with the attack on you, as well."

I knew this, of course, but I haven't let myself think about what it all entailed. It's all too raw, too much, right now.

Thankfully the car pulls up to a towering steel gate, a welcome distraction from the conversation about Ava.

Chris rolls down his window to punch in a code on a security box, then he rolls it back up and continues the conversation. "You'll most likely have to testify at Ava's trial, and the police need to compile a solid case to ensure a conviction."

"Right," I reply. "Yes. Of course. And I want that, too. I'll call." I glance at my world clock and hope for another reprieve. "It's almost eleven at night in the States, isn't it?"

"They're eight hours behind us, so yes, it's late, but apparently the detective works the night shift."

I sigh in defeat. "I'll call when we get inside, I promise." My attention moves to the window as the car pulls forward, and the glow of a new day allows me to see rows of white Haussmann-style buildings.

"We have a private residence," Chris explains as a large stone arched doorway with five steps leading up to it comes into view. "There are multiple homes in one building, but they aren't connected and there's no doorman. We own floors eighteen through twenty, along with a private garage that has a gym connected to it."

We. I love how he includes me. How he makes us "we."

"Twelve-twelve Foche Avenue," I read in the center of a black-etched circle on the concrete wall by our door, just before the car pulls into a private garage.

"Our address," he says softly.

An automatic light flickers on in the garage, casting us in a pale glow, and I look at Chris, search his face, and find the message he wants me to see. He knows how much I need to feel I have a home and stability. And he knows I'm still feeling the effects of our breakup, and feeling I didn't have a home in the not-so-distant past.

"Our address," I repeat, letting him know I'm as eager as he is to start fresh.

His lips curve slowly, approval sliding across his face, before he leans forward to talk to the driver.

He's telling me in every way possible that he wouldn't have brought me here if he weren't deeply committed to making us work, no matter what price there is to pay. *And there is always a price to pay,* I can almost hear Rebecca say in my mind. What is that price for Chris?

"Ready, baby?" he asks, and I am jolted to realize I was in such deep thought that he's already outside the car, offering me his hand.

Gathering my purse, I let Chris help me out of the car and he pulls me to my feet and against him, his fingers splaying possessively on my back. "No in between," he reminds me in a low, rough voice that tells me he feels what I do. He knows we're opening a door we can't close again.

My hand flattens on the hard wall of his chest, and I can feel the rapid heartbeat that tells me he's as affected by this moment as I am. "No in between." Our eyes lock and the warmth I'd felt when he took my hand is now heat simmering between us, wrapping us in anticipation. We are finally about to be alone.

"Pardon, monsieur, madam."

Our spell is broken by the driver, who is exiting the door off the garage, and I assume he's taken our bags inside.

"Oui, monsieur," Chris says, the French rolling off his tongue. "Je vous remercie de votre aide."

Thank you for the help, is my guess on that one, and when the two men shake hands, I'm certain I'm right. Maybe French won't be so hard after all. After some sleep, I might actually be able to learn some.

With a departing remark, the driver climbs into his car. As the sedan backs away I can now see the other side of the garage, where three classic Mustangs, two Harleys, and a silver Porsche 911 are parked.

I shake my head at Chris. "Different place, same obsessions."

"You're my obsession," Chris replies huskily, nuzzling my

neck. "Addictive in every way, and that comes with rewards. You get one of the Harleys."

I laugh. "Not a reward I'd choose, but okay." I point to the one that looks the most expensive. "I'll take that one."

The doors to the garage shut and Chris twines his fingers with mine and walks backward, leading me toward the building, mischief lighting his eyes. "You can ride with me, baby."

I roll my eyes. "You always have to be in control."

"You like it when I'm in control."

"I should deny that," I reply without hesitation. I'm way beyond censoring my thoughts with Chris.

He pulls me into the small foyer off the garage and punches the elevator button before wrapping me in his arms. "Should I prove how much you like it when I'm in control?"

"If you think you can," I taunt, melting just thinking about all the ways he might go about proving he's right.

The doors to the elevator slide open. "Shall we go upstairs and see if I can?"

I laugh. "Oh, yes."

He backs into the elevator and tugs me forward but I stop abruptly, determination in my sure footing. "I need to call the detective before we go up."

Chris's brow furrows. "Here?"

"I don't want what happens once we get onto the elevator to be clouded by what we've left behind."

Understanding and tenderness seep into his expression, and he steps out of the elevator. "Then we'll call here."

I fetch my phone from my purse and Chris leans against the wall, settling my back to his front. His hand rests on my stomach and I relax into him, the stupid nerves over this call I don't understand are more manageable now.

After punching a button, I listen to the simple but urgent message from a Detective Grant and then hit recall.

"Ms. McMillan," he says, clearly indicating he has caller ID and the way he's said my name reminds me of Mark to such a degree that I barely suppress a shiver.

"Detective Grant," I reply crisply.

"I understand you've left the country."

"I'm in Paris, yes," I say with remarkable coolness, considering I'm unraveling inside. Was I not supposed to leave? They never said a word about me not leaving the country.

"What was the rush to escape?"

Defensiveness flares inside me. "Escape?" I counter, and I feel the flex of Chris's fingers on my belly in response. "I'm not sure what that means, but I'm pretty sure almost being killed by a crazy woman justifies my need for a change of scenery."

"You needed it quickly, it seems."

Defensiveness begins to blossom into outright anger, tightening my words. "What is it you're alluding to?"

"You managed to take over Rebecca's job."

"Someone had to."

"Not everyone had her personal items and her deepest, most intimate thoughts." He hesitates and it's clearly for effect. "You ended up with her job and her boss. Really, her entire life."

My heart jackhammers and Chris molds me closer, silently telling me he is here, he is with me. He is all that keeps me from completely snapping. "I was almost killed last night," I repeat.

"That's a separate event from Rebecca's death."

"Ava confessed to killing Rebecca. She tried to kill me. That's pretty connected, if you ask me."

"She now says she confessed to protect Mark."

"Protect Mark?" I all but gasp and I turn to face Chris, my fingers digging into his arms. "She says *Mark* killed Rebecca?"

Chris's expression is unreadable, but I feel the muscles flex beneath my grip, and his hands settle firmly on my waist. His eyes find mine and hold, and I feel him beyond his touch. He is my rock, my strength.

"Ava says that you killed Rebecca and blackmailed Mark into silence," the detective informs me.

The darkness I've battled for hours now becomes a black hole, and the world seems to spin. A second later, my knees buckle and the ground is all I see.

Four

I blink and discover my hands are resting on the solid wall of Chris's chest. His arm is wrapped around my waist, anchoring me to him while he talks on my phone. My anchor. He is that and so much more, I think, as I realize I blacked out and now I'm back in this world. I've never blacked out before, and it's downright unnerving to realize I've lost all sense of time and reality.

"Did you tell her she couldn't leave the country?" Chris calmly asks into the phone. There's a short pause. "Then she's done nothing wrong." He listens again. "Yeah, well, for the record, I know she's innocent, too, and your 'just doing your job' could have waited until she got over the shock of last night, no matter how much you want to cover your bases. From this point on, you talk to her attorney, Stephen Newman. He'll be calling you." He ends the call.

I swallow, trying to find my voice, panic expanding in my chest all over again. "Chris, he . . . I—"

"You have nothing to worry about," he assures me, framing my face with his hands. "I've got this, and I've got you."

His eyes brim with warmth and promise, and I hope he knows something I don't. "He all but accused me of killing Rebecca."

"Ava and her attorney had to come up with a defense for her, and you were it. The police don't believe her, but to get an indictment they have to do due diligence. Our attorney will take care of this. And I'll take care of you."

There was a time when the idea of leaning on Chris would have totally scared me. After the way he shut me out over Dylan's death, it's still hard not to be a little scared—but it's also never felt as good as it does now, to be in this man's arms.

I look down to where my hands rest on his chest and they're shaking, but I can't seem to feel them shaking. It is as if my body and my mind aren't communicating. "I think . . . I think I'm not so good right now."

"Like I said. I've got you, baby." He punches the elevator button and scoops me up in his arms, and I sink against him, relieved. He has me. *I* have *him*. I choose to fully believe that right now. I need to believe that.

I rest my head against his shoulder and close my eyes. As silly as it might seem, I don't want to see what awaits us inside, in this state of mind. I want to wait and explore later, when the bad isn't tainting the good.

When I force my lashes to open a little while later, Chris is setting me down on a bathroom vanity. He kisses me, a quick brush of his mouth. "You okay?"

I cover his hands where they rest on my cheeks. "Only because of you."

"I say that about you every day since I met you, Sara. You do know that, don't you? When I was gone for Dylan's funeral, it was you that got me through. Knowing you were in my life—that's what broke through the darkness."

My breath escapes on his name. "Chris," I whisper, wrapping my arms around his neck and burying my face in his shoulder. Wrenching pain rips through me at the memory of finding Chris in Mark's club, screaming for the lash of a whip to beat away the pain of losing Dylan. "I love you." I can't keep the quaver from my voice and I don't try. I lean back and lift my gaze to his, opening myself up, letting him judge my words as he'd judged himself that night. "I love you so much, Chris."

"I love you, too, Sara. More than I've let you see, but I'm going to fix that." He brushes the hair from my eyes. "You take a hot bath while I make a few phone calls, then we'll get some rest."

"Yes, okay," I say and he stands there a moment, and I can't read him, but I think he wants to say something, or he expects me to say something. There is so much, too much, unsaid between us, but I'm unsure where to begin or even if now is the right time. He turns away, and the moment is lost. He walks to the tub, the epitome of grace and hotness, and bends over to start the water, but it's the act of doing something so tender and caring that truly makes Chris the man I love. He's both the man I found tied up and screaming for a harder beating, and the gentle, protective man he is right now, and the contrast sets me on fire and warms my heart.

I curl my fingers around the edge of the counter and glance around the bathroom, which is the size of a small bedroom. It has the same white tile as our San Francisco apartment, but there are gray accents and silver fixtures. It's luxurious, and so is the scent tickling my nose—musky and male, with a hint of spice.

Chris holds up a bottle. "My shampoo. It's the only way I can give you the bubble bath you like, until you can stock up on what you want."

"I like smelling like you," I say, remembering a time I'd worn his cologne and said the same thing.

He saunters over to me, all loose-legged sex appeal in his faded jeans and a blue AC/DC T-shirt, and settles his hands on my knees. *You're mine,* the touch says, and it is a welcome branding. Yes. Yes, I am his. "I like you smelling like me," he replies, his voice a velvety-smooth caress.

It's exactly what he'd said once before, and I react just as I had the first time. I'm out of my head and into the moment with him, my body alive, tingling all over. He's washed away the bad and left me deeply absorbed in him and all that he is. All that we have become together.

He brushes a knuckle down my cheek and I sense the shift in his mood. I can almost feel the dark, dangerously wicked side of Chris, ready to come out to play. My belly quivers with this knowledge and something raw and female begins to awaken inside of me, burning for satisfaction. I once denied how much I understood this part of Chris, and how much I am like him, but those times are past. I am who I am, even if I don't fully understand that person yet. But the idea that I will, and that Chris will accept nothing less of me, is downright arousing.

Chris steps back out of reach, and I'm cold where I was warm before. His fingers curl into his palms and the muscles in his arms are tight steel bands. My gaze lifts to his and his expression is hard, his jaw harder. But the storm erupting in his eyes speaks volumes.

He's carrying the world on his shoulders, including me. Despite every effort possible to save him, he lost Dylan to cancer. He and I had then almost lost each other. And now Rebecca is gone, after he tried to warn her to stay away from the club.

My stomach clenches with the possibility that he's blaming himself for her death; thinking he should have done more. I know he blames himself for his father's death, and maybe his mother's, too.

He needs me. Screw the police and Ava, and every piece of hell trying to shake me. I start to get off the sink and he takes another step backward.

"I'm going to walk through the house and make sure it's in order," he says and turns away, disappearing out of the bathroom and leaving the door open.

I stare after him, darn near twitching to follow him, but I fight the urge. And why am I fighting it? I wouldn't have fought it before.

My teeth worry my bottom lip. I know why. A piece of the darkness I've been fighting during our travel is all that's unspoken and undone between us. We'd only begun to find ourselves when losing Dylan, such a young, sweet child, to cancer had stirred the demons of Chris's past and nearly destroyed us. But I came here to fight for Chris, and for us.

My decision is made. I slide off the counter and go to the tub to turn off the water, then rush through the giant bedroom, catching flashes of brown leather and a balcony. I exit into a long hallway with shiny black wood floors that fork in several directions, but there's no sign of Chris.

My gaze latches on to the two flights of modern steel-and-wood stairs, one going up and one going down. Down seems the logical place for a kitchen and living area, and I head in that direction.

The steps twist and turn, and even open to another set of stairs that lead up. I continue down. When I'm nearly at the bottom I hear Chris's voice, a low, rough, displeased tone as he talks to someone. I anxiously follow where it leads. I all but vault the rest of the way down the stairs and into a breathtaking living room shaped like a circle, with modern leather furniture and sleek tables that match the stairs and floors.

I don't see Chris or hear him now, and my gaze goes to the stairs that go up to what appears to be the kitchen. As I start in that direction cool air washes over me, drawing me to the slight opening I'd missed in the balcony door. He must have stepped outside while I was on my way down the stairs.

I am at the door in a few seconds, and peek out to find Chris's back to me. "All I can say is, fucking make this go away for Sara. She doesn't deserve this crap. And if they need money and resources to find Rebecca and give her a proper burial, make it happen."

Air lodges in my throat and I know we are already in full

swing, facing his demons. I have no intention of letting them get an upper hand. All the weakness and fear I've let control me these past few hours evaporates.

Chris is putting on airs, pretending to be fine when he is not. He needs me. He needed me when Dylan died, and he's not shutting me out again.

Opening the door, I don't think twice about interrupting his call. The new day is cool, not cold, but my chest is burning. Chris turns at the sound of my steps, a dim overhead light illuminating the surprise on his face, the Eiffel Tower his backdrop. No, that's wrong. His pain is his eternal backdrop.

"I need to go, Stephen," Chris says. "Call me when you have news." He ends the connection and slides his phone into his jean pocket. "I thought you were taking a bath?"

I close the distance between us and wrap my arms around him, holding him tightly. His arms close around me and his hand slides down my hair. "What is this, Sara? What's wrong, baby? The attorney said—"

"I don't care right now," I say, tilting my face up to look at him. "I don't care about the detective or Ava or anything but you. Please tell me you aren't blaming yourself for Rebecca's death. *Ava* did this. Not you. Not Mark."

Surprise flickers in his face before the shutters come down and I can no longer read his reaction, but the way his muscles tense beneath my hands tell me I've hit a nerve. "I know Ava did this."

I shake my head, sensing the guilt in him he won't admit. "You don't know—you think you should have done more to get Rebecca out of the club. But you did everything you could, Chris. You did more than most would have done."

He stares down at me, his gaze hooded. We're adrift in a sea of silence and his reaction is impossible to read, and I'm not sure what to do next. Chris is a light switch away from dark and light, pain and pleasure, and I'm far from knowing how to navigate the bumpy waters of his darker side.

But I want to master it. *I* want to be what he needs, not some damn whip tearing him apart. I'm not yet, though. Should I push him to deal with what he's feeling, refuse to let him bottle it inside, where it can later explode? Or let it go for now?

He takes my face in his hands and searches my eyes. I have the impression he's looking for an answer to a question he hasn't asked, and I've never in my life wanted to be the answer to a question, the way I do when Chris is seeking one.

"What I don't know," he finally confesses, "is how I'll ever sleep again, after watching you almost die last night."

No one but my mother has ever loved me enough to worry this much, but with Chris that worry is complicated. I'm smart enough to see the writing on the wall, and I don't like what it reveals. While I was thinking about what comes next in Paris on the flight, Chris was rethinking it with Rebecca's tragedy as his guide.

"We aren't them," I tell him. "We aren't Rebecca and Mark. And I'm not going anywhere, so you might as well just let me come inside." I'm not talking about our house and we both know it.

I barely get the words out before his mouth comes down on mine, his tongue stroking against mine, awakening my senses, the taste of him pouring through me. Hungry for him, I want his passion, I want his pain. I want it all.

I tug at his shirt, running my hands under the material,

absorbing the feel of his naked, hard body beneath my palms. *Finally.* I've waited hours that felt like a lifetime to be this close to him, and I moan, part relief, part pleasure.

Chris tears his mouth from mine, tunneling fingers in my hair to hold me away from him, a struggle etched on his handsome face. "You passed out, Sara. I don't want to hurt you."

"I didn't come to Paris with Mr. Nice, Chris, so don't bring him out to play now. And I won't rest until we do this." I try to lean in to kiss him again.

He tightens his fingers in my hair and sends an erotic thrill up and down my spine. Oh, yes. Good-bye, Mr. Nice Guy. Hello, Chris.

"Gentle isn't how I'll deal with the kind of things going on in my head right now," he warns. "Why do you think I walked away in the bathroom?"

"I don't want gentle." I don't like what I see on his face, a battle between the burn to take me and what he thinks I'm ready to handle, and I won't let him decide for me. "I understand what it means to need more than that. I need more, Chris."

In a blink he's maneuvered me against a giant white pillar separating the iron gates, his hands framing my waist. "I used to think you didn't understand. But you do. Too well. And I blame myself for that, Sara. I didn't want this for you."

His guilt over Rebecca could so easily bleed into our relationship, like his fears over who he is and who he will make me become. "I told you. I'm not Rebecca, so stop going there, Chris. I read those journals. She changed who she was to be with Mark.

"You didn't turn me into who I am now. All you did was to help me to stop hiding from who I am, and I'm glad. Don't make me feel like I have to start again."

Seconds tick by as he studies me, before he asks, "Who are you, Sara?"

I lift my chin. "If you don't know that by now, I suggest you find out before it's too late to turn back."

I blink and Chris has turned me to face the banister, and I catch my weight on my hands to steady myself. His hand flattens between my shoulder blades and he steps close, framing my hips with his, his erection nestled against my backside.

"Do you remember what I promised you back in that Los Angeles hotel?"

"Yes: that you'd stop protecting me from you. But you haven't," I accuse, certain now that it's the right time, the right mood, to push him.

"Baby, I held back today to let you get over all you've been through. But don't let that mislead you. You wouldn't be here if I planned to protect you from me." His hand splays possessively on my stomach. "What else did I tell you?"

My lashes lower, heat slicing through me at the memory of lying in that Los Angeles hotel bed, his body intimately wrapped around mine. "That you'd own me if I stayed with you."

"Every part of you," he agrees huskily. "That means I know you completely. All of you. And it's time you understand what that means."

"Show me," I challenge, wanting him to own me, when no other man will ever come close to having this much of me.

When I never thought I'd want this much from a man. But this is Chris, and that's the only answer I ever need.

"Show you what?" he demands.

"How it feels to be owned by you," I dare to reply, and heat pools low in my belly at the many erotic things this might invite. "Because I haven't felt it yet. And I want to."

His teeth scrape my earlobe, his breath teasing the delicate skin there. "You will, Sara. You will." He steps away from me, leaving me cold and wanting. "Turn around."

I swallow hard, aroused by the possibilities his promise has stirred, relieved that we're taking our journey together, past the wall the loss of Rebecca almost erected. I tentatively turn and meet his stare, and instead of hot coals and burning embers, I find tenderness.

He lifts his chin at the doorway. "Walk inside, baby."

My heart squeezes at the soft endearment he uses often, and the message I read behind it. Whatever journey he's about to take me on, we'll still be just us when it's over.

He's not out of control. He's not even on the edge anymore. He's about to take *me* to the edge. And I want to go with him.

Five

It's warmer in the house than outside, but still a cool contrast to the heat burning inside me as I walk into the living room. Anticipation tingles along my nerve endings but my steps are slow, tentative. I do not know where Chris wants me to go or what he expects me to do, but I'm ready for anything.

"Stop," Chris commands when I'm standing beside the couch. I do and he adds, "Face me."

I turn to find him standing on the other side of a six-foot-long, cream-colored, high-piled throw rug. He crosses his arms in front of his chest, the brightly colored dragon tattoo stretching with the flex of his muscle. "It represents power and wealth, two things as a very young man I knew I wanted," he'd told me when I'd asked about the design. I burn to know what made him need those things. What he wants now.

"Undress."

My gaze snaps from Chris's arm to his handsome, unreadable

face, searching there for what he is thinking and finding nothing but wicked demand. I'm not surprised by his command; Chris has a thing about getting me naked while he remains fully clothed. It's about power and submission. His power. My submission. I haven't always given it to him willingly. Or maybe I have; maybe I simply haven't admitted it to him, or even myself.

I toe off my shoes, like I'm playing strip poker and I'm discarding the least intimate article of clothing first. I might be willing to be submissive, but that doesn't mean Chris as a dominant isn't a bit intimidating. And sexy. So damn sexy.

Next I reach for my jacket, and even now, as much as I want this, as much as I trust him, I feel vulnerable and exposed as I toss it aside. I want to understand why. But I'm also aroused by undressing for him. It seems that being vulnerable and exposed with Chris turns me on. On another occasion, undressing for him might be a seductive game to draw out, but this isn't one of those times. I'm ready to have it over with and to know what comes next.

I don't look at Chris as I quickly remove my T-shirt and then slip out of my velvet sweats. I'm left with a red bra and red panties, and I hesitate only a moment before I just go for it. I unhook my bra and toss it aside. My panties go next, kicked away with a brush of my bare foot. And now things are as Chris intended. I am naked and he is not.

His gaze does a slow, hot slide down my body, and I'm shaken by how intensely erotic it can be just having this man look at me. I've experienced it before, yet it's no less explosive when it happens. I'm aroused beyond belief, naked when he is not, and while this has bothered me in the past, it doesn't now.

It's part of his control, and he was right earlier. I not only like him being in control, I'm done trying to analyze why being at his command is almost a physical need. It simply is. And I like it.

"On your knees in the middle of the rug," he orders.

I go from aroused and confident to a spike of nerves and a racing heart. On my knees? This is like nothing he's ever asked, or rather commanded, of me.

I was completely at his mercy, naked and on my knees, in the center of a soft wool rug. The similarity between Rebecca's journal entry and this moment is striking, but it's the difference between the two that twists me in knots. Rebecca was writing about Mark displaying her in front of the club, about how that had upset her. I'm here alone with Chris, who I'm certain would never do such a thing. She wanted what I have.

"Sara," Chris prods softly, that tenderness back in his voice.

My gaze lifts from where it's fallen to the rug, and the concern in his face echoes what I've just thought. Chris would never hurt me.

"I'm good," I say, answering his silent question. "We're good." I step forward, letting the soft fibers twine in my toes and lead me to the center of the rug.

Chris's expression turns hot and dominant again, and my nipples tighten with his scorching gaze. Slowly, I lower myself, kneeling before him, his submissive in a way I have never been before this moment.

I'm certain whatever comes next will be some sort of dominant Master-type thing, like in Rebecca's journals.

But Chris steps forward and kneels in front of me, his palm

settling on my cheek, fingers caressing, and I blink at the affection in his eyes.

I cover one of his hands with mine. "I thought you had no gentleness in you today."

His lips curve slightly. "I guess you're corrupting me."

I smile at the reference to what I'd once said to him. "I like corrupting you."

"As I do you." Slowly, his fingers slide from my face, his palm caressing my bare shoulder. "Don't move."

Chris pushes to his feet and crosses to the curtain, where he removes a satin-like sash. My pulse leaps with the memory of the painting he'd done of me: naked, in the center of the floor, and tied up. My mouth goes dry. I know what he's going to do with that sash.

The instant he turns back to me, I see the hunger in his eyes. Gentle Chris is gone. A darker, more predatory Chris is present, stalking the woman in his sights. And my breath hitches, just thinking about being that woman.

He squats in front of me and his gaze rakes over my breasts. The imaginary touch is like velvet rasping over my skin. My nipples tighten with the invisible friction and I ache for the wild rush of his touch.

"Lace your fingers together in front of you."

He expects my hesitation; I see it in his face. I give him none, doing as commanded. His expression is unreadable; he simply wraps the long sash around my wrists and hands several times, then ties it off, leaving a long piece of the silk dangling to the ground.

He twines the dangling sash around his hand. "You're at my mercy, you know?"

"Is that supposed to frighten me?"

"No. It's not. And if it did, I'd untie you now."

"Isn't it you who told me the painting of me bound like this wasn't about bondage? It was about trust."

His eyes widen slightly, and then narrow. "I also said it was the kind of trust I don't have the right to ask for."

"You don't have to ask," I whisper. "You already have it."

"I know that, Sara. Now the question becomes, what will I do with it, and will you hate me when I'm done?"

"No." Despite the binding, my fingers find his hands. "I won't. I can't hate you."

"We both need to know if that's true."

"It is," I insist.

I want him to argue against or confirm my declaration but he gives me neither of those things. He simply leans in and kisses my forehead, a tender act that defies the way my hands are tied and what is surely to soon happen between us. And then he moves beside me and his fingers splay across my back. "Lean forward and put your hands in front of you on the rug."

I see the hard glint of challenge in his stare, and read the silent message he intends for me to see. If I can't handle this, I'll never be able to handle the dark secrets locked in his mind and in his past that he intends to reveal. And deep inside, Chris believes I'll hate him before this is over, whatever "this" is.

And so it begins. Test number one, of what's sure to be many.

My chin lifts in rejection of him assuming my failure. Then

I walk my fingers down the rug and stretch as far as I can. Chris's hand goes with me, a gentle weight that doesn't press. It's simply there, full of potential pleasure. For several seconds neither of us moves, and the sexual tension in the room crackles around us.

The rug tickles my nipples and the cool air caresses my bare backside. I am exposed. Swallowing hard, I wonder how Rebecca did anything remotely like this in front of an audience. Did she trust Mark the way I trust Chris? Or just love him the way I love Chris?

Chris caresses my back, and the erotic pleasure pulls me away from the grim place my thoughts have drifted. Sweet friction brushes down my spine with his touch, then over my waist, until his finger finds my tailbone and continues downward. In anticipation of where he will go next, my breathing is suddenly shallow, almost a pant. And when Chris begins the highly intimate, slow glide down the crevice between my cheeks, my sex clenches almost painfully.

"Did you like it when I spanked you, Sara?" he asks, his palm caressing my cheeks the way he had the night he'd actually spanked me.

My skin tingles beneath his touch and I can hear my breathing, short little pants I can't seem to control. "I . . . I don't know."

His hand stills, his fingers widen and tense. "Did you like it when I spanked you?" His voice is low, taut, filled with command.

Somehow my hair draped over my face and my arms tunneled around me are not protection enough from this soul-searching moment. I squeeze my eyes shut, aware that I've exposed more than my body to Chris. I've exposed a part of me that I burn to understand, yet can't seem to fully embrace. But I want to. No, I *need* to. I need to do this.

"Yes," I finally whisper. "Yes. I did." I hold my breath and wait for the reply that doesn't come. One second. Two. No words follow. I start to get up.

Chris's hand presses between my shoulder blades and holds me there, and the warmth of his breath teases my neck and ear. "Stay as you are."

Then he's gone, and a wave of unexpected, irrational panic overcomes me. It's all I can do not to sit up, and I take a deep breath and try to analyze what I'm feeling. I've just made a revealing confession that wasn't easy for me to say out loud, and the last thing I expected, or needed, afterward was to be left lying here, naked and bound.

This isn't what I expect from Chris. This is the behavior of the Master in Rebecca's journals. Of Mark. I feel insecure, uncertain. And damn it, I hate the deep insecurity that never seems to stop haunting me, making me question what I know of the man I love, who is nothing like Mark. He isn't. I know this.

I force another deep breath and repeat that reassurance in my mind, and then suddenly Chris is with me, touching me, and I feel his naked body aligned with mine. The tension inside me fades, warmth spreading over me where I've been chilled. He turns me to my side to face him, his erection thick between my legs, his hand branding my rib cage. His eyes meet mine, and the insanely impossible mix of wicked dominance and sweet tenderness melts away any remaining insecurity.

He strokes the hair from my face. "You do know that there's nothing wrong with liking it when I spank you, don't you?"

Heat floods my cheeks and I look down, taken off guard by the return to our prior, explicitly erotic, conversation. His fingers slip under my chin and force my gaze back to his. "It's just you and me, baby, and I'm not like anyone else who's ever been in your life. There's nothing to be embarrassed or ashamed of with me, ever. You can embrace who you really are, and we can be whoever we want to be together."

My gut clenches at the reference to the way my father and Michael tried to create me and control me; Chris has hit the sore spot. It is a testament to how much he's become a part of me that he sees_this in me, when I hadn't allowed myself to see it until this moment.

I burn to free my hands and touch him, yet at the same time I want them bound. I want to know where we will go next. "I know," I whisper. "I know, Chris, and it matters more to me than you can imagine that you aren't just saying that. You mean it. It's just going to take me some time to fully get them out of my head."

"We're going to strip away all the insecurities they put in your head, baby," he promises, and he slides his cock back and forth between my legs, sending darts of pleasure down my thighs and back up again. "You and me and a whole lot of pleasure."

I gasp as he presses inside me, stretching me, and I try to reach for him but can't, because of my bound hands.

He thinks my past is haunting me, so I can't handle more than straight-vanilla sex. He thinks that my shyness means weakness, and I want to tell him he's wrong. But with the feel of him inside me, the heat spreading through me, I can only manage, "What are you doing?"

"What does it feel like I'm doing?" he asks, nuzzling my neck. "I'm making love to you."

He squeezes my backside, and I moan at the erotic roughness in his touch as he pulls me hard against him, sinking his cock deeper inside me. Filling me completely. And this man does fill me completely, in all ways. I want to do the same for him. "But I thought you were going—"

"To make love to you," he finishes for me, and his cock is stroking back and forth, pumping in and out of me, driving me wild. "Yes, baby, I am."

"That's not what I meant," I argue weakly, nearly overtaken by pleasure. It's a struggle to simply keep my eyes open, but I fight the sensations overwhelming me to plead my case for my readiness for more. He thrusts hard into me, and I'm all but over the edge. Desperation rises in me and with no hands, I have no weapon but to blurt out my protest. "Chris, damn it. Stop. Listen to me."

His eyes meet mine, and this time I find hot coals and burning embers. He thrusts again, a wicked smile on his lips. "I'm listening. Can't you tell?"

I pant through the pleasure, determined to convince him I'm ready for that "more" we both crave. "Because I was slow to admit that I liked it when you spanked me, doesn't mean I can't handle it when you do. Please. Spank me now. I like it."

His fingers curl around my neck, dragging my lips a breath from his. "I'm going to do that and a whole lot more to you,

Sara. Just not now. Not tonight." His mouth closes over on mine, soft and sensual, but no less wickedly dominant.

I mean to resist, to finish arguing my point, but this kiss is laced with deep longing and passion, a kiss unlike any we've shared since I stepped on that plane hours before. He called me his addiction. He is my addiction, my passion. He's my reason to breathe, and when he begins to move inside me again, I am lost to the sway of our bodies, to the thrust of his cock. Lost to how much this man completes me.

He rolls me to my back and reaches for the sash around my wrists. Reality slams into me and my eyes snap wide open. "No," I say, folding my arms close to my chest. "I don't want you to free me. You didn't . . . we didn't . . . We've done slow. I'm done with slow."

He grabs the sash along with my hands, rough in that sexy way he can be rough, and I silently rejoice at a glimpse of this side of him. "What we did is called avoidance," he declares and his mouth lowers, lingering near mine, his breath a warm, wet promise on my lips. "And this, right now, is me savoring every second of making love to you. And in case you didn't know, you're the only reason I know what that means."

My breath freezes in my throat, the impossibility of how far we've come in such a short time overwhelming me. "I am?"

"You have to know that."

I'm instantly awash in emotions, and yes, still so intensely, wonderfully, overwhelmed by this man. "I do," I whisper. "I know because I feel the same way about you." I try to reach for him but can't. "I need to touch you."

He reaches down to untie my hands, and I swear I see him

tremble as he tosses the sash aside. With desire? With love? He's as affected by me as I am him, and it's this connection I never expected, and I never want to lose. Our eyes lock and hold, the air thickens around us, and words are not needed. We understand each other. We need each other. Chris is inside me, hard and thick, but this is much more than sex. He's right. It's making love.

His mouth slants over mine and his tongue presses past my teeth, stroking me at the same moment he curves his hand beneath me and lifts my hips. And with his actions, it's as if a branch snaps and we tumble into a wildfire of passion. The Chris I know doesn't lose control—but he has, we have, and I'm climbing out of my skin, trying to get under his. His mouth is on my mouth, my neck, my nipple, suckling and licking, and his cock is driving into me, slow and then fast, fast and then slow.

Time fades and Chris is merciless, punishing me with hard pumps of his cock, and sweet, wicked licks of his tongue. I am lost and found in this one place, in this one man, and I desperately try to hold back, to make this last, but can't do it. I dig my fingers into his back and I clench around his shaft, dragging him deeper, but never deep enough. This man can never be deep enough.

Release is sweet bliss, jerking my hips and stealing my breath. Every nerve ending in my body is alive and tingling with pleasure. Chris buries his face in my neck, his body quaking, and I feel the warm, wet heat of his release filling me. A new wave of pleasure washes over me, and it's far beyond physical. I'm overwhelmed by how right I feel with this man.

"I really do love making love to you," he murmurs, and when he lifts his head to stare down at me, I love the wildness of his hair and the sated heaviness of his deep green stare.

My lips curve. "Yeah?"

"Yeah," he agrees, and gives me a quick peck on the mouth. "Don't go away." He pulls out of me and stands up, and I gasp from the hollow ache of his sudden absence. He gives a wicked bark of laughter at my reaction, obviously pleased with himself.

I raise up on my elbow to watch him, and yikes, the stickiness between my thighs assures that I'll stay right where I am or make a mess. Oh, the joys of reality after hot sex. My gaze fixes on Chris's naked, sexy backside as he walks to a doorway on my left. Okay, so maybe reality is pretty darn good. Who cares about sticky? Chris disappears inside a room and comes back with a towel in his hand, the full-frontal view reinforcing my feeling lucky.

He grabs a pillow from the couch and then settles back on the rug, offering me the towel. I've barely had time to clean up when he pulls my back to his front, and we share the pillow. Sprawled on the floor together, naked, limbs twined together, I've never been happier. Chris is dark and damaged, and I think I'm far more damaged than I've ever acknowledged. But together . . . together I think we can find our way to the light.

"I am never going to look at this rug the same way again," Chris says, nuzzling my hair.

"That makes two of us," I agree with a laugh, but my smile fades when my gaze catches on the sash Chris used to tie me up. We're so close to finding true peace with each other, I don't want anything, especially my silent worries, to ruin it.

"Please promise me that my hesitation over spanking didn't make you doubt I can handle what you want to share with me." I force myself to dig deeper and face what is really bothering me. "And It's not because of Michael. I'm not fragile, Chris. I won't break because of some deep emotional wound, if that's what you're worried about."

He rolls me to my back and his hand settles possessively on my stomach. "Baby, I'm not about to sit back and let that man be what's in your head. I'll give you other things to fill the space. Good things. Pleasurable things.

"But Michael aside, there was no way I was spanking you after what you've been through the past few days. Not when there's a risk the experience might hit an emotional nerve. Sometimes a BDSM-type experience helps you escape. Sometimes it takes you deeper into the pain, and forces you to face it and deal with it. You're too new to this for that to be predictable. You don't know what you like, nor how you react to it, and neither do I."

I have a sudden memory of Chris tied up in the club, screaming for the woman behind him to hit him harder, and I know why he became the master of helping others escape. He can't give someone else control without the risk of them opening a wound and starting an emotional bleed. Not unless he goes to painful extremes. *Beatings.*

"We did exactly what I intended tonight," Chris continues. "We worked on trust, and you gave me enough to lie down naked in the middle of this rug and completely submit to me. Trust is everything, Sara."

He curls around me and I shut my eyes, absorbing the

sensation of being wrapped in his strong arms, and I hope that he can find the same trust in me, and us, as I have.

I blink into the beam of sunlight from the balcony and inhale the warm, musky scent of Chris, who is still wrapped around me. But rather than feeling warm and wonderful, there's a vague sense of unease inside me. Something feels off. Maybe it's the new place or the time zone change, and I wonder how long we've been asleep.

"Chris! Oh, Chris, baby, where are you?"

The female voice echoes from the stairwell, approaching quickly, and the sound is like a bucket of ice water. I go cold, aware that this is my source of unease and what woke me.

"Oh holy hell," the female says, and I can tell she's at the top of the stairs now, no doubt gaping at us where we lie on the rug. "Wow. Chris. A little early in this trip for female friends, isn't it?"

I flinch at her obvious meaning and try to sit up, but Chris's leg and arm shackle me. "Whatever you're thinking, it's wrong. Please, baby. Don't assume anything."

I don't *have* to assume—not when there's a woman who clearly knows him intimately enough to have access to his home standing a few feet from us.

Six

I can't lie naked on the floor like this one more second. "Let me up, Chris," I hiss.

"Not until you promise me not to jump to conclusions."

He shifts slightly. I try to push against him but he holds on to me. I growl low in my throat. "We are naked in front of her, Chris. *You* are naked in front of her."

He hesitates but lets me go. I twist around to my hands and knees to get up, and freeze. Standing at the top of the stairs is a striking, Barbie-doll-looking blonde wearing skintight black jeans and a tank top, with long, silky hair, a body to kill for, and tattoos on both bare arms. Her red "fuck me" heels are outrageously high, which on me would ensure a certain stumble, and a wave of nausea overcomes me. Why am I here? She is everything I'm not and can never be.

"What the fuck are you doing here, Amber?" Chris demands, then drops his shirt by my hands. "Here, baby."

I can't seem to move. *Amber.* An American name, and pretty. And Chris is *walking around naked* in front of her. I lean back on my heels to snatch the shirt and pull it on. When I try to stand I stumble, and Chris catches me, his hand closing on my arm. All I see is his bare foot and naked calf.

"Let go," I hiss again, and I manage to look directly at Amber, who glances from Chris to me with a gloating amusement in her eyes. I'm hurt. I'm embarrassed. I feel completely sideswiped and betrayed. There's so much more to this woman than Chris has told me.

"Sara." Chris has stepped close to me, his hip pressed to mine. His naked damn hip.

"Let go." I barely recognize the deep timbre of my own voice. "Now."

His hand slips away and I launch myself forward. Since forward is directly toward Amber, I regret my path, but I'll be damned if I'm backing down. I lift my chin and walk straight for her, and she smirks with her pretty pink lips and steps aside.

Of course she does. I'm leaving her with Chris. Who is naked. That fact keeps replaying in my head like a stuck record. *She has a key. He doesn't care if she walks in when he's naked. She's already seen him naked long before now.*

This doesn't compute with what I know of myself and Chris, but I won't be able to think straight until I'm alone. I'm not a confrontational person. I'm a "leave and never look back" person, and the possibility that I might have to leave forever twists me in knots.

I nearly run up the stairs and storm into Chris's bedroom. At this moment I can't call it mine, for fear that it, like him, will be stripped away from me. A gnawing worry that he never was mine in the first place begins to form, and I can't seem to move forward.

Stopping in the entryway, I fall against the wall and just stand there, breathing hard, the sound of my heart drumming in my ears. I expect some sort of outburst. I expect to cry, but I don't. Based on my earlier blackout, I'm fairly certain that not only am I on emotional overload, but that my mind and body are protecting me from complete collapse. It is almost as if I'm standing outside myself looking in, and seeing nothing but a gaping, empty hole. All I feel is a fear of what will soon be inside it.

"Sara."

I whirl around to face Chris. My gaze sweeps him from head to toe, as I'm sure Amber's did plenty of times. He's in jeans that aren't buttoned, bare feet and no shirt, and his half-dressed state is enough to make me combust. "I didn't come here to play with you and your tattoo-artist girlfriend, Chris."

"She's nothing more than a friend, Sara. A friend with piss-poor timing."

My fingers curl, my nails digging into my palms. "With benefits and a key? Is this how you define the trust you and I just talked about? Having another woman on the side, when you said there was no one? Or maybe I didn't ask if you had friends with benefits—so you didn't tell me about her."

I suck in hard-earned air and exhale painfully. "Damn you, Chris. I opened myself up to you. I gave you everything that I am, when I swore I'd never do that with anyone. I let you spank me." Pain nearly doubles me over, but somehow I hold myself upright. "I'm going home." I turn away, seeking escape.

Chris shackles my arm. I whirl on him again and tug against his grip, not about to let him pull me close and cloud my judgment. Judgment that's apparently impaired where he's concerned, or I would have seen this coming. "I want to go home, Chris."

"Home is with me, Sara."

"Seems that Amber thinks so, too."

He motions to the bed with his head. "Let's sit down and I'll explain."

His lack of denial carves an extra piece of my heart out. I shake my head, vehemently rejecting that idea. "No. I'll want to believe whatever you tell me, when that's obviously a bad idea."

My gaze rakes his shoulder, and the brightly colored tattoo she created, and anger burns in my belly. "Do you have any idea how much I hate that you were naked while you were down there with her? Which is crazy, since I know you've probably been naked with her more than with me."

His eyes flash, and it's all the warning I get. "That's it," he snaps. "You're going to listen to what I have to say." A second later I'm wrapped in his embrace and his long, muscular frame melds to mine, doing exactly what I'd feared. Distracting me. Working me over. Making me forget.

Big and strong, he easily maneuvers me to the bed, forces me to sit down, and bends over, his hands at my sides, effectively trapping me. His eyes meet mine and it doesn't seem to matter how hurt and betrayed I feel. I can't escape the familiar punch of awareness he creates in me.

"*You* are the only woman in my life," Chris declares, and the rough emotion in his voice creates hope in me. "You know that, Sara. I know you know that. You're reacting to the events of the past twenty-four hours, and even the past few weeks of hell we've gone through together."

Maybe.

Probably.

Partially—but I don't give him the hope he's given me. Selfish as it might be, I need it too much myself.

"And yes," he concedes, "I used to fuck Amber, but it's been years since I even thought about touching her. And a lot longer than that, since it mattered when I did."

"So at some point she was special to you."

"You took that out of context. We met in college and she pulled me into the BDSM lifestyle."

I'm shaken by his matter-of-fact announcement. She looks closer to my twenty-eight than Chris's thirty-four. I've never even thought about him going to college, let alone having it be when he'd discovered BDSM. He started painting before that, and I just assumed he'd gone straight from high school to art. I wonder what else I've assumed that I shouldn't have.

"Baby." Chris strokes my cheek and I feel the touch all over. Clearly my body is without the boundries of my mind. "Anything I had beyond friendship with Amber was a long time ago."

"But it's part of what defined who you are now, and she's still a part of your life."

"Yes. But where we've been is what brings us to the place *you* and I are now."

He's right. He's completely right. So why is this still such an issue to me? I bury my face in my hands. "I'm confused."

Chris pries my hands away from my face. "You are my present—and, I hope, my future."

"Then why does she have a key and feel free to just barge in?"

"I have her keep an eye on the place when I'm gone," he explains. "The security company told her I arrived and, since I came home without warning, she was afraid something was wrong. She's only a friend, Sara." His hands move to my legs. "Nothing more."

He's staring at me, willing me to see the truth in his eyes, and I do. I trust Chris. Even when I was downstairs in the midst of that hell, deep down, I trusted him. I reacted to the situation. And to Amber. "She still wants you, Chris. I felt it in the air."

"I know."

His directness stuns me, when it shouldn't. It drives home why I trust him, but the answer is hard to swallow. "And you don't see that as being a problem?"

He laughs. "All I am to her is a potential fuck who happens to be a friend. And she has no family. I'm it. I'm more a big brother to her than anything else."

My brows dip at that odd description. "Let me get this straight. You're a big brother *and* a potential fuck?"

"Yeah, well, *she's* fucked-up, and I know how to deal with all the cobwebs in her head." He pulls me to my feet. "Let's go make sure she knows you are the lady of the house." He starts leading me toward the door.

My eyes go wide and I tug on his hand. "Wait. No, Chris. It isn't necessary, and we have no clothes on."

He turns to stare down at me, his blond hair a rumpled, alluring mess. "It's not only necessary, it's mandatory. I want you both to be clear that this is *your* home, and *you* are the woman in my life."

I suck in a breath, touched deeply. "I know I am," I reply softly. "And you know I am. We're all that matters."

He encloses me in his arms. "You'll know even better, after we go down there and I introduce you to Amber."

I'd rather meet Amber later, when I'm on more even footing. "But I'm in your shirt and you're only wearing pants."

His lips curve. "If that doesn't make a statement, then I don't know what does." He motions to the door. "Let's get rid of her, then shower and go to bed."

The determined look in his eyes says it all. We're going to do this. "I'm not going to like this," I warn.

He smiles and kisses my nose. "It'll be a lot less painful than being naked on all fours in the middle of a rug while you stare at her."

I cringe and press my head to his chest before giving him a sheepish look. "I really did that, didn't I?"

"Yeah, baby." He grins. "And you looked good doing it."

I might have blushed at that comment, but the memory of why I'd frozen in that position hits me hard. I'd been stunned by the contrast of my dark hair and Amber's light blond hair, my untouched skin, her tattoos. "We're very different."

He runs his hands down my hair and captures my gaze with his. "That's a good thing, Sara." In his usual elusive style, he says nothing more. He simply laces his fingers with mine and pulls me toward the door.

Anxiety ripples through me as he all but drags me down the stairs toward the living room, but he pauses at the bottom of the stairs and we stare at the rug. My mind goes to the moment that I kneeled down in the center, naked and vulnerable, and completely willing because it was with Chris. Heat rushes up my neck and my cheeks flush.

Chris cuts me a sideways look, his eyes twinkling with the mischief I've come to expect from him. "Like I said. I'll never look at that rug the same way again."

His mood is contagious and I smile back. "It's a very comfortable rug."

His lips curve into a sensual smile. "It is with you on it."

I flush, and the gleam in his eyes says he notices. He leans in and brushes his lips over mine, his voice low and thick. "We have many rooms to explore together," he promises, and then motions me to our right.

The lightness in the air vanishes and my stomach knots, but I manage an agreeable nod. Reluctantly, and only because he is so adamant this is important, I let Chris lead me to the stairwell heading to the kitchen. Trying to remain composed on no sleep and a heck of a lot of emotional overload, I focus on everything but the potential Amber disaster before me, like how much I love the way the kitchen sits above the living area like a loft. I can't wait to explore the entire house.

I've taken only one step up when a whiff of the familiar scent of Chris's favorite French coffee hits me. Tension settles hard in my belly. Obviously Amber feels right at home here. I force down the negative feelings, reminding myself that this is not the day to make assessments. It's a day to go to bed and rest.

Chris and I reach the top of the stairs and my attention is riveted on Amber, sitting at a gorgeous stone island, her silky blond hair draped over her slender shoulders. She's the centerpiece of a gray and black modern kitchen, with stainless-steel appliances and a long line of gray-wash cabinets above the counters that have a splattered-paint look. She looks gorgeous, her pale skin pure perfection, and I'm excruciatingly aware of my day-old smudged makeup, and the heaviness of my dark brown hair that says I need a shower.

"I picked up freshly ground Malongo," she says of the coffee brand Chris loves enough to bring to the States with him, and lifts a white mug with steam rising from the top. "I'll pour you a cup."

She's looking at Chris and talking to Chris. This is not starting out well.

"We'll get our own," Chris says, pulling me around the island toward the coffeemaker and stopping by the counter. "I want to show Sara her new kitchen."

"Her kitchen?" she queries.

Chris turns toward her and pulls me under his arm, beside him. Her legs are crossed, her toes painted bright red to match her shoes. "That's right," he confirms. "Sara lives with me now. What's mine is hers."

Amber's gaze immediately goes to my finger in search of a ring, and a sharp pang of discomfort pinches my chest. I shove my hand behind my back, out of sight, but I feel sideswiped again at the idea of marriage. We've never even talked about it, and that hits me hard.

Chris snags my hand and pulls it between us. "I should be so lucky," he replies, as if Amber has spoken her silent question, his voice low and emotional.

Has Chris just said he wants to *marry* me? In front of Amber?

Seven

Stunned, I turn to face Chris, my hand settling on the warm wall of his bare chest. "What?" I ask, certain I've misunderstood. We've never talked about marriage, but I find I can barely breathe waiting for his reply. Chris as my husband? I've never dared to consider it really happening.

The look he gives me is both tender and hot at the same time, filled with the promise of far more than the next sexual adventure we both forever crave. "Don't look so surprised, baby."

"We just . . . You never . . ."

"We will. When the time is right, we will."

For one slice of an instant I see the trepidation in his eyes, and I understand. He's just made sure both Amber and I know how serious he is about me, but he doesn't really believe I'll ever marry him.

I press up to my toes, my hands flattening on his shoulders, and I whisper in his ear, "Nothing can change how much I love you." I lean back to let him see the truth in my eyes, and pure anguish flashes in his. He is touched by my claim but he doesn't believe it to be true. It's amazing how far we have traveled together, how the tables have turned. Not so long ago, I questioned if he could ever truly need me—and now, it's he who questions me in the same way.

I start to whisper his name, but his fingers slide under my hair and he brings my mouth to his, one sultry slide of his tongue licking into my mouth. The sound of Amber clinking things around loudly breaks through the passion spiraling between us and Chris pulls back, his fingers tracing a strand of my hair, the air between us thick with unspoken words. "We'll talk later," he promises. "Ready for that coffee?"

"Yes," I choke out, uncomfortably aware of Amber all over again. "Coffee is good."

He drapes an arm over my shoulder. "Then let me start by showing you our impressive collection of plain white mugs."

We turn toward the cabinet, but not before I catch a glimpse of Amber staring at us. No . . . *at me.* And the look is pure hatred, the kind of look Ava gave me weeks back when she'd seen me in the deli with Mark. I'd been stunned by the hostility in her face, since she'd always been friendly to me before. The comparison between that moment and this one shakes me to the core, and my nails dig into Chris's back where my hand has settled.

He glances down at me and his too-sexy mouth twitches, all signs of his darker side gone. "Save that for when we're alone, baby."

I glower at him, thinking there is a *lot* we should save for when we're alone. Amber hates me for sure now, and despite what Chris said, I'm pretty sure she's in love with him. "You were showing me the collection of white mugs?" I prod, my fingers pressing against the spot where I'd dug my fingernails, warning him to behave.

"I was," he agrees. "And who would want to miss that?"

Amber says something in French and Chris turns to her. "English, Amber. Sara doesn't speak French."

"Oh," she comments. "That's going to be fun for her."

Her. Like I'm not even here. I sigh inwardly, knowing I have to put a stop to this. Though I'm not confrontational, I left my doormat status back at my father's house.

I accept the coffee Chris pours me and set my cup on the island across from her, forcing her to deal with me. "I'll learn." And this time I mean it. I will not be crushed by a language barrier. "You're American, right? Surely at some point you had to."

Chris joins me on the opposite side of the island across from Amber and sets cream on the counter. "Yes, she was once as American as apple pie."

Amber's brows dip. "I'm still American, but unlike you, I've embraced French culture."

He loves Paris but he doesn't embrace French culture? I want to explore this, but Amber is already moving on. "Learning French sucked. I hated every second of it, but you really have to learn, to spend any substantial time here. Believe me, I found that out quickly."

Chris glances down at me. "She came here as a teenager,

like I did, and American students aren't welcomed with open arms."

"Kids are cruel," she agrees, surprising me by showing a vulnerable side.

I'm not sure I want to see her as human, which isn't nice. There's no healthy reason to feel this jealousy . . . aside from the fact that she's gorgeous and has a long history with the man I love. Oh, how I hate this insecure side of me.

". . . but that was ages ago," Amber says, finishing a sentence I didn't hear, standing at the coffeepot, all long, lean, and beautiful, filling her cup. "You need a one-on-one tutor if you want to learn quickly."

"She's right," Chris agrees. "We'll get you someone lined up, if you want?"

"I'd like that," I say, and I don't miss how he's asked me rather than ordered me, when only a short time before he was dominant and I was submissive. It's the balance of respect and dominance in Chris that makes him so very different from other dominant men, of whom there have been many in my life. "We need to find a really patient person who knows how to teach someone who doesn't learn other languages well."

"That would be Tristan," Amber suggests. "He teaches English. I'm sure he can teach French."

"No," Chris says and his eyes meet Amber's. "Tristan is not tutoring Sara."

"He's much better than some stuffy teacher who will cram rules and subject matter down her throat. He'll get her street-slanging it in a week."

"No," Chris repeats, and there is a low, dangerous quality to his voice.

Ouch. Who is this Tristan and why does Chris want me to stay away from him?

Amber returns to her chair. "She can't even speak to Sophie, Chris."

"Who's Sophie?" I ask.

"The housekeeper," she replies, surprising me when her deep blue eyes meet my light green ones. "She doesn't speak English."

"Amber," Chris warns, and he turns to me. "We'll get by the language stuff, baby. And Sophie only comes once a week."

The doorbell rings and Chris glances at his watch. "I guess I can't wonder who the heck would be here at this time of the night, since it's three in the afternoon here." He sets his cup down and glances at Amber. "It's more a question of who even knows I'm here."

She holds up her hands. "Don't look at me. I didn't have time to tell anyone."

I stand up as he heads down the stairs. "Don't you need a shirt?"

He glances over his shoulder. "Wanna give me that one?"

"Get your own," I call back, smiling, as he disappears around the corner. But as I turn back to the table and find myself alone with Amber, it fades quickly. For several seconds we just stare at each other and the silence eats away at the few nerve endings this day has left me with. I can't stand the empty space, so I blurt out, "Who's Tristan?"

Her lips curve like a cat that's about to capture a canary,

with me soon to be a feather in those lips. "A tattoo artist I work with," she explains. "A wickedly sexy, talented one. Customers wait for a good two months to get his ink."

This tells me nothing of why Chris wouldn't want me around Tristan. But I'm guessing it must be his connection to Amber, and maybe hers to the BDSM world. I want to be as far away from that topic with her as possible, and I say, "You did Chris's dragon. It's brilliant. You're quite gifted."

Her eyes register surprise and then pride. "Yes. I did it many, many moons ago, and it's still some of my best work. I was . . . inspired. It was a coming of age for both him and me."

"It certainly shows in the work," I manage, past a knot in my throat caused by her sentimental tone that reaches beyond sex to a deep history of friendship, and yes, passion.

She tilts her head and studies my face, and something flares in her eyes that I don't understand. Her gaze drops and travels over what she can see of my body, and the hot, sultry inspection is as far from hate as it gets. "You know," she purrs, her dark lashes lifting, "I could ink that beautiful pale skin of yours with a dragon to match Chris's. It would be . . . breathtaking."

I can feel heat spreading across my chest and up my neck. Is she coming on to me? No, that's pure craziness. I'm confused and uncomfortable. One minute she's looking at me as if she wants to kill me, and the next like she wants to strip me naked again.

My first instinct is to seek out Chris, but that might be exactly what she hopes for. I have to establish that I will not be pushed around, and do it quickly. Still, I sit there and say nothing. Me. The nervous rambler.

"I have a three-month wait, but I'll get you in right away," she adds, leaning forward to narrow the distance over the counter. "We'll surprise Chris."

We'll surprise Chris? Is she . . . surely not. Or is she? Does she want us to be a threesome? That's not happening. I don't share, and if I thought for a moment Chris did, I'd be on a plane back to the States. But she knows him. She's had sex with him. Kinky sex.

I swallow hard. *Past. Present. Past. Present.* I repeat these words in my head, feeling like I'll be using them a lot in the near future. "No ink for me," I say, my voice strained with discomfort. "Thanks, though."

Amber notices; I see the gleam in her intelligent eyes. She's smart, and that makes her dangerous. She pushes off her chair to stand, a good two or three inches above my five feet four inches. "Too bad," she says. "I could have told you all of his secrets while I worked on you."

I ignore the soft little rasp emphasizing "worked on you." She's definitely playing some head game with me, and I hate that it's working a little. Chris is the one to share his secrets with me, but still . . . *does* she know all the things about him I don't? Maybe. Probably. Some things, for sure. She's the one who lured him into the BDSM world. Well, he didn't use the word *lure*, and he isn't the type to be lured into anything. *Past. Present.* Maybe he had been the type back then? And Amber certainly is the type to lure someone into something. I almost laugh out loud. This is the man who, as a teen, responded to the French kids' teasing by beating the crap out of them and getting in trouble.

Amber rounds the island and walks toward me, and I am hopeful she is leaving. Instead, she stops beside me and shocks me by pressing her hand to my bare arm and running it up under Chris's shirt to close around my bare shoulder.

My gaze jerks to hers and it's all I can do not to pull back, but I've had enough people play intimidation games with me to know not to respond.

"Right here," she says, her fingers flexing on my shoulder. "I'll do a perfect duplicate of Chris's dragon. It would be delicious fun to re-create it." Her hand slides away and her lips curve. "He likes inked skin."

She's hit a nerve I do not want to exist, and I barely contain a flinch. I'm not the daring, beautiful creature that she is and, though I felt quite secure earlier, right now I fear I eventually won't be enough for Chris.

Her eyes gleam with satisfaction. She knows she's gotten to me, and I hate that she knows. "I have a feeling you'd be surprised at a lot of the things Chris likes," she comments, tucking a strand of long blond hair behind her ear. "You know, he's going to get called for one meeting after another by everyone and their uncle in the art world. That's what happens the minute he enters the city. You'll get bored. Stop by the shop if you like. I'm at the Script, off the Champs-Élysées. It's a short walk."

She smirks, and even that is pretty. I have a feeling she'd look good with the flu, while I look like something from a zombie apocalypse when I don't get enough sleep. Like now. "I'm sure Chris and I will get by that way."

"Come alone so we can talk about the tattoo," she encourages.

"Tristan will be there, too. He can give you a lesson." The cat-that-ate-the-canary look is back, and I'm sure she's not talking about a lesson in French.

She waves two fingers at me. "Later, *ma belle*." She walks down the stairs, and I don't turn to watch.

I have no clue what just happened. I only know that Amber isn't going away. Neither am I, so I'm going to have to find a way to deal with her.

I'm not sure how long I sit at the island in the kitchen, trying to figure Amber out, unwilling to risk another encounter with her before she is finally gone. Not even the idea of her fawning over Chris will lift me from my seat. Finally the need for a shower, and my curiosity over who was at the door and why Chris is taking so long, wins out.

I head to the living room and Chris is entering from a hallway on the opposite side of the room, wearing a white T-shirt and talking on the phone in French. I've never been so happy to see the man dressed.

Chris ends his call. "Let's go get a shower, order food, eat, and then sleep."

"I'm all for all of those things in that order," I agree, walking with him up the stairs.

"That was the security guy at the door who looks after our place and a few others around here. Rey is his name. He stopped by to give me a stack of messages." He runs a hand over his jaw. "One was from Katie and John, who'd heard about what happened on the news and kept getting fast busy signals when they called me."

I stop at the mention of his godparents. "Oh, no. We were supposed to be at the château today."

"Yeah," he confirms. We start walking again. "I feel like crap for not calling them."

"How did she know to call here?"

"Jacob told her we were here." His phone rings and he glances down and back up. "Speaking of Katie." He answers the call. "Hi, Katie. Yes, I'm okay. We're both okay. You're right. I should have called. I just wanted to get Sara out of there." We walk into the bedroom and Chris glances at me with a question in his eyes. "You want to talk to Sara?"

I nod and accept the phone from him. "Hi, Katie."

"Sara, honey, are you okay?"

I sink down on the bed and my heart twists. I don't know her well, but she has this motherly quality that stirs the emotions I've tried to bury deep down inside about the mother I lost, and who I'm not sure I ever really understood, and the loneliness that had followed.

"Sara, honey, are you okay?" Katie repeats.

I clear my throat and watch Chris slide open a long closet that covers most of the wall and matches the white finish. "I'm fine," I assure her. "I'm sorry we made you worry."

"I wish Chris had brought you here, not taken you to Paris. You're a fish out of water. How long will you be there?"

"Indefinitely," I tell her, and I'm surprised that I'm glad I'm here and not there. Katie and John are a part of Chris's past and present, but Paris is where Chris feels he needs to be to truly open up to me.

"Oh dear," Katie frets. "That's what I feared. Did you plan for this, or take off because of the problems here?"

"We'd started talking about it, but hadn't had time to plan."

"I can see why that felt important, but you're in for quite the culture shock. Some people do well, while others really struggle. Do you know how to speak French?"

"No, I—"

"That's what I feared. Okay. That's a big part of enjoying your time there. Don't fret; we'll remedy this. I have a friend who has a niece who's in school there to be a language instructor. Give me a few minutes and I'll see if she can tutor you, then I'll call you back. What's your direct number?" I give it to her and she adds, "Everything is going to be wonderful. We'll take care of you." She ends the call and I sit there stunned. This woman barely knows me, and she's already swept me into her family circle. I haven't had that since my mother died. Truthfully, not ever.

"Everything okay?" Chris asks from the closet, where he's hanging a shirt from his suitcase.

"Yes, fine. Good, actually. Katie is wonderful. She's trying to find me a tutor and then calling me back."

He scrubs his jaw, an amused look on his face. "And you thought I was a control freak?" He saunters toward me. "She's in another country, trying to line up your French lessons."

I smirk as he stops in front of me. "You *are* a control freak."

"So are you," he says, offering me his hand, then pulls me to my feet and wraps me in his embrace. "Which makes your giving it to me all the more meaningful."

The mix of hot fire and tender warmth in his eyes has my fingers flexing on the hard wall of his chest and my body relaxing into his. "Just remember, control is like a fortune cookie saying."

"A fortune cookie saying," he repeats, looking amused. "Right. It's meaningful only when you add 'in bed' to the end."

He laughs, and it's such a sexy laugh for all kinds of reasons. Yes, it's deep and masculine and warm and wonderful, but more than anything, it's relaxed. It's comfortable. It's a part of who we're becoming together.

"Let's go take a shower," he says. "I'll show you your closet. It's in the back of the bathroom and in desperate need of a whole lot of filling, because that little suitcase you brought isn't going to manage."

He's right. I packed fast and horribly. "I'm all for seeing the closet, but Katie's going to call back. I can't get into the shower until she calls."

His phone rings and Chris looks at the screen and sighs. "Thanks to one of our nosy neighbors, word has spread I'm back in the city. This is a major donor for my charity, who sits on one of the board of directors for one of the local museums."

"Take it," I encourage him. "I need to find my phone for when Katie calls back, anyway." I kiss him and head into the bathroom, loving the normalcy of the moment. We're just a couple sharing a bedroom and a bathroom, getting ready to shower, eat, and go to bed. Well . . . we also were almost killed by a madwoman who's accusing me of murder, not to mention that I confronted the manipulative, gorgeous ex named Amber. But I banish those events and focus on the here and now. I've had too little normalcy in my life, and I think Chris has, too. We need this.

Finding my purse, I dig out my phone. Satisfied that it has enough charge, I drain the cold water from the tub, then head toward the closet to check it out. The sound of Chris speaking French lifts in the air, the words rolling sexily off his tongue. I sigh. He alone could make me love this new language.

I flip on the light to find a completely empty closet the size of a small bedroom, with rows of built-in shelves and shoe holders that make my little suitcase full of stuff a joke. My cell phone rings and it's Katie. I sit down on a cushion-topped bench.

"Okay, you're all set," she says. "Chantal will be there at ten in the morning, and you'll adore her. She's actually graduated college and is starting a new job after the holidays, so this is perfect."

"Ten tomorrow," I repeat. "That's fast."

"I thought you'd need something to keep your mind off what's going on back here. And you aren't going to like being in a city where you can't communicate with people. Sure, there are some who speak English, but very poorly. And I know you're going to want to be involved in the art community and, before you blink, the various charity events Chris is involved with over the holidays."

"Oh, yes. I'm excited to be a part of the art community and the charity events."

"Of course you are. And charities will be a perfect outlet for your energy, since you can't work there."

My heart stutters. "What do you mean, I can't work?"

"You'd need to have gotten a work visa before you left, and

it sounds like you didn't have time for that; and getting a work permit approved is nearly impossible in France. The job market is poor, the art world competitive, and they're all about keeping the borders restricted. Of course you have Chris as an insider, but all the red tape still takes time."

How had I not thought of this? Of course I need a work visa, and now I know that is nearly impossible to get.

Katie continues, "It's going to be inconvenient to have to fly back after ninety days, then turn around and return for the Louvre Christmas event Chris always does, but I'm self-ishly happy about that. We'd like to see the two of you while you're here." Her voice softens. "I worry about Chris, Sara, and seeing the two of you together makes me happy. I wasn't sure he'd ever let himself connect with another person fully again."

"Again?" I ask.

"He's had a lot of loss in his life, Sara. It's not left him unaffected."

I draw in a pained breath. "Yes. I know."

"Take care of him, honey. Don't let him convince you he's so tough he doesn't need it."

"I don't plan to. You have my word."

The rest of the conversation is a haze, and when I hang up with Katie, I'm not sure what I feel. I'm thankful to be here, but I wish Chris had prepared me for the work situation.

"Hey, baby," Chris calls out, walking into the bathroom. "I'm afraid I just got cornered into a meeting tomorrow morning. It's at a café across the street from the Musée d'Art Moderne de la Ville de Paris, so you could go explore and I'll join you afterward." He stops in the closet doorway, gives me a quick once-over, and says, "What's wrong?"

"You said I could get a job and earn a living here, Chris."

Understanding washes over his face. "You can, baby. You just need an employer to sign off on your work visa."

"Katie says jobs are hard to find."

"You have two options. I can recommend you, and—"

"No." I shake my head. "I need to do this on my own."

"Or," he continues, "you volunteer where you want to work and prove yourself."

"And to prove myself, I'll need to speak French."

"It'll help."

"How am I supposed to earn a living?"

"Sara. Baby. You do realize we have plenty of money, right?"

"*We* don't have anything, Chris. It's your money. I have some money from my sales at the gallery, but that won't last forever. I have to buy a wardrobe here, and I—"

"Sara." His hands settle on my legs. "I know how hard it is for you to see my money as your money, and that you see this as depending on me. And I know very well that not only have the people you depended on in life let you down, but I also shut you out after Dylan died. That gave you reason to believe I'll let you down, too, but you *can* depend on me. And I fully intend to prove that to you."

Once again, he's seen what I haven't in myself. My old demons are back and they're breathing fire. They tell me that anyone I count on will simply go away at some point. I shove them down into the deep recesses of who I am and don't want to be anymore, and focus on what's important. Present. Not past.

"I trust you, Chris, or I wouldn't be here. You aren't like anyone else in my life—but that doesn't change the fact that earning my own living does help me feel that we're equals."

"We *are* equals. Money doesn't determine worth."

"It's about power. You yourself said that."

He grimaces. "I hate how your father and that bastard Michael made you feel like their money was a weapon in relationships. It's not, and it's going to be part of our life, because I intend to always have plenty of it." He sighs and shakes his head. "Look. We have a lot before us. Having money shouldn't be part of that equation, and your finding a job shouldn't be, either. I didn't talk about the work situation because I knew you'd find opportunities.

"Since we have money, you have the luxury of volunteering at the museums to work your way up to a full-time job if you decide you want it. Or you can buy and sell highly sought-after art from an office here in the house. You'd basically be doing what you did for Mark at the gallery, but as a consultant. Hell, you could even sell to Mark. Then we could travel, and you could use the trips to hunt for pieces you want to buy."

My apprehension quickly turns to excitement. "Would I need some sort of international license for that?"

"We can certainly talk to the attorney about it tomorrow."

"Yes. Please. I love this idea!"

"I'm glad you do, but remember that it's only one idea. You can explore your options, and you can't do that when you're worried about money. I do what I love, and I want you to do what *you* love. Believe me, it's going to take restraint for me to sit back and let you find your own open doors, when I want to open them for you. But I will."

Every time I think I can't fall more in love with Chris, I do. "Thank you. I do really need to know I have my own success."

"I know," he says, and his voice softens. "Sara. I need you to leave the money thing right here in this room tonight. There's plenty of other monsters in my closet for us to face, and I can't set those free if I can't even get past this."

I lean forward and frame his face with my hands. "You can tell me, or show me, anything."

His expression turns solemn. "I know, and I'm going to. And that's what scares me more than anything." He walks into the bathroom, leaving me to stare after him.

Eight

Chantal turns out to be a lovely, patient, twenty-three-year-old native Parisian. And considering it's nearly noon, and I've been sitting with my new tutor for two hours and I haven't learned much, she deserves my high opinion of her.

I lean back against the red leather couch in the amazing library on the same floor of our bedroom and drop the "word chart" Chantal has me using on the coffee table. The famous pieces of art Chris has on the walls are far more interesting than learning French. "You do know it's actually three or four in the morning for me? The time change has got to be affecting my ability to absorb the lesson. That's my excuse, and I'm sticking with it for at least a week. Then I'll come up with something else."

Chantal smiles her sweet smile, which brims with the kind of innocence that only one who hasn't been burned by life can possess. The kind of innocence Ella has. Or had. I wonder if these past few months have changed her. I wonder . . . No, I will not let myself think bad things. She is fine. Happy. Married and honeymooning.

"I've had plenty of people do far worse than you," Chantal assures me, sitting primly beside me in a black skirt and matching silk blouse, her long, light brown hair a perfect complement to her green eyes and olive skin.

I snort at her diplomacy, meant to comfort me. "In other words, I'm bad, but not as bad as the people who don't even speak their own language well."

She grins and says, "Exactly," and the playfulness in her expression really does remind me of Ella. *She* reminds me of Ella. Well, in personality. Ella's strikingly deep red hair and pale white skin are incomparable and, on her, enviable. A knot forms in my belly. Oh, how I miss Ella.

My cell phone rings and I run my hands down my faded jeans and grab it from the coffee table, assuming it's Chris with the good news that his meeting is over. "Hey," I greet him eagerly after seeing his number on caller ID.

"Hey, baby."

"Uh oh," I say, reading his weary tone. "Your meeting didn't go well."

"The museum is having some financial issues."

"They want your money."

"My money won't solve this. Not until they have someone who actually knows how to manage what they have. They asked me to take a temporary spot on the board to try to solve the problems."

"Did you agree?"

"I agreed to talk."

My concern is instant. "Please don't pull back from this because you're worried about me. I have a lot to learn, and plenty to keep me busy."

"I would prefer you do those things with me. That's why I brought you here. For us to experience Paris together."

I hesitate only a moment, conditioned to hold back, to fear being hurt—but I'm already all in with Chris. Holding back only hurts us moving forward. "I'm here to be a part of your life, to build one for us, Chris. It's a not a vacation. We have plenty of time."

"And yet I always have this sense it's never enough." There's a haunted quality to his voice that shades his words and I want to ask what he means, but he continues, "No matter what, it's doubtful I'll agree to sit on the board. My financial team and I came in and cleaned things up several years back for them, and they're in the same place all over again."

I've never given much consideration to Chris's business persona, and perhaps I should have. Despite his claim that he'd sold off his stake in the family cosmetics company, having no interest in sitting in a boardroom for a living, there's a reason why he's so rich. He manages his money. He doesn't just spend it.

"They want me to stay for meetings this afternoon," Chris adds wearily. He has to be as jet-lagged as I am, or maybe it's the situation. "Baby, I don't want to desert you your first day in Paris."

I shove aside a pinch of disappointment and firm my voice. "You need to stay. You said there were people involved who could contribute to your charity, right?"

"Yes, but I can still meet with them outside of this large commitment."

"You don't want a great museum to be lost, Chris, and neither do I. I'm completely fine. I haven't even explored the house yet, and there's shopping within walking distance. Chantal can direct me where to go for what I need."

"I can take you," Chantal offers eagerly.

"Perfect," Chris says, obviously overhearing. "I don't want you running around the city alone. It's a big city and you have a language barrier."

I look at Chantal. "Are you sure?"

"I have no plans, and I'd love to go shopping." She sounds genuinely eager.

"So there you go," I tell Chris. "I have an experienced Paris shopper as an escort. I'm set for the afternoon."

Heavy silence fills the line and I can almost hear Chris struggling with himself. "I'm really fine," I murmur softly. "Don't beat yourself up over this."

"Here's the thing," he finally replies. "I could throw every dime I have at children's cancer, and I won't beat it. It takes worldwide awareness and involvement to make progress. The museum supports the cause, and this donor is well connected in an international company."

"Then you need to do this, and if I can do anything to help, I will. So go fix what's broken and Chantal will keep me company."

"Tell her we'll pay her."

"I heard that," Chantal says. "And no. I'm not going to take money to go shopping."

I snort. "You'll deserve a big bonus if you find a way to get me to speak French."

"That bad?" Chris asks.

"Worse," I confirm. "Maybe some real-life situations will help."

Chris lowers his voice. "I might have to come up with a reward system for learning new words."

I bite my lip. "Be careful. I might not let the board have you."

"Please," he groans. "Don't let them."

"You're on loan only," I assure him.

"Fill that closet," Chris orders. "Make me feel like you want me for my money."

I laugh. "I do. You didn't know that?"

"I thought you wanted me for my body."

"Actually it's the Harley."

"Now you're just feeding my other obsession." I hear someone speak in the background. "I can still tell them 'no' and come home."

Home. *Our* home. I like that. "Don't. I'll be here when you're done."

"Be careful, and text me when you get back to the house so I know you're safe."

I open my mouth to make a "Yes, Master" joke I've made on several occasions, but snap it shut. The memory of Rebecca calling Mark that is just too fresh. Instead, I simply agree.

"He's a Harley guy?" There is an excited lift to Chantal's voice. While I've been on the phone she's been inspecting the rows and rows of books, many of which are interesting art and travel editions.

"Chris loves his Harleys," I confirm, and it's my turn to offer a cat-that-ate-the-canary smile. "And I love him on them."

Chantal sighs and walks back to the couch to perch on the edge of a cushion next to me. "There's something about a guy on a Harley. I think it's the whole 'bad boy who's so good but destined to break your heart' fantasy. Which doesn't sound like much of a fantasy when you put the broken heart part in the picture, but it is. It so is."

My gut tightens with that same damn memory of Chris showing up on his Harley after our breakup. It's a destructive memory and I will it to stop showing up. "Sometimes it's the ones who look the least dangerous who really are," I warn her, thinking of Mark in his perfectly fitted suits and with his perfectly chiseled body. "The suave, debonair ones."

Her eyes fill with longing. "I'd like to get my heart broken by both kinds at least once. But since I have no men in my life, I think we should go eat lunch and finish with macarons. Then we shop."

Her naïve welcoming of heartache is again so like Ella that for a moment I can only stare at her, and when I recover, lunch and shopping are the last things on my mind. "Would you know where one would get a marriage license?"

"Sure. City Hall. Are you getting married?"

Am I going to marry Chris? "I . . . No. Well, not right now."

"But maybe?"

I have to digest this question for a moment. Chris and I haven't talked about it any further, but I find myself smiling at the idea. "I'd say a very strong maybe, that leans toward yes." I don't let myself think about how painful it would be to embrace forever with Chris and have him shut me out again.

Chantal grins. "So hot Harley men don't always break your heart, huh?"

"No, they don't." *At least not intentionally.* "But that doesn't mean you should go chasing them. They aren't all like Chris."

"I know. I've never met him, but my mom says he's special. She's gotten to know him through Katie and John and a series of charity events." Chantal pulls her laptop from her briefcase. "Speaking of Chris, I think he might need to be with you if you're filing for a marriage license."

"It's not my wedding I'm interested in right now. I'm looking for a friend I lost touch with, who came here to get married. I thought the licensing office would be a good place to start to find her. What do you think?"

"You have to have a legal ceremony at City Hall before a religious one can take place, so if she got married here, a record would be there."

Hope fills me. I may be one step closer to finding Ella.

I don't like crowds. I think it comes from a childhood of being trapped in my house under my father's lock and key. Sitting in a tiny café across from City Hall with Chantal, I feel like the fellow patrons around us are sardines in the same can. My unease started when we climbed into a taxi to head toward City Hall. Maybe it's just eating out for the first time in Paris without Chris that bothers me.

I stare at the menu, which is all in French, so I can't understand it any more than I can understand the many conversations going on around me. "I'm assuming you chose this place to give me a lesson in ordering off French menus?"

"Actually, I brought you for the macarons. They're famous for them here." She looks hesitant and then reluctantly adds, "And I'm sorry to tell you this, but most of the restaurants will have French-only menus."

Oh. No. But of course they do.

"Don't look so distressed," Chantal says quickly. "A few streets from your house is the Champs-Élysées. Since it's a tourist hot spot, many of the restaurants there will have English on the menu. You'll also find a McDonald's and a couple of Starbucks there."

Just hearing that two American hot spots sit near my new home sends a rush of relief through me, yet the uneasy feeling hangs on. The nape of my neck tingles and I glance around, looking for suspicious characters. My progress is halted when my gaze catches on a waitress mixing up condiments with raw hamburger at the table directly to my left.

My gag reflex is almost instant and I return my attention to Chantal. "If you order raw meat, I'm leaving."

She laughs. "You do know tartare is very common here, right?"

"No, I'm not well traveled. I'm also not a huge fan of meat in general, though I eat it if it's nearly burnt."

"Hmmm, well"—she picks up the menu—"what about escargot?"

"I do not eat snails."

She arches a brow. "Too bad. It's another favorite for Parisians. How do you feel about duck?"

"They're too cute to eat."

She blinks at me, showing no signs of the impatience I deserve. "Fish?"

"Allergic. Do you eat pasta here?"

"It's not a French staple, but we have it. You will find a lot of American food on French menus, but I must warn you that most Americans dislike our attempt at their foods. Don't expect our versions to be the same as what you're used to." She sets her menu down and laces her fingers together. "We need to find things we do well that you will enjoy on a classic French menu. Our pastries and desserts are fabulous."

"A girl's hips can only take so many pastries and desserts."

"True," she concedes, and considers a moment. "Well, our quiches are amazing. It's the pastry crusts that make them so good, but they aren't calorie-friendly, either."

"Quiche is an option, though. I can eat that."

"We also do an excellent grilled ham and cheese. Also quite fattening, of course, since we drench them in butter."

Grilled ham and cheese? Is she serious? She grimaces at me and chides, "Don't look so appalled. They are our version of hamburgers and quite delicious. Our bread is homemade, and our cheeses are amazing. As you Americans say, don't knock it until you try it."

"I'm sorry." And I am. This is the food she loves. I need to frame my dislike with the diplomacy she's shown me. "I do love cheese, so I'll try the grilled ham and cheese. That is, if they have it on the menu here?"

"They do. Both quiche and the grilled ham and cheese are very common in our restaurants, so they can be your go-to orders. I'll teach you how to find them on the menu."

"I think that's smart." I manage to sound positive, though the idea that these are the only items that I'll eat is quite daunting.

"Okay, so 'Croque Monsieur' is the grilled ham and cheese." She shows me on the menu and I take a picture of it on my cell phone. "If you add 'Madame,' then you get a sunny-side egg on top."

My eyes go wide. "An egg on top of a grilled cheese?"

"Yes," she says, laughing. "You are really not enjoying this exploration into French cuisine, are you?"

"It's that obvious?" I ask, silently reprimanding myself for my continued bad manners.

"Very." As the waitress appears, Chantal says, "I'll order for us."

I would have tried to understand a few words of their exchange if not for the sudden prickling sensation on the nape of my neck again. The same sensation I'd had at the airport just before being welcomed to France by a pickpocket.

Instinctively I grab my purse, place it in my lap, and hold tight. Fighting the urge to turn to look behind me, for fear of being rude or seeing the man next to me eating raw meat, I shift in my seat. I'm in a new country, only days after Ava tried to kill me, just to name a few of my recent nightmares, and it's making me paranoid. That's all this is. Nothing more.

Except my urge to turn is intense—overwhelming, even.

The waitress walks away and I'm officially crawling out of my own skin. "I'm going to the bathroom," I announce, and push to my feet. I'll be able to check out the seats behind me when I return.

"Toilette," Chantal corrects, calling after me.

Without turning, I wave my understanding. Thankfully, I find the "toilette" easily. With no one else present in the two-stall facility, I press my hands on the sink and stare at myself, seeing a too-pale brunette who's the most uncultured person on the planet. I can't even enjoy a meal in Paris.

Worry threatens to go wild and explode into all kinds of unproductive directions. What if I hate Paris, when Chris loves it and wants to live here? Even if I convince him to come back to the States, will he feel like I do here? No. No. He likes the States. But still, he wants to be here.

I shake my head. This is nuts. I'm overreacting. Just because I'm not immediately falling in love with Paris doesn't mean I won't fit in or I won't like it. I'll like it with Chris. I'm sure of it. Very sure.

Needing to hear his voice, but knowing that isn't possible right now, I dig out my phone to text him. That way he can answer when he has a break from his meeting.

Do you eat tartare, aka raw meat?

Hate it, comes his instant reply.

My shoulders relax and I smile at the fast reply and his answer. Snails?

Not a fan.

Fish?

Depends.

I'm allergic, I type, not sure I've ever told him that.

My phone rings and I feel guilty when I see Chris's number. "I'm sorry. I shouldn't have bothered you."

"You aren't bothering me. I needed a break from the egos about to blow the doors off the conference room. Where are you?"

"Some restaurant I can't say the name of. I also can't read the menu, and I don't think I'd like it any more if I could."

"No worries, baby. We Americans living in Paris know all the places to go to get the food we like. It'll be better when you're with me."

He's right. It will. The part where I'm with him will be wonderful. The rest, though . . . "I know. You're right."

There is a brief pause and he says, "You don't know, do you?"

"I do."

"You aren't convincing me."

"I just don't love the food so far. It's nothing more."

"I don't love the food, either."

I watch my brows knit together in the mirror. "You're so confusing sometimes." Actually a lot of the time, but I keep that to myself. "If you don't like the food, why do you want to live here? Food is such a big part of life."

There is a heavy silence, and then, "Sara—"

He stops at the sound of a male voice speaking rapidly in French. I hear Chris reply to the visitor with a tone that says he's not pleased, and guilt twists inside me again. I feel shallow and selfish for bothering him about unimportant things.

"Sara—" he starts again, but I don't let him finish.

"I'm sorry. You need to be taking care of business and I'm interrupting you."

"You aren't bothering me."

"I am and I love you, Chris, and I don't care about raw hamburger. I care about you. Your involvement there means great things for the museum and for your charity. I believe in what you're doing and in you. Go. Work."

He hesitates. "You're sure?"

"Absolutely positive."

"I'll take you to eat someplace you'll like tonight. Then I'll take you home and show you how much I missed being with you today."

Take me home. Oh, how I love those words. Home. Home. Home. I have one, and it's with Chris. I smile into the phone. "Sounds perfect." Then I toughen my voice. "Now go kick some big egos around, and make them listen to reason."

"I will." The relief in his voice tells me he was far more worried about my reaction to Paris than I'd noticed. "I'm not sure what time I'll get out of here. I'll call you when I know. I love you, baby."

We say a quick good-bye and I put my phone away, lean on the sink, and look at myself in the mirror again. This time I see a woman in love, who is eager to explore the world she hasn't seen with the man in her life. I head back to the table to eat my grilled ham and cheese, which thankfully has no egg on top. When I glance at the two tables positioned behind my chair, they're empty and complete with place settings. No one had been sitting there. I silently laugh at myself for my jittery mood. There was never anyone watching me.

Nine

⁓

I know why Chris is drawn to Paris when Chantal and I walk through the main entrance of the Hôtel de Ville, or City Hall, a spectacular building resembling a castle that spans several blocks. This very building and the city itself are a celebration of the art Chris and I both love.

In awe, I step to the side of the doorway and pause to absorb what surrounds me. Everywhere—from the antique furniture and the masterpieces on the walls to the marble floors—there is beauty. What really steals my breath, though, is the spectacular architecture woven with art. White pillars, archways, and finely crafted trim work are frames for intricately drawn paintings on the ceilings and walls.

"This is even more magnificent than the outside," I murmur. Far more than what I expected of a political office with a public affairs division.

"There's a museum here, too, but you have to schedule tours."

"Really?" I ask excitedly, tearing my gaze from a mural to return my attention to her. "What do you know about it?"

"I hear it has Picassos, but I'm not really into art so I've never visited."

Picasso. I'm in the same building as a Picasso. Just across the city in the Louvre is the *Mona Lisa*. Oh, yes. I do think Paris can grow on me.

"This way to the marriage license office," Chantal says, pointing to an elevator.

Fifteen minutes later, after being sent to several different offices, Chantal and I stand at a counter in a large public room that resembles a registry of motor vehicles in the United States. "What's your friend's name?" Chantal asks after speaking in French to the prim, fifty-something woman behind the counter.

"Ella Johnson," I offer quickly, eager for answers.

Chantal speaks to the woman, who then keys information into the computer and shakes her head. My stomach plummets to the floor. "What about the intended husband?" Chantal asks me.

I tell her and then hug myself as I wait for the dreaded next head shake. A few keystrokes later that's exactly what I get, but the woman goes on to explain something to Chantal.

"She says," Chantal relays, "that you have to have established residence in France for forty days and post a public notice before the wedding. Most foreigners do that at thirty days, but she sees no notice or application. Has it been at least thirty days?"

My stomach rolls violently. "Yes. She was only planning to

be gone two weeks. She had to be back to work and she never showed."

"Oh no," Chantal replies, looking appalled. "You didn't tell me. I had no idea." She turns to the woman and they exchange a rapid back-and-forth before Chantal casts me a grim look. "There just isn't any chance she got married. They'd know. Maybe she and her fiancé were overzealous and didn't do their research. They could have gone out of the country to get married since two weeks isn't enough time here."

Except there's no record of her leaving, but I don't say that. "Thanks, Chantal. I'll look into other options." I fight the urge to call Chris and tell him what I've discovered. "I need to go to the consulate in the morning. I lost my passport and I want to ask questions about my friend. Could you go with me as part of my lesson?"

"Of course." She reaches out and squeezes my hand. "Don't fret. I'm sure she's fine. In fact, I bet she loved the food so much, she decided to move here and they've planned a spectacular wedding event once they've settled in."

My laugh at her joke is instant, and I embrace her suggestion with enthusiasm, hungry to believe Ella is safe and happy. "Maybe she even likes tartare," I joke.

She grins her approval. "I know what you'll like." She loops her arm in mine. "Let me show you what 'chocolate' French style is, and do some shopping. It'll make you feel better."

"Chocolate" turns out to be a hot-cocoa-like drink served with whipped cream on top at a little café off the Champs-Élysées. Absolutely decadent, it's so incredibly rich that even the chocolate lover in me can't manage more than one small cup. After our stop in the café, Chantal and I spend an hour shopping at name-brand stores and I struggle with the returned sense of being watched. I'm beginning to think this creepy feeling has more to do with being in a wholly unfamiliar place than anything else.

I've just settled in a chair outside a dressing room while Chantal tries on a sexy red dress for a date she has Saturday night, when my phone rings. It's Chris calling during a short break in meetings.

"How's shopping going?" he asks.

"No luck yet."

"Sara." His voice is filled with part reprimand, part disappointment.

Why is he pushing me so hard on this? "I'm looking, I promise."

Several seconds tick by. "I'm not your father."

My lashes lower and I struggle with the history he's hit me with; with a father who'd tried to hold me captive with his money. With my fear of becoming my mother, who was more my father's subject than his wife.

"I know, Chris." My voice is barely audible.

"Do you, baby? Because you aren't convincing me."

"Yes." And I do. Chris is exactly what Chantal had said: special. "There's no comparison."

"You aren't going to get used to having money again and then have me disappear on you. I'm not going anywhere. I made that mistake once. I won't make it twice."

"I don't care about the money. I care about us."

"Then get what you need and what you want. That's good for us."

I hear only sincerity and love in his voice. "This really means a lot to you, doesn't it?"

"It's part of us creating a new life, Sara. You have to be able to let go of the past." He pauses. "And so do I."

He's right. And coming here was part of that, for him and me.

Unbidden, Ella slides into my mind. Maybe leaving her job and even me behind was the only way she could embrace her new life?

"I'll find something I love," I promise. "How is it going there?"

We chat a bit more and we're about to hang up when Chris says teasingly, "Spend money. That's an order."

To which I reply, "Or else?"

"You don't want to know."

Yes, I do. "Oh, now you're just tempting me to burn this black AmEx you gave me."

"Sometimes, Sara," he says, his voice all sandpaper rough and wickedly suggestive, "the reward is better than the punishment." He hangs up and I laugh, biting my bottom lip as potential rewards play in my mind.

Chantal exits the dressing room, a sexy vision in the clingy red dress. "Ooooh, that's a devilish laugh you just gave. I'd love to have been on that call to hear what Chris said."

"My lips are sealed." I give her a once-over. "You're looking pretty devilish yourself. I wonder if they have that in my size?"

Her expression lights with excitement. "Finally! Let's get

you out of denim and into red silk before you change your mind."

Two hours later, Chantal and I exit one of many stores we've visited, and though it's only five thirty, we're greeted by darkness, and the chilly weather makes me wish this black leather jacket was a bit thicker.

With seven bags of various sizes and weights now to my name, I am following Chantal to the entrance of a lingerie store, appalled to discover there is not a Victoria's Secret in Paris, when Chantal's phone beeps with a text. Chantal fishes her phone from her purse, her brow furrowing as she reads the message. "My mother's sick with a stomach bug and needs me to look after my grandmother." She looks up at me. "I'm sorry. My grandmother had a stroke last month and she's just come home from rehab."

I can't believe she's apologizing. "Your grandmother is a million times more important than I am."

"I feel bad deserting you, though. Do you want me to walk back to your house with you?"

"You are too kind, but no. I'm fine."

And I am. It hits me that I haven't been feeling watched for a while now, proving my theory that I get that sensation when feeling off-kilter. "I'll see you off and shop a bit more before heading home."

"If you're sure, then"—she glances toward the road—"I need to cross the street to grab a taxi."

We dart across the road together to a line of several taxis and Chantal flags the first one in line. After tossing her bags in the back, she pauses. "It was loads of fun, Sara. I'm glad Katie called my mother and brought us together."

I'm quick to agree. I like Chantal, and finding a friend this early in my move to Paris is comforting. "Me too." I grin. "Even if you do eat snails."

She snorts out laughter and the funny sound has us both grinning. With a quick wave, she starts to get in the car. "I'll see you in the morning. Oh. Wait." She pauses halfway inside the taxi and straightens. "I've started to ask this all day, and we keep getting off the subject before I do. Is there someone else helping you look for your friend?"

My brow furrows at the unexpected question. "We do have a private eye who's been helping, but he's not been able to get much information."

"Oh, okay then. I guess he just crossed efforts with you today. The lady at City Hall said someone else had been by yesterday inquiring about Ella." She disappears into the car with a final wave.

Stunned, I stand there long after the taxi pulls away, my mind chasing Chantal's words around in circles. Blake is in the States. He didn't go by City Hall yesterday. Chris mentioned hiring someone here as well, but I'm certain he has no one on this yet. Did Blake go above and beyond and hire someone here we don't know about? That has to be it.

A horn honks and shocks me back to the present. Shifting the numerous bags in my arms, I turn toward the row of shops and restaurants behind me. Squinting, I'm almost certain I see the green lady sign that would be my coffee destination.

A white mocha and a place to sit down and call Blake to see if he did indeed hire someone is perfect. I'd like an update on Ava anyway.

Ava—how have I managed to forget that she accused me of killing Rebecca? My only answer is self-preservation: my brain decided I can handle only so much at once.

I start walking, and almost instantly my skin prickles and the hair on my nape stands up. My steps quicken with that damnable sensation of being watched, and I glance around the busy sidewalk, surveying the people hurrying to and from destinations, and identify no obvious threat.

And why would I? This is just the control freak in me struggling with the unknown of a new city, paired with the stress of the past few days, triggered by thoughts of Ella and Ava. Nothing more. I think. I hope. My reasoning isn't comforting.

I'm three stores from Starbucks, counting the doors to a safe public place.

One more door and I'm at Starbucks, about to go inside, when I stop dead in my tracks. In disbelief, I blink at the sign hanging above the next store: THE SCRIPT. Amber's tattoo parlor. The door to the parlor starts to open, and adrenaline surges through me.

Acting on pure instinct, I dart inside Starbucks, desperate not to be seen. Inside, warm air washes over me along with a strong dose of relief. I glance around the tiny café with limited seating, like everywhere I've been in Paris thus far, and I go to the counter.

"English?" I ask the tall, dark-haired man behind the counter, and receive a highly accented, "Yes. English."

"Oh, thank you." My stress level lowers instantly, my shoulders relaxing and my pulse slowing. It's amazing how a little thing like ordering my favorite drink in English can be so immensely comforting. "White Mocha. Nonfat. No foam."

I glance at the glass case by the register, delighted to find all my favorites from back in the States. I've had macarons and chocolate today and don't need anything else, but my finger has a mind of its own and points to an oversized sugar cookie with icing.

The employee speaks my silent language even better than English, and I'm quickly handed my cookie in a bag.

Once I've paid, I scoot to the end of the bar, juggle my bags, and somehow manage to gobble—okay, inhale—my cookie while I wait on my drink. I analyze why I was so desperate to escape an encounter with Amber. No, why I'd run away from one.

My lips twist in disapproval of my actions. What am I doing? Sure, Chris doesn't want me around Tristan and I'm not a fan of Amber, but really? Running away? Hiding? If there's anything Chris has helped me see, it's that I have a tendency to run and call it avoidance, and it doesn't work. By the time my coffee is set on the counter, I'm completely angry with myself for being a coward.

I glance around at the wooden tables and there are none available. I sigh and conclude I have to head home to call Blake, assuring myself the decision has nothing to do with a worry that I might run into Amber. Nevertheless, I pause with my hand on the door and steel myself for the highly unlikely chance I might run into her.

I step outside and immediately head toward the Script, past the window painted with a collection of tattoo-like graphics, and I don't know why, but I stop. Cement seems to form around my feet.

I know Chris doesn't want me to meet this Tristan guy. Actually, he expressed concern at him being my private tutor. Absolute disapproval would be a more valid description, but meeting him and having him become my tutor are two different things.

My fingers curl around the bag handles. I'm justifying standing here, and I know it, and I force myself to admit the real temptation that has me frozen in place. What I'd really been running from when I'd rushed into Starbucks. I want to go inside.

I want to know who Amber is, and what she once was to Chris. I want to know what this place was to him, what it might still be to him. But in my heart, I know Chris wants to show me these things himself. I know he won't like that I'm here.

That's all that matters. *He* matters. My decision becomes cemented in my mind.

I'm not going in.

I glance forward, and realize home is back the other way. I turn around to depart.

"Sara."

I hear Amber's voice and pause, more of that cement sucking the movement from my feet. If I were an artist, I would paint myself in a box. Instead, I'm a fool who's just ensured trouble for myself with a certain famous, sometimes cranky, painter of my own. I can't walk away from this encounter without potentially coming off weak, and thus more of a target to Amber than I already am.

Cringing, I turn to face her. "Amber," I manage in greeting, and her name sounds as bitter as it tastes on my tongue. "Hi." Before I can stop myself, my gaze sweeps her very different appearance today, taking in the red streaks woven into her blond hair that match the shiny red pants she's paired with black knee-high boots. Her heels are so high they could be registered weapons, and I sure as heck will think twice about ticking her off.

Her lips twist into a knowing smile that says "caught ya," and I assume she means checking her out, but I'm wrong. "Changed your mind about coming inside, I guess?"

Of course she'd seen me in the window. How could she not have? "Actually, I was trying to remember which direction my house is." I lift my Starbucks cup, attempting a fast recovery. "An addiction I'll indulge in frequently here, I'm sure. I need to be able to find my way from it to my house on a regular basis."

"Right. Well, you're here now. Why not bring your American addiction inside and see my place?"

Let me count the reasons why not. Chris. Chris. And Chris. Repeat ten times.

But Amber's watching me, her expression filled with a challenge that can be about only one thing, or rather, person, to which the same answer repeats itself. Chris.

"For a minute," I agree, walking toward her, still in the establishing backbone territory with her. "I'm meeting Chris for dinner soon."

Her gaze cuts to the side a moment and I am shaken by the

blast of emotions waving off of her and into me. Pain. Resentment. Jealousy. Affected by the magnitude of what I sense in her, I stop next to her and actually have to fight the urge to comfort her, reminding myself these are the same emotions that led Ava to very bad, very dark actions.

Her head turns sharply, icy blue eyes locking with mine. "Maybe I'll join you for dinner."

A shiver races down my spine at the hatred I'd seen for an instant in the kitchen last night. "We'll have to set that up sometime." Memories of what jealousy did to Ava soften my tone far more than Amber's five-inch heels ever could.

I head inside the Script and find myself in a warehouse-like, modern-looking open space. Wall-to-wall frames are filled with tattoo designs, and saucer-shaped silver lamps dangle over two shiny white tables with curved edges sitting side by side. Behind them is an open doorway leading to what appears to be a room filled with numerous tables and leather chairs.

I make a beeline for a chair in front of one of the tables, when a man appears in the open doorway, and it's all I can do to keep walking. Dressed in black leather pants and a T-shirt, he is tall, with wavy raven hair to his chin, and perfect, masculine facial features. But it's not his looks that have me ready to stumble over my own feet. It's the way he oozes the kind of power Mark does and leaves me with two certainties. He is Tristan and he is a Master.

He leans against the wall directly across from the table I've stopped at, crossing his heavily tattooed arms in front of his broad chest. I stare at them, expecting some fizzle of female awareness like I get from Chris's, and find none. Huh. I'm still not a tattoo girl. I'm a Chris girl. The idea makes me smile in-side. Yes. I am definitely a Chris girl.

"Hello, Sara," he says, his voice a deep, rich, highly accented tone, his intelligent eyes assessing me with far more interest than I'm comfortable with.

I set my bags down and claim the chair in front of the table, instinctively playing the power game Mark has taught me to engage in so well. "Hello, Tristan."

His lips quirk. "You know who I am."

"You know who I am."

"Amber described you quite well," he assures me, a bit too much suggestiveness to his tone.

Considering Amber has seen me naked, I really don't want to know what that means.

Amber sits behind the table in front of me. "I left out the more intimate details," she says, clearly reading my mind, before rolling her chair over so that she can see both of us.

My cell phone rings and I dig it out of my purse and, rather than my normal pleasure at the sight of his number, my heart plummets when it's Chris calling. I close my eyes and push the answer button. "Hey," I say, and my voice sounds as tentative as I feel.

"Hey, baby. I just turned onto Champs-Élysées. Where are you? I'll pick you up so we can go eat."

I inhale deeply, the breath splintering through my lungs like shards of glass. He isn't going to be happy, but I have to tell him the truth. I've had a lifetime of people lying to me. I won't lie to Chris. I won't do that to our relationship. "I stopped at Star-bucks, and—"

"You're at the Script, aren't you?"

His voice is tight, hard, and I can barely find mine. "Yes," I whisper.

"Is Chantal with you?"

"No. Her mother was sick and she had to leave."

There's a dreaded tense silence before he says, "I'll be right there."

Ten

❧

"Chris isn't happy you're here," Amber comments before I've even had time to stick my phone back inside my purse.

"Why do you say that?" I sound as defensive as I feel.

"Sweetheart," Amber purrs, "I read your expression like it was a book."

"Le Professeur."

My attention lifts to Tristan, still leaning against the wall, and who logic tells me has just said "teacher." I have the distinct impression his oddly timed insertion into the conversation is an effort to deflate the situation before war breaks out.

"Teacher," he confirms in English. "I hear you need one."

There is a message buried in the heaviness of his stare that tells me he isn't talking about French. "No. I have a teacher I'm quite satisfied with."

Amber snorts. "He's teaching now, is he?" Bitterness tinges the clear insult.

My gaze lands hard on her, and I open my mouth to defend Chris, planning to hold nothing back—but in the process my attention lands on her arm, which is resting on the table. The material has climbed up enough for me to see more of her skin, and my lips part at what I find.

Without conscious thought, I grab her wrist to hold her in place and see the familiar marks I once saw on Chris's skin. The marks made by a sharply landed whip.

Ice slides down my spine. Suddenly, Amber is so much more than a bitter ex-girlfriend of Chris's. She is damaged like him, like *me,* someone I relate to. Someone I understand.

My gaze lifts to hers and my throat is thick, my words hoarsely spoken. "What happened to you?"

Shock registers on her face, and I know she knows what I mean. Her lashes lower, blocking out my inspection. When they lift she meets my stare, and contempt pours from her, but it does nothing to hide the pain I now know runs far deeper than a mere breakup with Chris.

"He isn't much of a teacher, if you don't know what happened to me," she finally grinds out between clenched teeth.

I flick a look at Tristan. "I know he did this to you." I don't wait for his reaction or hers, watching Amber as I clarify as if she doesn't understand when she does. "I didn't ask how this happened to you. I asked *what* happened to you." What horrible something she was hiding from inside her pain.

Her glare is a mix of fire and ice that would intimidate someone else, but not me. Not someone who understands burying pain as damn well as I do. "Chris happened to me," she hisses between her teeth, and yanks her arm back.

Chris happened to her? Tilting my head to study her, I try to read what's deeper than the surface.

"Sara."

Chris's voice surprises me, and I guiltily jump to my feet as if I've just delved into some sort of secret territory. And maybe I have. I don't know.

He's standing to the left of Tristan, by what must be a back entryway. Did he hear the exchange? I think he must have. All I know for certain is how completely he has stolen every ounce of energy in the room, how the air crackles around him, and I'm struck by how easily this occurred. Casually dressed in his standard faded jeans and a T-shirt, he owns the room, where Tristan needs his leather and tats, and Mark his custom suits.

"Chris," I say because, well, it's all I seem to be able to think to say.

"Let's go," he orders, and the room pulses with the push of power behind the softly spoken command and, yes, the anger.

Tristan says something in French, and I'm not sure if he's speaking to Chris or Amber. I think Amber.

Chris's stare lingers on me several seconds before he casts a hard look on Tristan. Tristan gives him a nod. "Long time, man."

"Maybe not long enough."

Tristan smirks. "You say that every time you come home."

"Because you're always here."

Holding his hands up, Tristan laughs. "You're the one who keeps coming back."

They begin speaking in French, and a subtle tension builds. They don't hate each other, but Chris simply doesn't want me around Tristan. I have the sense that he's making sure Tristan is just as clear as I am on that point.

Hating that I can't understand what's being said, I reach down to grab my bags. Chris is there to help before I have time to gather them. Our hands collide, warmth climbing up my arm, and my eyes meet his. His stare is a pure, possessive demand that once would have set my defenses into overdrive. Now I see beyond his surface to the acid I've stirred to life with my actions. If I could turn back the clock fifteen minutes and change my decision to come here, I would.

"Chris—" Amber starts.

"You've said enough, Amber," he snaps, not even looking at her. I realize he hasn't looked at her since he arrived and I wonder what that means, but, honestly, I don't care. I shouldn't have come here. There's plenty about Amber I have to learn, and as impatient as I feel to know those things, Chris needs to decide when to tell me.

Still watching me, Chris bends and claims my last bag, leaving me with my purse to hold. "Anything else?" he asks.

I shake my head, unable to speak for the guilt eating me alive. I did this. I made him feel whatever bad thing he's feeling. I don't care about anything Tristan and Amber could show or tell me, but he doesn't know that. So I haven't done a good enough job of showing him how much I love him, or he would.

I step to his side and we head for the back door, and he motions me in front of him to exit down a long, narrow hallway. He reaches around me to open the door, and for a moment his hand lingers on the surface, his body close to mine but not touching me. I want him to touch me. Seconds tick by and I hold my breath, waiting for what he will say, but there's only silence. He opens the door, and disappointment fills me at the lingering tension between us. But this isn't the place to clear the air—not with a potential audience.

Outside I find a parking lot that holds only six cars, and Chris's silver 911 is one of the three present. I quickly head for the passenger door, eager to be alone with him and explain myself. Impatiently, I wait while Chris places my bags in the backseat.

He turns to me, his jaw set hard and a reserved look in his eyes. "Get in the car, Sara."

I decide now isn't the time to get through to him. "All right, Chris—but not because you bark a command at me. Because I want to be far away from here when I make you hear me out." I fold myself into the leather seat.

He just stands there, staring down at me, but I don't look at him. Sometimes, I'm not sure he knows how to digest my responses to his demands. Sometimes I don't, either, but this time I do. No matter how much I might deserve his anger, he isn't my Master. So my snapping back at his orders shouldn't surprise him.

He joins me in the car and we are closed in the darkness and his wrist settles on the steering wheel, but he doesn't look at me. I sense him struggling with himself and I think he's going to say something, but he doesn't. And I don't. He starts the engine and puts the car in gear. I'm pretty certain the next few blocks are going to feel eternal, and I'm right. They do.

Feeling the stuffiness of both the car heater and our pent-up emotions, I've taken my jacket off by the time we pull into the garage at our house, and Chris is out of the 911 almost instantly. He rounds the car and opens my door, but he doesn't look at me. I grind my teeth. One incident, this easily, and he's shutting me out. It cuts like splintering little pieces of glass in my heart.

I step back to allow him to retrieve my bags, and fight the instinct to emotionally withdraw myself as well, to protect myself. I'm still fighting that feeling when we head toward the elevator entrance, neither of us looking at each other, still locked in a silence I can barely stand.

He punches the elevator button and I stare at his profile, wisps of blond hair framing his handsome face, and I watch the pulse of a muscle in his jaw. I sense his distance, his withdrawal, and suddenly I'm angry all over again.

I've traveled across the world for Chris. I came here to fight for us, and I intend to do just that. He is *not* shutting me out and tearing us apart over one stupid mistake. I won't let him do this to me or us. Never again.

The elevator opens and he waits for me to enter, and I do. I rush inside and whirl around to confront him. He stalks forward and this time he doesn't avoid looking at me, his expression etched with pure determination and some raw, dark emotion I can't fully name. I don't get the chance to try.

Before a word is out of my mouth, the bags he's holding hit the floor and Chris has pressed me back against the wall. My purse tumbles from my arm and his powerful thighs encase mine; his hips mold my hips. I gasp with the rough tangle of his fingers in my hair and the blaze of his eyes as they capture mine. I am angry with him. I am aroused. And when his mouth claims my mouth, his tongue slicing past my lips with a delicious lick followed by another, demanding my response, I am at his mercy.

My fingers curl around his T-shirt and I press away the tiny space between us, molding myself against him. He owns me and, considering how the past thirty minutes have gone, this terrifies me, but I'm all in with Chris. I decided that long before Paris. I am his to command, moaning with the taste of him, sultry and male, on my tongue.

His hand sweeps up my side, fingers flexing over my ribs, palm covering my breast. My nipple tightens in anticipation of the tug that follows and I moan, my need to touch him almost unbearable. I reach for his shirt, intending to push beneath, but he doesn't let me.

Chris's fingers close around my wrist and I know he is in that dark place, where he doesn't let me touch him—but I am in a dark place, too, on edge, ripe with my anger and unwilling to be submissive to him. Challenging his silent message of control, I reach for his shirt with my free hand. He shackles that wrist as well and tears his mouth from mine. Our eyes lock, the sound of our heavy breathing filling the air and the motion of the elevator swaying our bodies. The floor vibrates slightly beneath our feet and I sense, rather than see, the doors behind Chris slide open, but still we stand there, still we stare at each other.

"They don't get to tell you who I am." His voice is a rough growl, low and tight. "I do. I tell you and I show you, so you get the truth—not their fabrication of it." A muscle in his jaw flexes. "Understand?"

My anger and fear dissolve instantly. He's not pulling away

from me. He's angry that Amber and Tristan might taint my view of him, when he's already convinced I'll hate him before this discovery process is over.

"Do you understand?" he demands when I apparently don't answer fast enough.

This time I don't fight the bark of his order, understanding the desperateness beneath its surface. "Yes. Yes, Chris. I—"

His fingers tangle in my hair again, tugging my head back in that deliciously rough way he does. Dark Chris calls to me and I no longer fight answering. "Do not go there without me again." His voice is raw, like the emotion I've seen in his face and tasted on his lips.

"It wasn't what you think it was, Chris."

His eyes flash with disapproval. He isn't pleased, or accepting, of what I've said, and his mouth closes down on mine, punishing, controlling. His tongue thrusting and tasting before he repeats his words, his fingers stroking my breasts, teasing my nipple. "Do not go there again without me, Sara."

"I won't." The words come out a hoarse groan as his hand strokes a path up and down my side, and back over my breast. His touch is heavy, the air thick, and I'm certain he isn't convinced. "I won't go back without you."

His fingers curl around my neck and he stares down at me, searching my face with such intensity it feels as if he's seeing straight to my soul. And I welcome the invasion. I welcome him. Seconds tick by, and I have no idea what he sees or doesn't see in me, but he drags my mouth to his and kisses me.

The silky hot stroke of his tongue is a shot of adrenaline and desire that spikes through my body and creates a tingling sensation from head to toe. I shudder with pleasure and drink him in, tasting the bittersweet hunger in him, the anger and torment. I burn to touch him beyond where my fingers rest on his chest, to feel hard muscle flex beneath my fingers.

But control is his outlet of choice when there is no whip, no pain. And I'm no longer angry, no longer rebelling against his demands. No longer fighting his need for an outlet I have long ached for him to know that he has with me, in me.

I tremble with the caress of his hand over my waist, traveling to my hip, and curving around my backside to firmly pull me hard against his thick erection. His palm skims upward to the small of my back and flattens, molding me even closer. I moan into his mouth and he groans in response, his tongue delving deeply, hot with growing demand, with a palpable urgency. And his hands are everywhere, touching me, stroking me, caressing me, driving me wild and, before I know what's happening, he's shoving my jeans down my legs. I blink and my boots are gone, and I'm half naked in an elevator with the doors locked open.

Chris turns me to the wall and his hands slide, slow and firm, possessively down my waist and over my hips. Feeling his gaze rake over my body, I am wet and weak in the knees. He cups my cheeks from behind and steps forward, pressing his lips to my ear. "Tonight I want to spank you, but I won't. Not when it would be punishment. I won't ever do that to you. But don't think that means I won't want to."

I understand Chris. I don't know how or why, but deep in our souls we connect, and I know what he is doing. He's showing me a hard exterior, but all I see is vulnerability, a need that tonight has sparked to show me a darker, more dangerous side of himself, and have me not run for cover.

"You can't scare me away, Chris. So throw all the words you want at me. I'm still here. I'm not going anywhere. And in case you forgot, I liked it when you spanked me."

His hand finds my stomach and then presses deeper between my legs, until his fingers tease my clit. "Maybe this time I'll tie you up and flog you."

"Do it." His fingers stroke into the silky wet V of my body, and I am panting, barely able to speak, but I swallow and somehow finish my challenge. "The more you push me, the more I push back, Chris."

He nips my earlobe and I can feel him unzipping his pants. "So you say," he murmurs.

"So I know." Throwing caution to the wind, I press onward, trying to unleash the pent-up energy in him he always bottles up until it explodes. "Only one of us is running. Only one of us is afraid of what I have yet to discover, Chris."

The air crackles and his hand goes to my waist, fingers flexing into my flesh, and I revel in the certainty I've succeeded in taking him to the edge. "You think I'm running?" he demands.

"No. I think you're trying to make *me* run, so you can blame me if we fail."

His cock presses between my legs. "Does that feel like I want you to run?" He enters me, driving hard inside me without any prelude. "Does that?" And then he is thrusting, reaching around me to meld his hand to my breast, holding on to it, and me. He thrusts again, burying himself, with a fieriness that outreaches pure physical need.

Oh yes, I have made him angry and I'm glad. I want this side of him; I want all of him. And damn it, he keeps trying to deny me. He keeps trying to hold back and, yes, he keeps trying to make me run.

Pressing my hand to his, I meld it to my breast, holding him there, never planning to let him go. Pleasure splinters through me with each thrust of his cock, each moment he's buried deep inside me. Sensation after sensation begins in my sex and rushes through nerve endings. I am lost in how he feels, how I feel, and I arch into him, my muscles clench around him, and then I can't breathe. My orgasm takes me by surprise, enveloping me, consuming me. I rise to the top of it far too quickly and come down far too hard and fast, but just in time to feel Chris shudder, his body tensing with his release. He stills, burying his face in my neck, and his body slowly relaxes. For several moments he holds me there, and I'm not sure either of us breathes, let alone speaks or moves. I'm not sure what to say or do next.

Abruptly, he pulls out of me, and I don't know why, but an unusual sense of complete, utter emptiness washes over me. The "why" is answered when I start to turn to find him already headed out of the elevator. I stare after him, knots balling in my stomach. Maybe I pushed the wrong buttons. Maybe I pushed him to far or too hard. Maybe I made a mistake.

Saturday, July 14, 2012

I'm sitting on a plane, heading back to San Francisco, and I'm nervous and excited. I'm not completely sure why I'm nervous and I'm going to spend some time on the flight thinking about that. It's not logical. Especially since I know why I'm so excited. And it's not just about going back to "him," either.

It's home. Traveling isn't what I crave. Maybe one day I will. Maybe one day I will want to see the world beyond the eyes of the many famous artists I admire. Right now, though, I need stability. I need what I can count on. I need a sense of who I am. I hope he is a part of who I am, but I think our time apart was good. As much as I missed him while I was away, as eager as I am to return to San Francisco, this trip helped me finish the process of finding myself again. Of knowing what it means to be Rebecca Mason, not just "his."

I hope he and I truly will find each other again. If he means what he promised, that things will be different, then maybe they

129

will. If we don't, though, I believe in myself enough again to be willing to leave him behind. This brings me back to the nerves. I guess I know what they're about after all. If he and I are going to be together, we have to define what that means. I'm not sure he can be himself when I'm truly me, but I have to know. And, I think, so does he.

Eleven

⚜

Staring after Chris, it takes me all of sixty seconds to decide that being half naked is not the best way to pursue him and demand a conversation. I need a bathroom to pull myself together first. I stuff my pants and boots in a shopping bag, gather the rest of my haul along with my purse, and go into the hallway. Rushing toward the bedroom, all too aware of my naked backside I worry Chris will be there waiting for me and I'll be at a disadvantage. Pulse racing, I enter an empty room. The relief I expect to feel is no more in sight than Chris. What if he left the house through the front door? Where would he go? When would he return? And why am I worrying, when he might simply be somewhere else in the house?

By the time I'm dressed, I'm at the top of a curve on a roller-coaster ride of emotions that started the day I met Chris and has yet to end. The room is empty without him, and my mind is already going wild with the possibility of finding him gone. I tell myself it will mean nothing; he'll be back. We'll be okay. He thinks I betrayed him by going to the Script, which hurts, but I think he's hurting, too. The idea of hurting him when he's lived a lifetime of pain is too much to bear.

I dart for the hallway and all but run up the stairs leading to the upper level of the house—the location of Chris's studio, which he'd planned to show me tonight. If he's still home, my instincts tell me, he'll be there. At the top of the landing I discover two halls leading left and right, but the towering, castle-like silver arched doorways are what hold me spellbound—but not just for the unique artistic statement they make. For the unique artist I just know is beyond them. A sharp twist tightens my belly. This is his castle and, like my new home, I'd wanted to explore it in a positive moment, not in the midst of emotional havoc.

Creaking open the door, I find towering ceilings and darkness pierced only by the warm glow of natural moonlight radiating from a window or skylight. Awareness fills me instantly and I feel Chris before I see him, his presence pouring through me like warm sunshine on a cold, lonely day.

As I step fully into the shadows, my attention is riveted to where Chris is leaning with one hand on the wall, his back to me, looking out of a ceiling-to-floor archway window resembling the doors behind me. He doesn't turn or speak, but the subtle shift in the air tells me he's aware that I'm here.

My hesitation is a brief moment before I dart forward. I simply don't have it in me to ride this emotional roller coaster for a few more turns, and I'm not sure Chris does, either. My impatience to end the tension between us is so extreme that

I don't stop when I'm right behind him. I place myself in the small space between him and the wall and blink up at him.

He stares down at me, his lashes a veil shielding his eyes, and he says nothing, does nothing. I know this man as I have never known another human being, and he's waiting for me to say or do the right or wrong thing. And the only right thing I know is to be honest.

I close the small space between us and settle my hands on his waist, relieved when he lets me. Unsurprised when he doesn't touch me. "You asked me to hear you out last night. Now I'm asking you to do the same of me. I didn't intend to go to the Script."

"And yet you did."

His tone is flat, hard, but at least he's talking. "I went to Starbucks, not Amber's place."

"And the temptation to go next door was too much."

"I won't lie and say I wasn't tempted to discover what was inside." My hand moves to his arm, splaying over his dragon. "This is part of you, and I don't know why, but it feels almost a part of us. Yet she created it. So yes. I'm curious about her and it, and I don't even know if it was done at the Script."

"It wasn't. And if you want to know about my past, you ask me."

My hand flexes on his arm, and I have to warn myself to fight one battle at a time. He says ask him, but he gives me pieces, not complete stories. "I didn't ask her about you. Not one single question."

"We both know you don't have to. She's more than eager to share her version of who I am."

"I, of all people, understand where you're coming from. I remember how much I needed to tell you my past in my way. Michael stole that from me by showing up at the charity event. I won't do that to you."

His hand goes to my wrist at his waist and I'm certain he's thinking about removing it. "Apparently that memory didn't dissuade you, considering you went inside anyway. And you knew she'd open up doors I wasn't ready to open."

My fingers curl around his shirt, clinging to the material and with it, him. "That's not true. Or it is, but that's not what I was thinking at the time. She came outside as I was walking away. I felt trapped. She tried to intimidate me, Chris. If she's going to be around, and clearly she is, I felt I couldn't show her any sign of weakness."

"So you disregarded how much I don't want you there." It's not a question.

"You never said you didn't want me there."

His eyes turn as steely as his voice. "I didn't have to. You knew, Sara."

He's right. I knew. "I was weak." I feel my bottom lip tremble and my chest feels like it's going to cave in. "I should have walked away."

"Yes." He reaches down and drags my hands from where they rest to settle them between us. "You should have."

"I tried. I just . . . I had one of those 'who has the bigger, ah, sword' encounters you and Mark have but deny." This half joke gets me nothing. He just keeps staring at me with hard eyes.

I drop my head to his chest, knowing what I haven't said and have to admit. "I can't believe I'm going to say this out loud." I draw a breath and force my chin up. "Right or wrong, I needed her to know I could and would protect what is mine."

Seconds tick by before he softly asks, "Which is what, Sara?"

The husky quality to his voice gives me courage. "You," I whisper. "I needed her to know you belong to me now."

He studies me for what feels like an eternity, not denying or confirming my claim. His expression is still so damn unreadable. I am going insane waiting on his reply until finally he asks, "That's why you went inside?"

"Yes, it is. I just . . . couldn't help myself."

Slowly, the corners of his mouth lift and his body relaxes. A moment later, his strong arms wrap around me and he buries his face in my neck, the earthy, wonderful scent of him tickling my nose. "I love you, woman." He strokes my hair from my face and leans back to stare down at me. "And you can claim me as yours any day of the week. I plan to claim you."

"You're not upset anymore?"

"If it had been Mark, I'd have done the same damn thing."

I scowl. "If? You *did* do the same damn thing on numerous occasions."

He laughs. "Okay. Maybe I did." His hands settle possessively on my hips. "Remember. I do own you, baby."

"In bed," I amend. "The rest of the time, I own me." I smile. "And you."

He grins. "I suggest we debate both points after dinner." He pauses for effect. "In bed."

Thirty minutes later Chris and I are sitting side by side, our legs molded intimately together, in a surprisingly spacious Mexican restaurant at a table for four, rather than a saucer-sized table for two. Apparently seating two people at a larger table is some kind of cardinal sin in Paris—unless the price is right. Chris tipped the waiter what I assume was a healthy chunk of change and we scored our happy seat.

Finishing off a chip, I am rather impressed with the food. "If the meal's as good as the salsa, I'm going to be a happy girl."

"It is," Chris assures me. "I told you. I know all the American hot spots."

I lean against the wall, angling my body in his direction and he faces me as well, setting a hand on my knee. "Does finding the American hot spots keep you from missing the States?" I ask.

"Spending a lot of time in the States keeps me from missing the States."

My curiosity over his desire to be in Paris continues. "How much time do you spend here versus in San Francisco?"

"It depends on my charity commitments."

An unpleasant thought hits me. "If I get a job here and you have commitments in the States, I'll have to stay here without you."

He sets his beer down and settles both his hands on my knees. "I don't want to go anywhere without you, Sara, which is why I suggested you start your own art business. Call me selfish, but I'd like you to travel with me. I also don't want to pressure you to do anything but what you want to do. If you want a job in the art industry here, or anywhere for that matter, I have no doubt your love and knowledge of art, along with your charm, will allow you to get whatever job you want."

Hearing Chris Merit say this about me is an amazing feeling. Yes, he's the man in my life, but he is also a brilliant, respected artist who doesn't give away meaningless compliments. "Thank you, Chris."

"Thank you?" His brow furrows and he takes my hand. "For what?"

I brush a wispy strand of blond hair from the healing cut on his forehead and repeat what I'd told him at the airport. "For believing in me, but most of all for being you."

There is a flash of some unreadable emotion in his eyes; then his deliciously sexy mouth, which I can think of any number of ways to put to use, curves into a smile. "I like it when you say that."

"I like that you want me with you. And I'm excited about the idea of starting my own business and, despite flying, traveling with you."

His smile is brilliant, free of any conflicting emotions. "You'll get used to flying, and I have no doubt you'll make your business a huge success."

He's happy. Happy that we'll have more time together, and happy for me to have a career of my own. I wasn't wrong to come here with him. I was more right than I've ever been about anything in my life.

"I ran the business idea by the attorney today," he continues. "You just need to call him and do the basic setup."

Attorney. I stiffen, remembering Ava's accusations against me. I have no idea why I need a reminder, how anyone puts this kind of thing aside for any amount of time. But I have and I did. It's like my mind turns certain things on and off at certain times, to keep me from going into overload. I swallow hard. "The same attorney who's talking to the police for me?"

"No. Two different people, but I talked to both today."

My heart begins to race. "Why didn't you tell me? Did he talk to the police yet? Do I have to go back to the States? Please tell me you aren't trying to protect me from some epic melt-down, because—"

He kisses me, his warm lips lingering on mine for several seconds, and miraculously my heartbeat begins to slow. "Easy, baby," he murmurs. "Everything is fine. If I knew anything, I'd tell you. Stephen and the detective played phone tag all day. He called me just before I went to pick you up at the Script, and they have a phone conference in about an hour. Stephen's going to contact us afterward."

He removes my hand from my chest, where I've balled it into a fist, opens my palm, and laces his fingers with mine. "I'll have you talk to Stephen to give you some peace of mind. He's very good at his job, and you'll know it when you talk to him."

I lift our hands and press his to my cheek. "I just want this to be over."

"I know, and I hate you're worrying yourself over this. It's going to blow over quickly."

"I hope so." An idea hits me. "Can we call Mark? Maybe he's heard something about the police investigation?"

Chris's lashes lower and he sighs before leaning back in his seat. "Yeah, well. Mark. There's another story altogether. I talked to him."

I tense at his bleak tone. "When? What did he say?"

"Today. He's in New York. His mother's in the hospital, and he's by her bedside."

My lips part at the horrible timing. "Oh, no. What's wrong with her? Please tell me it's not serious."

"Breast cancer."

Unbidden, I see a flash of Dylan's frail, cancer-sickened body, and the vision punches me in the chest. Certain Chris must be thinking of him, too, I lace my fingers through his. "How bad is she?"

"Stage three. They caught it early. She's having a mastectomy tomorrow, and since it's a Friday he's staying the weekend and flying back home Monday to meet with the police. He's pissed about Ava twisting things in knots and pulling him away from his family right now. He told me to tell you he'll deal with her." He smiles. "And you know Mark. If he says it, he means it. So stop worrying. Between me, Mark, and Stephen, you have a lion, a tiger, and a bear on your side."

Amused, I ask, "Which are you?"

"All three when I have to be—and for you, baby, I'll do it all."

My hand closes over his tattoo, thick muscle flexing beneath my palm, his expression turning alluringly sexual. My body tingles to life with my ability to affect him with a simple touch. "I'll take the dragon." I don't try to hide how much I want him. "Just the dragon."

His eyes gloss slightly, his lashes lowering, but not before I see a flash of the same emotion from a few minutes before. I cup his face, urging him to look at me.

"Monsieur Chris," a man says from beside our table.

Chris and I both turn to inspect our visitor. Recognition flashes on Chris's face and he pushes to his feet to shake the hand of a short, dark-haired man who looks to be in his fifties, and introduces him to me as an employee of one of the many galleries in Paris. I listen as the two talk and laugh, and I understand nothing they say, but I can see how much the man likes Chris. Everyone likes Chris, and so few know the haunted man beneath the surface. But I do. Or do I? He doesn't seem to think I do. With all I've seen, all we've been through, what could possibly still be bad enough for him to dread sharing it with me?

Our visitor departs as our food arrives, before I can let my mind run too wild with possibilities that can only do more harm than good. My worries slide away as plates filled with delicious Mexican food are set in front of us. Chris rubs his palms together and pats my leg. "You're going to love it."

I smile at his contagious enthusiasm and do exactly as he suggests. I dig into my cheese enchiladas while Chris watches for a reaction, and their spicy, yummy flavor explodes in my mouth. "Mmm," I manage as I swallow. "It's terrific." I scoop up some of the sauce and swallow. "Really terrific."

Chris scoops up a forkful of his chicken enchilada and holds it to my mouth. "Try mine."

I accept the bite and he slowly removes the fork from my mouth, watching me, his eyes brimming with hunger—and not for food. "Good?" he asks, and his voice has a soft, velvety quality.

"Yes." My voice is raspy, and not from the spicy heat of the food. "Very good." But not as good as him.

He eases closer and brushes his mouth over mine. "It tastes better on your lips than mine."

I blush as he leans back again. I never understand how he still makes me blush, but he does.

He's smiling at my reaction, his expression pure male satisfaction. "Now do you believe you can eat well in Paris?"

I'm pretty sure everything will taste better with Chris around. "I do believe you've convinced me."

Our eyes collide and our laughter fades. The air thickens and something I can't name sparks between us, tingling through my body. "I wouldn't steer you wrong, Sara," he says, and there is a rasp in his voice where there had been velvet before. He's not talking about food anymore, and the sincerity in the depths of his stare touches me deeply.

"I know," I whisper. And I do know. I really, really do. This man has all of me, or . . . no. That's not true, and it hurts to admit this, even to myself. He has almost all of me. It's hard not to hold back a small bit, when I know I don't have all of him.

Twelve

The attorney calls Chris during our ride home from the restaurant and, as promised, Chris has me talk to him directly. Despite having little new to tell me, Stephen does make me feel better, assuring me the police efforts are just due diligence and I have nothing to worry about. And no, I don't have to leave Paris.

I actually relax and Chris and I plan our exploration of the city together. We debate which exhibits we want to visit first, and I decide I'm a *very* lucky girl. I am going to view famous art with a famous artist as my guide. It's a dream come true.

"My only commitment is a boys' sleepover camp for disabled kids Friday night, at the Louvre," Chris says as we turn onto Foche Avenue near our house.

"No meetings?"

"No meetings," he confirms. "Which means I'm free to take you to some of the museums and introduce you to some important people in the industry."

"Who I won't be able to talk to."

"There's plenty of people who speak English." His phone rings for the third time since we've been talking, and he glances at the screen before declining the call. His attention turns back to me, a subtle tension in him that hadn't been there moments before. "This whole city feeds off tourism, especially from Americans. There are more people who speak English than you might think here."

"I still want to break down the language barrier," I say, though I'm wondering about the two unanswered calls. Whoever it is, he doesn't want to talk to them in front of me. I think it's Amber. She knows he's pissed, and my womanly instinct says she won't let what happened earlier at her shop pass without contacting him.

We pull up to the gate of the house, and Chris rolls down his window to key in the entry code. A moment later we're pulling into the garage attached to the house.

His house. I'm never going to fully feel like I'm at home until these secrets stop dividing us.

Inside, I make my escape to a hot bubble bath, intending to pull my jumbled thoughts into some kind of order. I'm not going to let myself think about Chris returning his calls to . . . whomever, since I'm liable to let my imagination run wild.

I've barely buried myself in bubbles to my chin when Chris saunters into the bathroom with a glass of wine in his hand and sits down on the edge of the tub. "This'll help calm your nerves," he says, offering it to me. "I have an extensive cellar outside the city that my father left me. I keep a few bottles here for guests."

Wine his father, the wine expert who drank himself to death on wine, left for him.

Uncomfortable with the thought, I set the glass on the other side of the tub.

I grab his shirt and wrap my wet hand around it, tugging his mouth near mine. "Thanks, but I don't want it. I just want you."

He looks at me knowingly. "The past is the past. I'm putting it behind me, and us."

Unease stirs inside me. This fits into his need for control in some way, but I'm not sure how. "The past is a part of you and us. You can store it away someplace different, but you can't make it go away. And you can't even resolve it until you, we, face it."

"What do you think I'm trying to do?"

Maybe this isn't about control at all. Maybe it's about losing it. Maybe bringing me here, exposing himself to me for what I believe he sees as judgment, is doing a rare number on him. Am I selfishly pushing him too hard and too fast? Stripping him naked too quickly? "Chris—"

His cell phone rings and he squeezes his eyes shut. "I should check it in case it's important."

"I know." I wish I could throw the phone in the tub.

He doesn't move, lingering as if he feels the same way. The ringing stops and his lips twitch. "I guess it wasn't important." He leans in closer, and my heart begins to race with the promise of his mouth against mine.

The phone starts ringing again.

Chris curses and starts to move away, and I reluctantly release his shirt. He stands up, tugging his cell from his jeans pocket, his face impassive as he looks at the number and hits "end." There's an instant pinch in my chest, and I quickly roll to my side so Chris can't see my reaction. At least he's still declining the call. Apparently he didn't return the prior calls while I was running my bath. Or maybe he did and "the person" is calling back.

"Amber."

My stomach clenches at her name and I roll back over to face him, feeling exposed, thankful for the bubbles still brimming to my neck. "What?"

"You want to know who's calling. It's Amber."

"Oh." My reply lacks finesse, but considering the edginess of his mood, it's better than the "I know" I almost said. "Why don't you take her calls?"

He runs a rough hand through his hair, leaving it in sexy disarray. "Because right now I'd tell her to stay the fuck away from you, and I won't say it as nicely as I just did."

I'm taken aback by how angry he is. Too much, it seems, and I wonder why. "She didn't lure me into a trap." I have no idea why I'm defending a woman who'd stomp me with her spiked heel in a heartbeat.

"She cornered you."

"And I let her. A mistake I regret."

"You don't know what Amber is capable of. I do."

Chris happened to me. My gaze drops to the water as Amber's words replay in my mind, carved in one part pain, one part elusive backstory. Did he hear what she said to me? Does the accusation I'd sensed have anything to do with his anger? Yes. Yes, I think it does.

I glance up, seeking some kind of answers, only to blank at the sight of Chris stripping off his shirt. "What are you doing?"

The hard lines of his face fade into amusement at the less-than-brilliant question, another one of his rapid shifts of mood. "Getting naked. Got a problem with that?"

My gaze slides over his deliciously sculpted body, lingering on his rippling, sexy abs, and my mouth goes dry. My questions about Amber slide away. "No problem," I assure him. I sound aroused. I am. "What took you so long?"

He tosses one of his boots. "I was trying to be Mr. Nice Guy again and let you enjoy your bath. It really doesn't work for me."

"I'm so glad you figured that out."

As he tosses his other boot away, his cell phone rings again.

Exasperated at Amber bursting inside my barely realized little fantasy, I say, *"Again?"*

Chris glances at his phone. "Blake this time."

"I need him!" I sit up, bubbles flying and water splashing. "I have to talk to him, right away."

Chris's gaze rakes over my naked breasts, then lifts to mine. "This is not the reaction a man wants his woman to have for another man."

I sit up on my knees. "Don't joke. Answer the call, please, and put it on speaker so I won't get the phone wet."

Looking baffled, Chris hits the answer button and says, "Hold on. Sara wants to be on speaker." He sits down on the tiled seating area of the tub and places the phone closer to me. I sink back into the water and curl my knees to my chest in front of the phone. Chris arches a questioning brow at me and I give a nod before he says, "You're live, Blake."

"You two are giving me performance anxiety," Blake drawls over the line. "We Walker men don't like performance anxiety, or to let down a pretty woman, but I have no news. You know what they say, though. No news is good news."

"It's not about Rebecca this time," I say, thinking of Ella's silence, insanely worried about what it means. "I went to City Hall today to check on Ella's marriage certificate."

"What?" Chris asks. "When?"

"This morning. Chantal took me."

He opens his mouth, then flicks a look at the phone and clamps his lips shut, obviously deciding what he has to say is better said alone.

I continue: "When Ella came here, she told me she was eloping and would be back in two weeks. But you can't get married here unless you've established residency for sixty days."

"Maybe her doctor was caught up in romance and forgot to check the laws," Blake suggests.

Chris adds, "I'm a resident and I didn't know about the sixty-day rule. Maybe she just decided to stay longer."

"Maybe," I concede, my voice tight. "But most people file a required public notice of their intended marriage—and there's no record. She's just disappeared without a trace."

Both men are quiet, the heavy silence telling me they both know it sounds bad.

"I'll find someone there to help," Blake says. "In the meantime, my staff will do what we can do from a distance."

"Good," Chris says. "I'm going to talk to Rey, my security person, and see if he has any suggestions, too. I'll check in tomorrow."

"Wait," I quickly say. "Before you hang up, Blake. The lady at City Hall who helped us today said someone else had been by to check on Ella's marriage license yesterday."

Chris's brows dip. "Did she give you any details on this person?"

I shake my head. "We were gone by the time Chantal told me. I didn't have the opportunity to ask questions."

Chris doesn't look happy. "I'll go back to City Hall, Blake. You just get on this and let me know what you find out. So you have nothing new on Rebecca?" he finishes.

"Nothing new." Blake hesitates. "Ava's sticking by her claim of innocence."

"You mean her claim of my guilt." My tone is flat and I drop my chin to my knees.

Chris spares Blake an answer. "Call me tomorrow with an update."

"Will do." Blake adds, "It will work out, Sara." Then the line goes dead.

I can't seem to make myself move. I let my lashes lower, and my chin sink a little heavier onto my knees.

Chris doesn't offer me words of comfort, and I'm glad. Somehow, he knows I've reached my limit with words. I just need a moment of silence to calm a dark something brewing inside me before it has a name. I just need . . . a minute.

Then his hands come down on the edge of the tub in front of me. "Look at me, Sara." His tone is pure dominance and authority, and it hits a button in me that snaps my gaze to his. "Stop. No more."

I blink. "What?"

"Fear is controlling you and it's tearing you up inside. If you think I'm going to sit by and watch you do that to yourself, you don't know me as well as you need to."

My rebuttal is instant. "I'm not. It's not."

"You are, and it is. Focus on what you can control. That's what I meant about limits, on the airplane. Know what you can bend to your will, and don't waste energy on what you can't. It'll suck you dry, like it is right now."

"We're talking about pending murder charges, and—"

"There are *no* pending murder charges. The police are simply making a case against Ava that rules out her using you as a defense later. And you're here, where you don't have to endure that process like you would in San Francisco."

My defensiveness bristles into high gear. "It's not just the murder charge. Most important, Ella is in trouble. I know she is—just like I knew Rebecca was dead." I choke on the last word.

"And worry helps her how?"

I gape. He sounds so damn cold. "I can't even believe you're saying this! I'm not going to stop worrying about Ella."

He squats down in front of me, and I'm captured by his commanding stare. "I'm not telling you not to worry. I'm telling you to face that worry, and then put it in the same box you put your father and Michael. Because it's no more worthy of your heartache than they are."

Those words punch me in the chest. Fear and denial have

always been my poison. When I fear, I deny. But I can't deny anything that's going on now, and I don't know what to do with that. Yes, my father and Michael are tucked inside a box, but the lid is so freshly sealed that I'm not sure how I managed to do that.

"We'll hire the best of the best to find Ella," Chris promises, his tone gentler, "and I'll do everything I can, too. But you have to focus on what you can control, not what you can't." He strokes a thumb from my cheek to my ear, and goose bumps rise as if he'd touched me all over. "We attack the problems. They don't attack us. And we do it together."

I look deep into his eyes and find myself wrapped in the familiar connection we share. It streams through me like moonlight on a bay, glistening through my soul. I sigh deep inside, tingling and warm, and I dare to admit what I've feared has left me too vulnerable, too easily hurt. Chris is how I opened, and then shut, my proverbial box to seal away the past. He made it possible. "I love you, Chris." And I love how easy it is to say the words, how safe I feel to say them.

"I love you, too, baby. We have this under control. I promise."

I reach up and let my wet fingers drag across his jaw. "Ah, my beautiful, talented artist. *You* have it under control. You always do." I envy him that, but it feels good to know I'm getting there myself, and that I don't have to do it alone.

He captures my wrist, his eyes twinkling with amusement, his seductive lips hinting at a smile. I like making him smile. "Beautiful?"

He makes me smile. "Oh, yes."

A sexy mix of heat and mischief seeps into his eyes, warning me I have a wicked, wonderful surprise coming my way, before he lifts my hand, presses his lips to my palm, and draws a circle with his tongue. I gasp at the unexpected, incredibly erotic act, and he leans back, dragging my wet hand down his neck before he stands up.

Biting my lip, I watch him take his pants off, and vow to call him beautiful more often if this is my reward. Chris watches me watch him and, when he is gloriously naked, my eyes gobble up every last inch. He is hard. Everywhere. I like how hard he is everywhere. And I am now hot when the water no longer is, but I don't think I'm going to care in a minute.

He steps into the tub and pulls me down so that we're facing each other on our sides. "Your stitches are going to get wet," I warn, touching the bandage on his arm.

"I'm allowed to get them wet after twenty-four hours." He wraps his leg over mine and settles the thickness of his erection between my thighs. "Ever had bathtub sex before?"

"No. Never."

He begins to playfully tease my nipple with his finger. "Me, either."

Surprised, my eyes go wide. "I'll be your first."

He pulls me on top of him and brings my mouth near his. "You're the first for a lot of things."

I smile and then moan as he presses between my thighs and smoothly enters me. I suck in a breath as he thrusts deeply, burying himself as far as he can; then he stills and stares at me. "About those limits. You'll find you don't get any with me."

"I wasn't aware I'd asked for any," I say.

He rolls to his back and pulls me on top of him. "Ride me, baby."

It's one of the rare moments he's let me on top, given me control, and considering how scorchingly hot I find his dominance, I'm surprised by how much I like it. His eyes rake over my body, and the heavy-lidded, lust-laden expression on his face says he likes it, too.

I revel in my ability to make this amazing man, this beautiful, seemingly always in-control man, lose himself to passion—and I gladly obey his command. I ride him and the fantasy that I never seem to make reality, but he does. The one called control.

Saturday, July 14, Layover, Los Angeles

I hate sharing. I hate being shared. This is what is on my mind as I sit in the airport, so close to home but feeling so far away. It seems important as I return home to know what I will and will not accept in my relationship with "him" if we are to have one again. He knows I won't sign another contract, but I want something that runs deeper than ink on the page. He says he's ready for that, but is he capable of the commitment I crave? This is a man who brought others to our most intimate moments, who brought her to our bed when he knew it upset me. She hates me. It's in her eyes every time we're near each other, but I still had to endure her touching me. And him. I had to watch her touch him.

I shiver just writing about it, thinking about it. The only reason I endured it, and I can forgive it as the past, is his reason for doing it. Or what I believe in my heart to be his reason. He was hiding from a real connection with me and I know, I just know, that's why he brought her to our play when we grew closer. She was his wall. His protection. Can he let down his walls? Can he let me see the real him? Can he love me as I love him? I only know that I can't settle for less. It's everything or nothing . . .

Thirteen

Morning comes way too soon, considering I'm still on San Francisco time and wrapped in Chris's arms. Apparently feeling the same way, Chris moans at the sound of the alarm, burying his face in my neck. "What time is it?

"Early." I reach to the marble-topped nightstand and hit SNOOZE on the alarm clock.

Chris lifts his head and glares at the display. Six thirty. "Why exactly are we waking up this early? I don't have to be at the museum until ten."

"Chantal's taking me to the embassy to get my passport, and she thinks we need to be there when they open at eight thirty." I roll toward the edge of the bed and Chris's big leg shackles mine, holding me in place.

"You aren't going to the embassy without me. I'll take you on Monday." His voice is absolute pure authority, the voice I find so utterly erotic, it can sink me to my knees on a rug.

This morning, I bristle at his command and roll to face him, my hands going to his bare chest, his eyes sweeping my bare breasts. My nipples pucker and I'm irritated that my body betrays me.

"Stop trying to distract me," I snap.

"You're the one distracting me. You're not going to the embassy without me."

"I don't need you to escort me to the embassy, Chris. There will be plenty of English speakers there. Besides, Chantal will be with me."

"Ella is missing and some stranger is looking for her. I don't want you running around on your own."

"Running around?" I demand. A frustrated sound escapes my lips. "I'm taking care of business, Chris. And whoever was asking about Ella was looking for her, not me."

"There's a connection to you now since you've been asking around about her. I'm not taking a chance. Wait for me."

"Last night you told me to take control of my circumstances and stop wallowing in fear. Now you're telling me to hide in the house. That's a double-edged sword you don't get to use. Talking to the embassy about Ella is action, not fear, and I don't want to put this off."

"You're not going, Sara."

Unbidden, old demons begin to stir inside me. "Yes. I am."

He stares at me for several intense seconds. I stare back. He reaches across me and grabs his cell phone from the end table.

"What are you doing?" I demand, certain that whatever it is won't please me.

"Canceling my meetings."

My eyes go wide. "No!" I roll to my back and cover the phone with my hand. "You can't do that. What you're doing at the museum is too important."

"Then wait for me."

I open my mouth to argue, but a glimpse of some deep, dark emotion in his eyes seals my lips. I remember seeing this look when he'd confessed fear for my safety. Suddenly my past, where my mother and I were more property than people, feels inconsequential compared to how deeply death has touched Chris's life.

Copying the familiar, sexy way he reaches behind my neck and pulls me to him, I slide my fingers under his hair and bring his mouth to mine, letting our lips linger until I feel him relax into me. Intimate seconds tick by where his very existence tingles through my body and nestles deep in my soul. When our mouths finally part, I stare into his gorgeous green eyes. I will never get tired of looking into those eyes. "Thank you for worrying about me. I'll be okay. I promise. I won't go anywhere else. Straight there and back."

The hard lines of his handsome face soften, his mood doing one of the dramatic shifts I've come to expect from Chris. "You're never going to be good at taking orders, are you?"

I grin, and go where I once never would have dared. "I thought I did pretty well on the rug the other day."

Surprise and hunger register in his stare, and he drops the phone on the nightstand. "Yes, you did," he agrees huskily, settling his heavy, perfect weight on top of me and pressing my thighs open. His thick erection presses into the V of my body. His arms settle by my head and wispy strands of blond hair brush his brow. The hunger in his eyes has turned outright ravenous. I am breathless. "Maybe," he suggests silkily, "I should take you back to the rug right now."

Liquid heat pools between my thighs and I wrap my arms around his neck. "And risk Chantal walking in on us this time?"

"If she wasn't on her way"—his head dips, and I feel his warm breath against my cheek, my lips—"would you want to go back to the rug?"

The idea, mixed with the seductive way he presses a kiss behind my ear, sends a surge of desire pulsing through me. "Yes," I admit, breathless. "I would want to go back to the rug."

He goes still for a moment before he smiles against my cheek. "I wonder what it would take for me to make you agree to that this morning?" His hand sweeps the curve of my breast, trailing down to my waist, and then pressing to my belly and lower. A burning sweet spot between my thighs aches for his touch. The alarm goes off again and I want to scream with the injustice of the timing, with how close he was to that spot.

Chris reaches over and hits the snooze button. "We're being timed." He slips his fingers into the silky heat of my body, parting me, and pressing the pulsing thickness of his erection against me. Anticipation burns through me as he adds, "So I'd better not waste any time." He thrusts hard into me and I gasp. "Maybe this will make you do as I say."

"Don't count on it," I taunt, but my defiance fades into a moan at the way he slides his cock left to right, stroking nerve endings to life.

His cheek caresses mine, lips brushing the delicate skin of

my neck, then my ear. "There's a price for making me worry, Sara,"

"What price?" I manage in a whisper.

"There are all kinds of ways I could make you pay," he assures me, tugging roughly at one of my nipples. I bite back a moan and my sex clenches around him. His head dips and his teeth scrape the stiff peak before he suckles it deeply. My fingers twine into the silky strands of his hair, urging him to continue, but he abandons my nipple to nuzzle my neck, denying me what I want. "The price you pay today is putting up with another man. Rey's going with you to the embassy."

Unbidden, Rebecca's journal entries about the many ways Mark shared her with another man, and how much it hurt her, rips through my mind. The pain she must have felt. The pain I would feel if Chris tried to do this to me. I'd be torn into tiny pieces, never to be put back together again.

"Sara, I would never, under any circumstances, share you. Not the way you're thinking. Not with a damn soul."

I blink and find Chris staring down at me. "What?"

"I don't know what set it off, but you're thinking about the journals, and how Mark shared Rebecca with other people."

I'm amazed he can read me so easily. It's true. I'm haunted by Rebecca's life and now her death.

"Remember your own words," he continues. "I'm not Mark and you're not Rebecca. You know me. You know I don't share. You're mine, Sara. Only mine. "

His possessive words radiate through me and warm the chill of my memories. I wrap my arms around his neck, blocking out everything but the warmth in his eyes and the feel of him inside me. "I like being yours."

Pure male satisfaction flashes in his eyes. "Then you'd better accept that I'm going to protect you, whether you like it or not. Either Rey is going to take you to the embassy or I am."

I give him a playful frown. "You're being overwhelming again."

He nips my bottom lip and licks it. "I'll make it up to you." And he does. Oh, how he does.

Chris pulls on light blue jeans and a white T-shirt with the museum logo on it and heads downstairs to brew coffee. I choose a black skirt, a V-neck black silk blouse, and knee-high black boots and brush my freshly washed long hair into a silky mass around my shoulders. Satisfied I look passport-worthy, I head for the kitchen, jitters overtaking me with the thought of leaving for the embassy. It's a silly energy drain when I'm simply replacing my passport, but it's hard to completely ignore Chris's paranoia. I don't see how anyone here could connect me to Ella. Could they?

The instant I step into the living room, my nostrils flare with the rich aroma of coffee beans, and the idea of sharing a cup with Chris brings a smile to my lips. Hurrying up the stairs, I'm still smiling when I see Amber, with her back to me, decked out in an orange shirt, black leather pants, and high heels, and pouring herself coffee. My smile disappears, stripped away with the shock of her presence like a sticky piece of tape ripped from my mouth.

She turns and smiles at me. "Morning, Sara." Her gaze

sweeps up and down my body, sending discomfort through me before she meets my eyes. "You look nice today."

"Thank you." I wonder if she really means to compliment me or frame the obvious. Amber has this Barbie-gone-biker kind of beauty that's striking in every way, and I'm . . . just me. It's hard to believe we'd draw the same man's attention. I'm suddenly ready to be rescued from this conversation. "Where's Chris?"

"Letting Rey in."

I barely contain a sigh of relief at what is sure to be his short absence. In the meantime, I do . . . what? I glance toward the coffeepot, remembering how she'd touched me the last time we were here. I'm not so sure I want coffee, after all.

Amber watches me eye the pot and lifts her cup. "Would you like some coffee?"

As if I'm the guest, not her. It might be innocent, but I don't think it is. I don't think anything Amber does is innocent.

I force myself to cross to the coffeepot. "What brings you here so early?" But I know why she's here. Chris wouldn't take her calls last night, an action I regret now. I suddenly wish he'd just talked to her.

"I usually stop by a few mornings a week when Chris is in town," she replies, implying she plans to continue the pattern.

I freeze with my back to her and the coffeepot in mid-pour. With extreme effort, I beat down how fiercely territorial I feel of my new home and my man, reminding myself why Chris keeps her in his life. She has no family, and the wounds on her arms, combined with the haunted look in her eyes I'd seen last night, indicate her story is more nightmare than fairy tale.

Despite the discomfort Amber stirs inside me, I love Chris all the more for being the kind of person who won't shut her out. And if he won't, I won't.

Finishing the task of filling my cup, a new attitude in place, I return the pot to the burner and rotate around to face Amber. "Cream, right?" she asks, and offers me the bottle on the island beside her.

I feel ridiculously unsettled by her being attentive enough to remember how I take my coffee. Trying to shake it off, I reach out to accept the creamer. "Thank you."

Her hand closes over mine, a scalding vise that makes my heart race. Her eyes are flat, almost hard, and she lowers her voice to a near whisper. "He's good at shutting people and things out. Too good." She cuts her eyes sharply away, like she had back at the Script, then flicks them back to mine. "I won't be one of those things."

I'm shaken both by how she's called herself a thing, not a person—and by the truth she's stated. Chris is good at shutting people out.

Footsteps sound behind us and she jerks her hand away from mine. "It could be you, just as easily as it could be me, that he suddenly blocks out. Remember that."

Stunned, my lips part and I don't move away.

Amber grabs her purse and rushes toward the stairs. "Off to work," she announces as she passes Chris and the man behind him, whom I assume to be Rey, on the stairs.

"Amber," I hear Chris say, halting her with the short command. I take the short delay to compose myself, turning away from the stairs. The creamer and my cup of coffee are still in my hands. I set them on the counter and steady myself by leaning against it.

"Don't forget what I told you," Chris reminds Amber, and I don't even care what he's talking about. Amber has sliced open the memory of Chris leaving me and all but kicking me out of his apartment, and it's still too fresh not to bleed.

Footsteps sound behind me and I hear Chris and the other man speaking in French. Drawing a deep breath, I turn to face them, avoiding Chris's stare for fear he'll read how shaken I am. But I feel him. Every time he enters a room, I feel Chris in every pore of my body, in every inch of my existence.

Rey, who is somewhere around Chris's age, and a good two hundred pounds of hard body and dark, edgy good looks, inclines his head and greets me with "Ravi de vous rencontrer, Mademoiselle Sara."

The pull of Chris's stare willing me to look at him is magnetic. Somehow, though, I blink Rey into better focus and repeat his words in my head, pleased at my understanding of a basic greeting. "Nice to meet you, too, Monsieur Rey, and thank you for escorting me today."

Rey smiles approvingly and flicks Chris a rather amused look. "I thought you said she doesn't know French."

Afraid I've encouraged him to test my French rather than sticking to his well-spoken English, I say, "Understanding a few small phrases and speaking them are two different things. I speak the French language about as well as I do English after three shots of tequila."

Both men laugh, and at the sound of Chris's rich, sexy chuckle, I finally look at him. His eyes meet mine and the tender concern in his wraps around my heart and begins to seal the wound Amber has opened.

Chris runs a hand over his jaw, looking thoughtful. "I seem to remember sounding like I'd drank a bottle of tequila back when I learned."

"I find that hard to believe."

"Why do you think I got into so many fights at school?"

Rey shakes his head. "I wish I had an excuse for the ones I got into. At least I chose a job that gives me a way to use my aggression in a positive way." His eyes land on me and the humor fades from his expression. "Chris told me about Ella."

I shoot Chris a questioning look and he explains: "Rey has some connections he's going to use to help us find her."

Eager for answers, I step closer. "How? What does that mean?"

"My brother is a military gendarmerie," Rey reveals. "That's the French police in more rural and border areas."

"The towns outside the city are popular escapes from the city so they're important to cover," Chris adds. "Aside from his brother, Rey's going to hire an investigator to ensure no stone is unturned here in the city."

"It would help to have a picture of Ella and any data you have on her," Rey says. "And it would be a good idea to take the picture with us to the embassy, in case one hasn't already been given to them."

I'm flustered by the request, kicking myself for not being prepared. "I don't have a picture with me."

"We can arrange to get her United States driver's license through my brother," Rey offers. "But a better picture would be helpful."

Chris offers a quick suggestion. "Would the school have a picture of her?"

"Yes." My voice lifts with my approval. "That's a great idea. If I can't get a staff photo, someone will be able to give me a yearbook shot, for sure."

The doorbell rings. "That must be Chantal. I'll let her in, then call the school before they close."

I dart forward and Chris shackles my wrist. "Let Rey get the door," he says softly.

Rey speaks to Chris in French, then his feet hit the stairs.

Finally, we're alone.

The burn of the recent heartache he caused me explodes into my words. "Amber can only get to me because you haven't told me whatever it is you need to tell me."

He gives me a heavy-lidded stare. "What did she say to you?"

"Nothing I didn't know. And what she said isn't the point, Chris. Or maybe it *is* the point. She's talking, and you aren't."

"What did Amber say to you, Sara?" This time there is steel in his voice.

I grimace with defeat. He's in stubborn alpha-male mode, where "no" isn't an option. "She said you're good at shutting people out, and she doesn't plan to let you do that to her. And she's right: you *are* good at shutting people out. No one knows that like I do."

"Sara—"

"It's the past. I know." I touch his cheek. "But Chris, if there is anything I fear, it's you judging yourself through my eyes, like you did after I saw you in Mark's club, and judging wrongly." My breath hitches. "I can't go through that again. I can't."

His gaze lifts to the ceiling, and he seems to struggle before he fixes me in a burning stare, and not the kind I crave on a cold winter's night. He's angry again. "This is what I get for letting her in this morning. I should have known better."

Exasperated, I shake my head. "If you don't want me around her, and you knew she was going to be present in our lives here, why are we in Paris, Chris?"

"If we didn't have to be here, we wouldn't be. This is where this has to happen."

In his haunted eyes I see the demons of his past, and the damage they've clawed into his soul. "Chris—" I start, but stop abruptly as I hear Chantal's and Rey's voices downstairs.

Chris reacts to our limited time, cupping my head and pulling my forehead to his. My hand settles on the solid wall of his chest, and his heartbeat is a steady, soothing thrum beneath my palm, the way he is to my soul. The way I want to soothe his.

His fingers gently tease the hair by my ear. "There is a right place and a right time. You'll understand what I mean—soon, I promise. I'm asking you to trust me on this."

My heart squeezes with the rough quality of his voice, at the vulnerability I doubt anyone else knows he's capable of experiencing, let alone exposing. But he lets me inside the walls I once thought I'd never tear down.

"As long as you promise to trust in *us,* Chris." I sound as affected as he did and I'm not sorry. I want him to understand how much he means to me.

He leans back and looks at me, and for a mere moment, his eyes are intense, probing. They soften then, warming me inside and out, amber flecks flickering to life in their depths, beams of sunlight in what has become a storm cloud of worry. "You know what I'm going to say to that, don't you?"

I relax with him, my lips curving, my fingers teasing his smooth jaw. "That I wouldn't be here if you didn't."

His hand settles possessively on my lower back and molds me closer. "That's right." And then his talented tongue is licking into my mouth, drinking me in with one long, seductive stroke, followed by another and another. I moan as his equally talented fingers caress up my waist and over my breast to tease my nipple. A delicious ripple of pleasure travels directly to my sex and I wrap my arms around his neck, pressing closer to his hard, lean body.

He deepens the kiss, caressing my backside—a firm, deep touch—and I welcome the stir of erotic memories. The room fades away and I am back on my knees on the rug in the living room, naked and exposed for him, as I have never been for another man. Slick heat forms between my thighs where I want Chris. Where I want him now.

Chantal's laughter lifts in the air, louder now, and my eyes pop open. I've totally forgotten we aren't alone. I try to pull away but Chris holds me to him, leaning in to nip my earlobe and whisper, "That's how trust tastes, baby. I'll show you how it feels tonight." He releases me, leaving me weak-kneed.

"Good morning, Sara!" Chantal sounds sweet and innocent as she approaches.

"Morning," I all but croak out, backing against the island counter for stability. I don't turn to face her. What if I have lipstick smudged all over my face? I quickly inspect Chris's, finding him free of my pale pink shade, and reach up to wipe my mouth.

Chris steps close again, his body radiating heat into me as he uses his thumb to swipe around my upper lip. The friction of his touch sets off an eruption of goose bumps and I lean harder into the counter.

"She's right," he says. "It is a good morning." But there is absolutely nothing resembling Chantal's innocence in the way he says it or in the wicked, possessive way he looks at me. But there is more in his eyes; a glint of something I can't identify. And then, with a quirk to his sexy lips I really want somewhere on my body right now, he turns to greet Chantal and Rey, but I find myself suddenly taken aback by what my lust-laden mind had missed. What just happened between us wasn't a simple seduction; it was cause and effect. My reaction to Amber's visit triggered his need for control. And driving me insane in a minute flat and making me wait for satisfaction was his way of claiming it, and me.

By the time Chris walks us to the black sedan Rey's driving, I've decided I have to put my insecurities aside and give him space. Regardless of what he means by the "right time," it may never be the true right time for him—or us.

Chantal slides into the car and Chris wraps me in an embrace. "I'll see you tonight." His voice is soft velvet I feel like a caress stroking my body. "All of you."

I trace his lips with my fingers. "As long as I see all of you." He might take my words as another push, so I quickly twist them into a double entendre. "I like you better without clothes." I slip from his arms and slide into the car, with his husky, satisfied laugh following.

Fourteen

With Rey and Chantal on either side of me, I enter the embassy feeling pretty darn glad to be alive after Paris's insane rush-hour traffic. I might not be happy with my bodyguard situation, but the way Rey avoided a number of crashes earns him a lot of respect. In fact, if I wasn't in so in love with Chris, I might fall madly, deeply in love with Rey, if only until the adrenaline rush of near death completely faded.

Inside the building, which looks like any administrative building in the States to me, Chantal and I slide off our hooded jackets, and we all wipe away remnants of the cold rain. Being a macho kind of guy, Rey of course isn't wearing a jacket at all.

The passport office turns out to be an oversized waiting room with rows and rows of steel chairs, and a line of window booths at the front. We're directed to a line. A very, very long line.

I sigh. "Why don't you two go get some coffee or something? I don't want you to have to stand in line."

Rey axes the idea instantly. "I need to stay close to you, in case you need anything."

I press my lips tightly together to bite back an instant retort. He's inadvertently hit a nerve called "anything to do with my father." All through my childhood, a security guard accompanied me and my mother at outings. As a child I'd simply thought it part of having a powerful father who loved us. As an adult, it became evident he was just protecting his property.

Rey reaches for my jacket, pulling me back to the present and the crowded, stuffy room. "Why don't I take this for you?"

I blink at him and release my jacket. "Thank you." Rey isn't my problem; my father is. And Chris isn't the problem, either. Unlike my father, his desire to protect me has nothing to do with a power trip or personal gain. It stems purely from a mixture of Ava's attack and a lifetime touched far too intimately by the hand of death.

"I could give you a French lesson in line," Chantal offers.

"I'm too distracted to learn French right now," I reply, slamming my mental box shut a little harder.

She waves off my excuse. "Nonsense. This is time we can put to good use. When you are speaking French, you'll thank me for pushing you."

Rey reaches for Chantal's coat, his attention sweeping over her determined expression, and there's both amusement and a hint of male appreciation in his face.

When he steps into the line with us I frown. I can deal with him being here, but not hovering. "I thought you were going to go work on a backache in one of those steel chairs?"

His lips twitch. "A backache. Yes, I can't wait." To my surprise, he saunters away.

Chantal watches his departure and sighs wistfully. "He can be my bodyguard any day."

I roll my eyes. She's been casting him shy, admiring looks since she arrived at the house. "Go talk to him. Get to know him."

She purses her lips. "You're just trying to get out of French lessons."

"No, I'm simply putting off making a fool of myself in public when I butcher the words. You can join me when I'm close to the front of the line."

"Oh, no." She shakes her head, and you'd think I'd told her to dive off the roof without a parachute, for the panic on her heart-shaped face. "I'm afraid we'll just sit there in complete silence, and I'll drool on myself and he'll have to wipe my lips."

I give her a serious look. "Not if he does it with his tongue."

She blinks at me and we both burst out laughing. My cell phone goes off with a text and I retrieve it to read his message.

Are you there yet?

Yes, I reply. The line is long. This could take hours.

Where is Rey?

Generally hovering, as you instructed.

For your own good.

Hmmm . . .

What does hmmm . . . mean?

It means . . .

I consider a short, text-worthy way to state what I feel.

I love you, Chris.

I love you, too. Going into meeting. Text me before you leave so I can meet you at the rug.

I'll bring the pink paddle, I type, and my cheeks burn with my boldness.

It's in my suitcase.

I bite my lip. Is he serious? Did he really carry it through customs?

I stuff my phone back into my purse, and I swear my backside tingles.

Chantal's laughter cuts through the decidedly lusty sensation I'm feeling, and I turn to find her in conversation with a woman in line behind us. The instant she notices I'm free, she ends her chat and pulls a small flip chart from her purse. Evidently unconcerned about my embarrassment, she starts drilling me, her expression returning to her previous determined one. I respond with a groan and a laugh, accepting the inevitable, and dutifully repeat a phrase in horridly spoken French.

Thirty minutes later the front of the line is finally mine, and I head to the window—only to be given reams of paperwork to fill out. Chantal and I join Rey, and I wade through pages of forms.

Chantal seems to have the opposite problem to mine. Where I ramble when nervous, she doesn't speak at all. It's awkward, just as she feared, and I can't focus on my paperwork.

Finally, I can't take the silence anymore and I glance at Chantal. "Can I convince you to find coffee somewhere? My treat. I've got a chill from the rain I can't shake."

She pops to her feet, seizing the escape. "Absolutely. Coffee sounds great." She glances at Rey. "Would you like some?"

His lips twitch and he answers her in French. I have no idea what he says, but she blushes, looking exceptionally young in her pale pink sheath dress, with her light brown hair curled sweetly on the ends.

I watch Chantal leave and a pinch of protectiveness overcomes me. Rey's a good ten years older, and far more worldly than she. I cock my head and study him. "What did you say to her?"

"If I wanted you to know, mademoiselle, I'd have said it in English." He delivers this statement in a completely deadpan voice, but I have the distinct impression he's trying to get a rise out of me.

I narrow suspicious eyes at him. "How long have you known Chris?"

"Seven years."

"So he trusts you, even though you're a smart-ass." My tone is as perfectly deadpan as his had been.

He stares at me a long moment and then lets out a deep, hearty chuckle. "Yes. I suppose he does. And I guess the same applies to you."

This time I laugh and, unlike Chantal, I'm comfortable with the silence we fall into as I complete my forms. I instinctively like Rey, even if he does refuse to tell me what he said to Chantal.

I complete the forms and head to the desk to turn them in, hopeful the process will move quickly from here.

It doesn't. For the next hour the three of us wait, and Chantal thankfully begins to loosen up with him. Both of them drill me on my French, laughing at my pronunciation—and I do, too. At some point, I relax into what I believe to be new friendships blooming, and with them, connections to this city and to Chris.

When finally my name is called, my mood and my steps are lighter. A plump woman behind the counter with a thick accent asks my name. She keys my information into a computer and studies her screen a moment, then she begins to speak in highly accented English and at lightning speed.

"Can you repeat that, please?"

"Denied," she states flatly. "Your passport is denied." She hands me my paperwork and a form written in French.

My pulse leaps. "Denied? What does that mean?"

"Denied is denied. No reissue. You want answers, go see Special Services."

"Where is Special Services?"

She points to my left and I see a "Special Services" sign over a door. Blind to the rest of the room, my heart thundering loudly in my ears, I rush toward the sign and find a small office with four steel desks, only one of which is occupied.

A man in a dress shirt and solid navy tie, with streaks of gray in his neatly trimmed brown hair, gives me an expectant look.

"English?" I ask hopefully.

"Yes, madame." He sets down his pen and rests an elbow on the desk, looking rather miffed at the interruption. "What can I do for you?"

I cross to his desk and hand him my paperwork. He glances at it and then at me. There is a new sharpness to the way he looks at me, cutting and almost . . . accusing. I tell myself I'm being paranoid, but adrenaline is pouring through me and I barely keep my voice normal. "What's the problem?" I demand, when he says nothing.

He picks up the phone, using his other hand to point me into a chair in front of his desk. The silent command provokes another surge of adrenaline and I have to inhale slowly to calm myself before I sit down.

I've barely settled into the seat when he hangs up the receiver. "Please stay here, Mademoiselle McMillan. We need to ask you some questions."

My heart skips a beat. "About what?"

But I know. This has to do with Rebecca.

"Just wait here." He delivers his clipped command as he pushes to his feet and walks away, exiting out of a back door several feet behind his desk.

I spring into instant action, unsure how long I have to enlist help before he returns. Fumbling with my purse, I pull out my cell and dial Chris's number.

The three rings feel like a dozen before he answers, "Sara?" His voice is rich, warm, soothing, and oh so welcome.

"I need you here," I breathe out. "I need you at the embassy."

Chris immediately starts speaking in French to someone else and I hear several voices communicate with him before he's back on the line with me. "I'm already walking to my car."

I close my eyes in relief. He hasn't asked why I need him. He's simply leaving a meeting without an idea why. Guiltily, I think of how I'd allowed Amber to rattle me earlier and I'm reminded of all the reasons I shouldn't worry about Chris shutting me out. All of the reasons why I should, and can, count on this wonderful, amazing man.

"Talk to me, Sara. What's happening?"

"They denied my passport and said they need to ask me questions."

He curses under his breath. "Don't answer anything until I get there. I'm calling Stephen. I'll call you back."

"Okay."

"Sara. It's going to be fine. It's an administrative flag, nothing more. A misunderstanding we'll clear up."

But I'd heard his initial reaction, his curse, and we both know it's more than an administrative flag. "Just hurry, please. I need you, Chris."

"And I'm here for you. I'll call you back after I talk to Stephen."

We hang up and I sit, my foot tapping nervously. Chris wouldn't have to call the attorney if he truly believed this was just a passport flag. And what does that even mean? Why is my passport flagged?

"There you are!" Chantal exclaims, and I turn to find her and Rey headed toward me. I'd forgotten about them completely, and I cringe at the idea of them discovering me being accused of murder. What will they think of me? Or worse, of Chris?

I push to my feet and step around the chair to meet them, trying to hide the trembling of my hands by running them over my hips.

"What's going on?" Rey asks, and he doesn't look pleased. "And why didn't you tell me you were coming in here?"

"They need to ask me some questions. I'll be out as soon as I'm done."

"Questions?" Rey looks baffled. "About the pickpocket?"

I hesitate and almost laugh. Could it be as simple as that? Could I be overreacting? Oh, *please* let it be about the pickpocket. "Maybe."

"Maybe it's about Ella," Chantal suggests, and she glances at Rey.

The door behind the desk opens, and Rey's gaze goes past me. I turn to find three men entering and, before I can stop her, Chantal charges toward them.

Rey steps to my side and whispers, "What's really going on, Sara?"

"Chris is on his way here now. Please, if you want to help, get Chantal out of here."

He shakes his head. "I can't leave you."

"Sara," Chantal says, and I turn to find her standing beside me, looking exceedingly pale.

"What is it?"

She whispers, "Is there some kind of investigation in the States?"

"I . . ." I do not want Chantal to know about this. "What did they say?"

"I didn't understand, really. I asked about Ella, and they started questioning me about some investigation in the States."

My hand goes to my throat. "Were they . . . talking about Ella?"

"I . . ." She looks flustered. "I don't know."

I grab her arm, my fingers digging into her delicate skin, and the room spins around me, fading in and out. What if Ella had returned to San Francisco after we checked her passport and Ava had killed her to spite me? It seems impossible, but then so does Ava really killing Rebecca.

"Sara." Chantal's voice rattles along my raw nerve endings, her very existence a reminder of Ella's sweet, trusting nature, and neither of them would stand a chance against Ava.

My gaze darts to Chantal and I blurt, "I need to know if the investigation involves Ella. I need to know if they mean Ella. Ask them now."

Fifteen

Is Ella dead?

I hug myself, trying to control the shaking my adrenaline rush has created, holding my breath as I listen to the French exchanges erupting around me. For an eternal moment, I listen to the murmurs, understanding nothing but a random reference to "Ella", and still I don't get an answer to my question. *Is* Ella dead? Is she dead? No one is talking to me. No one is talking in English. I can't take it. My heart is going to explode in my chest.

"Is Ella dead?" I all but shout. The room is instantly silent, all eyes on me, and I think maybe I actually *did* shout, but I don't care. "Is she dead?" This time I whisper. This time I have their attention.

The first man I'd spoken to leans across his desk, fists pressed on the steel surface, to bring himself eye level to me. "We don't know who Ella is, but we intend to find out."

The accusation in his voice is pure acid, but I process only what is important. They have no clue who Ella is or where she is. *Ella isn't dead.* The men in this department don't know who she is.

"We have questions for you, Mademoiselle McMillan," the man adds, and I swear the other three men are hovering behind him worse than Rey does with me.

Before I can stop myself, I reply, "And I have questions about the missing-persons report on Ella." It's been weeks since Blake contacted the embassy about her. Weeks!

He gives me a piercing look before glowering at Rey and Chantal, speaking to them in French. I have the overwhelming urge to yell again. I'm really getting damn tired of people speaking French when they know I don't understand it.

Rey glares at whatever the man has said, responding in a rough, fast rampage of French. I might not know the language but I recognize "pissed off" when I hear it.

Chantal's hand comes down on my shoulder; a gentle, comforting touch. "They say we have to wait outside, Sara. I don't want to leave you."

These men have told her they want to question me regarding an investigation I'm attached to in some way, and she doesn't want to leave my side. I can only hope that means they didn't use the word "murder." Still, she should be running. I'd be running. But she, like Ella, is too naïve to know this. She, like Ella, could too easily end up vulnerable and in trouble.

Protectiveness rises in me and I rest my hand on her shoulder, promising myself I will soon do the same with Ella. "I'm okay. You go with Rey and get out of here. Thank you for all you've done today."

"We'll be outside the door," Rey states, and I find him in a glare with the man behind the desk. "*Right outside* the door if she needs us." His attention shifts back to me, his tone softening for my ears only. "I can't risk being escorted out of the building by refusing to leave or I would, but don't talk to them until Chris gets here."

"I won't," I assure him, and my phone rings. "That's probably Chris now."

"Mademoiselle—" the man begins, and Rey immediately cuts him off with some sharply spoken statement in French, and, intended or not, he's created a window for me to take my call. I climb through.

I dart toward the opposite side of the room and perch in an empty chair. "Chris," I answer and glance up to watch Rey and Chantal being escorted from the room.

"Stephen says not to talk to anyone."

"Does he know what's going on?"

"He doesn't have any answers yet, but his answer would be the same. Tell them you aren't at liberty to talk without counsel, or simply buy time and I'll tell them."

"Mademoiselle McMillan," the man behind the desk says, a sharp bite to his words.

I hold up a finger. "One more minute."

He grinds his teeth. "One only."

"I heard that," Chris says. "He's just trying to intimidate you. Pretend he's Mark trying to get under your skin. Lift that little chin of yours and stand tall."

Mark couldn't put me behind bars. I change the subject before I run out of time. "Please tell Rey to take Chantal home."

"Not until I get there."

"Please. I don't want them to hear the accusations against me. How can I make a life here with you if everyone you know thinks I'm a . . ."—I can't say *murderer*—"criminal?"

"No one is going to know about this."

"They already told Chantal there's an investigation in the States. Please. Get them to leave."

"I have to know if they take you somewhere, Sara. And I'm almost there. I'm hanging up to focus getting to you. Don't speak to them about anything." He hangs up before I can argue.

I squeeze my eyes shut and draw in a thick, hard-earned breath, before sliding my phone into my purse and turning toward the men on the other side of the room. Crossing the distance between us, I pause in front of his desk. "Monsieur . . . ?"

"Bernard," he supplies.

"Monsieur Bernard," I repeat. "Can you direct me to the toilette?"

He studies me a moment. "Can't it wait?"

His tone verges on rudeness and I reply with sticky-sweet innocence. "I'm feeling quite queasy. Something I ate, I believe. Tartare. I thought to spare your desk a mess."

He openly scowls and speaks to a man over his shoulder, then to me again. "Monsieur Dupont will escort you."

I'm such a criminal they need to escort me? The man, bald and in his midfifties, with a hard, round face, approaches me.

Chris's words from last night play in my head. *We attack the problems. They don't attack us. And baby, we do it together.* I inhale deeply. *We do it together.* And it hits me then that "together" doesn't mean handing over my life to Chris. It means sharing it. Unlike others in my life before him, Chris is trying to make me stronger. Hiding in the bathroom until he arrives is not stronger.

Straightening, my chin lifts, and while the uneasy sensation in my belly remains, I *am* stronger. I walk to the chair and sit down. Surprise flashes on his face. "You're ready to answer questions?"

"No. I'm not ready at all. I'm waiting on a call from my attorney." I lean forward, resting my hand on the desk, my voice as steady now as his. "And, Monsieur Bernard, if you slander my name with anyone, especially my friends outside, you will know my name far better than you wish you did."

The surprise he'd shown seconds before morphs into a stunned expression. It matches what I'm feeling. Where did that come from? His brow furrows. "You are quite defiant for a woman accused of murder."

I raise my eyebrows. "Accused by the very woman who tried to kill *me* two nights ago—so, yes, you bet I'm defiant." And why haven't I been before now? I'm innocent. I'm a victim. I'm furious that I'm being questioned.

"Then why did you flee the country?"

"I did not flee the country," I state calmly.

"She came with me."

I twist around to find Chris standing in the doorway, his hair a damp mess, droplets of water clinging to the black Harley jacket he wears with the same ease he does his power. The entire room seems to suck in a breath at the same moment, waiting for what will come next. Waiting for him.

185

His attention fixes on me, and it's as if no one else were in the room. He sees me. He's dismissed *them*.

"I told you I was close, baby," he drawls, seemingly unaffected by the situation. He saunters into the room, and while he's all casual coolness and sexy swagger, there is a lethal, primal quality just beneath his surface. I might be trying to take control myself, and I want to, but it's a beautiful thing watching Chris be Chris.

He stops beside my chair and holds out a hand. His eyes are gentle, yet somehow still glinting with hard steel and pure dominance. Holding his gaze, I slip my purse onto my shoulder and press my palm into his. A warm, tingling sensation dances up my arm and I see Chris's eyes dilate, awareness seeping into his unwavering stare. He feels it, too—this crazy, impossible attraction between us that's contained by nothing, not even the jerks watching us. I love that about us. I love us.

His fingers close around mine and he pulls me to my feet. "We're leaving. We have museums to visit."

Bernard speaks in rapid, agitated French.

Chris flicks him a bored look and says something in reply. Maybe two sentences. I'm dying to know what; I really have to step up my game.

I glance at Bernard, whose peeved expression is pretty darn telling—as is the defensive way he crosses his arms in front of his chest. Whatever Chris has said, Bernard officially has his panties in a wad, and I almost laugh.

Obviously entertained by the man's reaction, Chris's lips twitch and he motions me to the door. We're halfway to the exit when Bernard calls out to us. Chris stops but doesn't turn, as if the man is unworthy of his attention. He answers the man, sounding rather amused, as if whatever power Bernard believes he has is a joke. Then we start walking again and we don't stop.

We travel briskly through the waiting room, where people cluster like ants. Halfway to the exit the hair on the nape of my neck prickles, as it had when I was shopping yesterday. Fighting the urge to look behind us, I try to erase the sensation with a rub of my hand. It has to be Bernard watching our departure, and I cast Chris an anxious glance. "Can we just walk out like that?"

"We just did."

Right. We just did. The prickling sensation deepens and I rub harder; I can't get out of here soon enough. "What about Rey and Chantal?" I ask when we finally step into the main corridor.

"I had Rey take Chantal home."

"They don't know about—"

"No. You can relax. I questioned Rey on the phone before I got here."

Relief washes over me. "Have you talked to Stephen?"

"Long enough for him to tell me to do what I'd planned on doing anyway, and get you the hell out of there."

Having my freedom blessed by our attorney is cold comfort, considering I'm still without a passport and being questioned about a murder I didn't commit. "You know," I say through my teeth, "these accusations are really starting to piss me off."

Chris looks down at me, approval glowing in his eyes. "About time you got mad."

Yes, I think as we approach the exit. *About time.* I guess I have Bernard to thank for my coming around. It's time I remind everyone I am a victim, but not the kind I've acted like. Ava tried to kill me. They should be helping me, not attacking me with her.

We join a half-dozen people near the exit, all staring at the sheets of rain coming down outside. I cut Chris a hopeful look. "I don't suppose you have an umbrella under that jacket of yours?"

"'Fraid not," he replies, shrugging out of his jacket to wrap the heavy weight around me. "Let me pull the car as close to the door as I can get it. Watch for me at the curb, but it's still a pretty good run."

An image of me slipping and falling flat on my face is not a pleasant one, and I take off his coat, wishing I hadn't left mine with Rey. "No, it's too heavy for me to run in. Really. I'm no Grace Kelly, Chris. I will fall. I'd rather just leave now with you." I shiver and hug myself. "I want out of this place."

"I'm parked too far away. Wait for me. I'll come back to the door with something to cover you up."

"Fine. If you want to play Mr. Good Guy. I'll wait. But please hurry. I don't want Bernard cornering me again."

Chris shoves an arm back in his coat, and the prickling sensations on my neck return. Uneasily, I glance around the lobby, and I'm instantly drawn to the profile of a man leaning against a nearby wall. He glances up and I gasp with shock at the familiar face. The man straightens instantly, preparing to bolt, and I grab Chris's shirt. "It's the pickpocket from the airport. He's here."

"Where?"

I point.

My pickpocket has dashed for the door in a full sprint. Chris turns to me, hands solidly planted on my shoulders. "Stay here. And I mean *stay here,* Sara." Then he runs for the door.

Sixteen

I'm running before Chris is even outside. There's no way I'm staying inside when he's chasing a criminal who could easily be armed.

Shoving my way past the doors, struggling to slide my purse across my chest, I burst outside, and I might as well have been sprayed in the face with a fire hose for the fierceness of the cold rain attacking me. Shoving my soaked hair from my face, I desperately scan for Chris, and find him in a hard run to my left. Instantly I am in motion, wishing my thin silk blouse was warmer and my heels lower. Wishing even more that I dared have my phone ready in case I need to call for help, without the downpour ruining it.

When I am a half a block from the embassy, Chris is another half block ahead of me, and the rain is torture. I swipe the water clinging to my face, as if that will really help. I blink again and panic when I can't find Chris. One minute he was in front of me, the next he is out of sight. Panic assails me, and my heart jackhammers. Thunder crashes above me and I nearly jump out of my skin, but I keep running.

At the end of the street I scan wildly in all directions and cut left, the path without a street to cross and the logical choice, praying it's the right one. I'm another block down, doubting I've chosen correctly, when a swinging gate catches my attention and instinct stops me in my tracks.

Cutting around the corner, I see a small, deserted courtyard and gasp as I discover Chris and the pickpocket in a physical scramble. My fingers curl around the metal gate and I barely contain a scream as Chris is shoved against the wall and punched in the face. A second later, the pickpocket is against the same wall and I watch as Chris throws a blow himself, followed by another. And he does it with his painting hand.

I don't think; I just act, running toward them. I have to save his hand. "No!"

"Get back, Sara!" Chris shouts at me, and I cringe as my distracting him results in him getting a knee in the gut. Chris punches the guy again.

"Your hand!" I scream, closing the distance between us, and latching on to his elbow. "You're going to hurt your hand!"

Chris curses and holds off a kick from the other man. "Damn it, Sara, back away!" He punches the guy again, and this time the man slumps.

Chris leans in close to the other man and says something I can't hear, let alone understand. The man's reply is muffled, a near growl. Chris knees him in the gut and the man starts talking. When he stops, Chris releases him, grabbing me and pulling me behind him.

The stranger darts off through the gates and Chris whirls on me, his fingers digging into my shoulders, rain plastering his hair onto his face. "Wait means wait, damn it!"

Blood rushes in my ears. "Your hand. Let me see your hand."

His expression is pure fury unleashed, and instead of showing me his hand, he grabs mine and pulls me back onto the sidewalk and into a mad dash. Two briskly covered blocks later, we rush into a bar, rain dripping off our clothes and forming puddles on the hardwood floors. Chris doesn't look at me. He doesn't have to. Anger crackles off him, and I have the distinct impression he's barely contained.

He asks the big guy at the door, "Toilette?"

We receive a finger point and a one-word reply, and we're on the move again, my hand still firmly in Chris's. The adrenaline readying me for our soon-to-come confrontation is all that keeps my aching feet and chilled body in motion down a flight of stairs to a tiny hallway with one door at the end.

Chris shoves open the bathroom door, and drags me inside with him. A second later I'm in a space barely big enough for one, and Chris is locking the door. Another second later, and I'm pressed against the wall. For once, his big body is pressed against me and I'm not wet from arousal.

"What part of 'wait' did you not understand?" he growls at me.

"Someone had to call for help if you got into trouble."

"I said wait, Sara, and I damn well meant wait. You have to listen."

"Chris, I—"

"Don't push me, baby," he warns, water tracking the angry lines of his face. "You won't like the results. And if you think you've heard that one before, think again. This is all new territory."

I'm shaking inside and out, and not from the chill of my wet skin. "Don't threaten me."

"Then don't fucking give me a reason to be this damn pissed. Nothing is worth risking your safety."

"You are!"

His lips thin. "I'm not giving you the chance to repeat today. This ends now. We're going back to the States."

"What?" The one word is all I can manage, all that can cut through the clawing pain of my heart being ripped from my chest.

"Stephen said a week in the States, and we can end the Ava fiasco."

We. He's saying "we," and for a moment I cling to the meaning, but only a moment. If I go back now, he'll shut me out. He knows it and so do I. "Did Stephen say I have to come back?"

"He said it's a good idea. He'll work out the passport situation."

He's shutting me out before I can hurt him. "Did he say I *have* to return?" I ask again, unable to control the tremble in my voice.

He presses his hand to the wall, his body lifting away from

mine. His silence is damning, and my mind slides down a water-fall into the icy waters of nevermore. I'm sinking, and I have to escape before I drown. I try to duck under Chris's arm.

His leg shackles mine, holding me in place. "I'm trying to protect you."

"Don't even go there, Chris. I'm sick of that excuse. If you want out, then say you want out. Let me by."

He's a solid, unmovable wall, his expression infuriatingly indiscernible. "That man back there was hired to follow you in hopes of finding Ella."

My lips part in surprise. "What? Why? By who?"

"Ella has found her way onto the wrong radar screen."

"Whose radar?"

"Garner Neuville, a very rich, very powerful man who's nothing but trouble. The kind I want you nowhere near."

"Why would he be looking for Ella?"

"Exactly. Whatever she's into is bigger than marrying some small-time American doctor. I want you out of Paris."

Icy fingers crawl up my spine. I'm no better off than the night I sat on Ella's bed, willing her home, and wishing for Chris. They're both a million miles from my reach and I haven't a clue how to find them.

"But sending me back to the States isn't about Ella, is it? It's about your fear that I'm going to go off and die on you." He jerks away from me and it's as if a door slams shut, and I almost flinch with the impact.

But I keep going, I keep pushing. I'm worried about Ella. I'm angry at Chris. I'm hurt. "Well, you know what I fear? *This* is my fear. This moment when, once again, you shut me out and I'm alone. If you were going to leave me alone, you should have walked away before now, when I still knew how to breathe without you."

We stare at each other and all he gives me is more of his damn silence. I've said the things we don't say, and he doesn't even react.

I begin to shiver. I can't stop shivering.

Chris shrugs out of his coat and steps closer, our gazes collide, and the regret I see in his eyes carves a piece out of my soul. I'm going to lose him, and it's going to destroy me. And I think it's going to destroy him, too.

He moves toward me and I hold my breath, preparing for the impact of his touch that never comes. He wraps the jacket around my shoulders and I huddle into the dry, warm silk on the inside, but I don't look at him.

"I'm going to get the car," he announces softly. "I'll pull up to the door."

My gaze snaps up as he reaches for the lock on the door, and I have this horrible feeling that if I let him walk out now, it's done. We're done.

"I'm not leaving," I say, and my voice is steady. "I won't leave without Ella, and I won't leave without you. All of you, Chris."

He stands there, more stone than man, more distant than present. Then he opens the door and disappears into the hallway.

We don't speak on the ride to the house, the soft hum of the car heater filling the empty space. Once we're inside the garage, and outside the car, Chris wordlessly takes his jacket from me and hangs it over one of his bikes to dry. I'm mostly dry, thanks to my thin blouse and skirt, and the blast of the heater.

At the door we pause to remove our boots, and Chris takes off his socks as well. I can't bring myself to remove my thigh-highs, and it's the first time in a very long time I've felt awkward with him. I think he feels it, too. It's in the air. We aren't right. We aren't even close to right.

Inside the house, we wait for the elevator doors to open. More awkwardness fills the air and it begins to twist me in knots. Finally the elevator arrives, and Chris waits for me to enter. We lean against opposite sides of the car, facing each other. Chris lets his head drop backward against the wall, and his lashes lower, wispy strands of half-dry hair teasing his forehead and cheeks. The wet cotton of his T-shirt outlines his hard body and dried blood outlines a two-inch cut on his cheek, which doesn't look like it needs stitches. I hope the injury to his hand is equally minor.

The car begins to move and Chris doesn't look at me. I have this sense that he believes if he does, the walls he's convinced himself to erect between us will fall. I burn to tear them down myself, to grab him and hold him, and promise him I'm not going anywhere. That's what he wants to hear: that I'm not going to die. He wants the impossible.

I can't take not touching him, not talking to him. The elevator stops moving and I step toward Chris. At the same moment, his head lifts, his eyes crashing into mine, his face carved in hard lines and shadows, no rainbow in sight. We're still living the storm. No surprise there.

I resist flinging my arms around him and reach for his hand, glancing down at his slightly swollen knuckles, and back up at him. "Let me clean the cut and bandage it for you." I back out of the door, gently tugging him with me, encouraged when he follows. I lead him to the bathroom and he immediately tugs his shirt off, and hangs it on the side of the tub before sitting on the edge himself. The sight of his dragon flexing with the hard lines of one shoulder and arm does funny things to my stomach. It's a part of his past I will never know, if he has his way.

I look up to find him watching me watch him. Emotion tightens my throat. "Where would I find bandages?" I don't even know where anything is in my home, which might not be my home soon. Why does that feel so much worse now than ever before?

"Under the sink." It's the first time he's spoken since the bathroom in the bar, and the sound of his voice is silk soothing my raw nerve endings.

I turn away from him, gathering my supplies while I also gather my emotions. Part of me is ready to regret becoming this attached to Chris, but I squash the idea. Chris is feeling enough regret for both of us. One of us has to be willing to put it all on the line for this relationship.

When I turn back to him, Chris moves to the toilet seat to allow me to sit on the edge of the tub. Still feeling a bit too emotional, it's my turn to avoid eye contact. I sit down and tap my leg for him to put his hand on top of it. He doesn't hesitate. His fingers splay on my upper thigh, palm resting in the center, and I am instantly, achingly aware of the touch in every part of my body.

I study the cut on his knuckle, surrounded by rapidly forming bruises. It's impossible to tell if there is any serious injury unless X-rays are taken, which I'm sure he'll refuse.

"I don't know how to love you and not protect you," he says, and my eyes lift at his soft confession. My heart thunders as he adds, "And I don't know how to protect you and not overwhelm you. I'm always going to be on edge. I'm always going to think . . . too much."

"No one knows what tomorrow brings, Chris. We have to live for today together."

He runs his uninjured hand through his drying hair, leaving it a wonderful mess. "That's just it, Sara. I can't do that. I'm never going to be able to do that. I can't do *this*."

He pushes to his feet and he's gone, leaving me alone.

Seventeen

I'm remarkably calm when I snap out of my stunned reaction to Chris's declaration. I'm not sure how long I've been sitting on the tub, but my body is stiff and cold.

When I finally stand up, I strip off my clothes and turn the shower on to scorching before I step inside. I need to think, and once my mind is working again, my perspective on what he's said changes.

Chris loves me. I believe that. He told me I'm what got him through losing Dylan, even when I wasn't with him. So, while my first thought was that his reference to not being able to do "this" meant us, me and him, I don't think that now.

I think he means the pain, the worry, the fear. I believe that it's the moments when he's felt "I can't do this" that he's ended up tied up and screaming for someone to whip him until he feels nothing else.

My poor damaged man. So brilliant and wonderful, and he

201

can't see it. He wants to leave Paris to protect me from more than outside danger—he's still afraid I can't handle who he is. This hurts far more than his reactions today. I'm not leaving. *We* are not leaving.

The hot water is cooling, and I get out and dress in my favorite soft black sweats and a pink tank. Once my hair is dry, I resist the urge to look for Chris. He left here feeling out of control, and I need to give him time to get it back. Pushing him won't get me the results I want.

Grabbing my laptop, I head to the leather chair by the window in our bedroom. I open the blinds of the massive arched window, so like the others in the house. Rain patters against the panes and I curl one of my bare feet beneath me. Needing a connection to at least one of the two people I wish were with me now, I begin my search for Ella by googling the name "Garner Neuville."

Two hours later, the everlasting rain a soft hum on my rattled nerve endings and I'm lost in thought. What does one of the richest men in Paris want with Ella, who has no family and no money? I've tabbed through pages and pages about the thirty-two-year-old billionaire who inherited a fortune and turned it into a bigger fortune, and have to figure out an answer. I have no idea why Chris thinks this man is trouble, but I don't doubt he knows what he's talking about.

It makes no sense that Neuville would be looking for Ella, so this has to be connected to her fiancé. I never liked David, never trusted him.

I set my computer on the floor and stare at the bedroom

door, willing Chris to appear. It doesn't work. I can't just sit here. I have to attack the problems, not let them attack me.

I push to my feet. I'm going to find Ella, and talking with this Neuville person is a good start. But I'm not doing it without Chris. He's had enough time alone, and so have I.

Now it's our time.

The door to his studio is open when I arrive at the top of the stairs, and I hope it's an invitation. The hard, dark song reverberating off the walls isn't as encouraging: "The Bottom," by Staind. The words grind through me, inescapable, intense. Emotional.

You suffocate, you cannot wait for this to just be over. The song is the voice to Chris's feelings. The window to how deeply he hurts. And I hurt for him all over again. If I can't stop his pain, I'm at least going to be with him, through it.

I step inside and see Chris on a stool directly in front of the archway window, leaning toward the canvas resting on an easel. His hand, bandaged but apparently functional, moves easily with the brush he holds, and he's changed out of his wet jeans. He's now dressed in a dark blue pair, but he bypassed a shirt and shoes, and his hair is soft and spiky, like it's been freshly washed. He showered in another bathroom, avoiding me while I've been wishing he'd appear.

The song lyrics remind me that every masterpiece he's ever created has been done to music to match his mood, and this song has a clear message. He's suffocating. He wants this to end. He doesn't mean us, I remind myself. He needs me, like I need him.

Suddenly, I have to know how this song relates to what he's spent two hours creating on the canvas. I push away from the door and start walking. Chris doesn't turn and I don't think he knows I'm here. He's intensely into his work, deeply involved in what he's creating. I stop as soon as I'm close enough to see the canvas, but not close enough to disturb his concentration.

And my heart skips a beat. He's painting me. Draped in his leather jacket, my rain-drenched hair plastered around my face. I'm pale and my eyes reflect such anguish that I can barely breathe. He's captured the moment I confessed I was living my biggest fear, of him shutting me out—and he's done it with such brilliance that I'm reliving it, my heart bleeding from the pain.

He'd said nothing after my confession, shown no reaction, but he'd felt one. He feels one now.

Chris might not have been physically with me these past two hours, but he hadn't shut me out. My heart swells, and I burn to go to touch him. But it's not the right way to reach him right now—it's not the right thing to do.

I walk past him, toward the window, winging it, hoping I'll read Chris and understand what he needs right now.

I know the instant he comes back to this world and me. My skin tingles and heats with the weight of his eyes following me. I step directly in front of the window, several feet from where he's been working. Turning around, I'm surprised to see him standing on this side of the canvas now. His hands are by his sides, his jaw tense, his eyes as haunted as mine are on his canvas.

I stand there and I wait. I'm not sure what I'm waiting for, but I wait. I don't speak and neither does he. We've been good at this silent thing today. Too good. I can't take it. I think I suck at waiting.

"Paint me," I say. I've refused his request to do so in the past; I was afraid of what he would see. When I had secrets I didn't want him to discover. "The real me, not the one from your memory." I tug my tank top off, which leaves me naked from the waist up, and I toss it aside. It's important that he knows I'm willing to be naked inside and out for him, and I quickly slide my pants and panties down and kick them aside. There's a ledge that leads onto the wide windowsill, and I climb on top of it so that I'm inside the frame of the archway.

Chris moves toward me with a slow, sensuous stride, dominant but not predatory. The desire etching the hard lines of his face encourages me. He is coming for me, and I am his. I've held back until now, but no more. My personal demons just need to go to hell and stay there. They aren't dragging us down with them.

I came to Paris for him, for this. Today was about his secrets, his past. His heartache and fears. Neither of us thought those things would be easy to face. And I don't need easy. I need Chris.

Finally, he stops in front of me and my nostrils flare with his musky, wonderful scent. I want to wake up smelling like him every day of the rest of my life.

He looks down at me as the song loops and replays, echoing what I see in the dark depths of his stare. I catch a portion of the song, something about waves washing away scars. I want to be the waves that wash away Chris's scars. I want that very much.

Slowly, his gaze lowers, lingering on my mouth, and then doing a lazy sweep downward over my breasts, my stomach, my sex, and I feel it like a caress. By the time he begins traveling upward again I am liquid fire and anticipation, slick between my thighs and tingling all over. I need him to touch me, but when he's on edge, I know better than to touch him before he's ready.

He reaches above me and my gaze follows as he hits a button on the archway. An electronic blind begins to slide down over the window. I almost laugh at the craziness of the moment. I'm naked, standing in front of the glass, watching a blind lower, and I don't care. I just want Chris to touch me. He hits the button again and seals the shade into place a full foot over my head. Still exposed to the open glass, I wonder what the point of lowering the shade was. I find out when he reaches for a cord connected to the center of it.

"Hands over your head," he orders, and finally hearing his voice is sweet honey. It pours over me and into me, and my heart slows its pounding beat.

I willingly lift my arms, aware of how my breasts are now eye level and thrust closer to Chris. He steps onto the sill with me, in front of me, his big, perfect body cradling mine as he backs closer to the glass but not against it. His touch arouses me even more, and I'm already on fire. My nipples nestle in the crisp hair of his chest and I can't stop the arch of my body into his, or the soft moan that escapes my lips. I'm so lost in how much I need him that I'm barely aware of him knotting the cord around my wrists.

He steps off the sill, leaving me aching from the loss of his body, and I'm certain he's about to tease me and drive me wild.

Then an anxious thought takes over. How many women have been here like this for him? Has Amber?

Chris wraps his arms around me, molding me close. "No to what you're thinking," he says. "I don't bring anyone else here. Only you."

My lips part. "You . . . you knew what I was thinking?"

"Yes." He traces my jaw. "I knew." His lips brush mine, a gentle whisper, before they caress over my cheek to my ear, then to my neck. The tenderness of his touch is unexpectedly erotic. Goose bumps gather on my skin, and my nipples tingle and tighten.

I thought this was about control—and it is; I'm tied up. But it's a softer shade of dominance. He vibrates with desire, his lips traveling to my shoulder, his hand to my breast, my nipple, and back down my waist to my backside. He is touching me everywhere, kissing me everywhere. Tender, wonderful nips and bites and licks that travel lower and lower, until he's on his knees pressing his mouth to my belly.

He lingers there and his eyes lift to mine, promising me delicious pleasure. His hands divide and conquer, the fingers of one tracing the intimate seam of my backside, the other stroking between my thighs where I'm slick and aching.

"Do you have any idea how wild it drives me, to know you get this wet so easily for me?" he asks, his voice laden with desire. For me. Because of me.

I try to laugh, but it comes out choked. "It drives me pretty wild, too."

He smiles, and it's as beautiful as watching him flatten that room of stuffy suits at the embassy. His tongue dips into my belly button, teasing me with where it will go next. I moan when his hand firmly cups my backside, before he lifts one of my legs, and then the next, over his shoulders. Caressing a path from one of my knees to my backside, he orders, "Hold them there."

I nod and swallow hard as his thumb teases my clit, flicking it gently before his fingers press inside me. Gasping, I squeeze my eyes shut. His mouth closes down over me, and aah—I can't think. Everything seems to go into kind of a soft haze of pleasure.

My head drops back and I have a fleeting out-of-body moment where I see myself in the window, my hands tied above my head with my legs wrapped around the neck of Chris Merit, while he does delicious things to my body. I laugh in disbelief that this is my life. His tongue is doing something incredibly perfect to me, and his fingers . . .

I gasp and arch my hips, shocked as my sex clenches around his fingers without warning. Ripples of pleasure radiate to the rest of my body, and Chris uses his skillful fingers and tongue to bring me from the peak to the valley. Slowly, the scream of pleasure within me becomes a hum, and I'm panting from the impact.

Chris kisses up my thigh to one of my knees, then gently lowers my legs to the floor. He wraps his arms around me and presses his cheek to my stomach, holding me there as if he feels like he's about to lose me.

As seconds tick by, he starts to scare me.

"Chris?" His name is a whispered plea.

His hands begin traveling upward as he stands, cradling me

to his body. "I can't breathe without you, either, Sara," he says, in a low, gravelly voice, replying to what I'd said in the bar. "And that's the problem."

"Just stop trying," I whisper. "Untie me. Please. I need to touch you."

He kisses me instead, unwilling or unready to give away control, but there's a softness about him, about how his tongue caresses my mouth. I taste his passion, his hunger, but there's something more. Something that still tastes like good-bye.

I stroke his tongue with mine, trying to kiss it away, but it doesn't work. I try to burn it away with heat and fire, but it won't fade. So when he tears his mouth from mine, I don't give him time to speak.

"I'm not going anywhere. You can try to send me away, but I came here for a reason. I believe in us and I'm not going away."

His hands frame my face. "If you tried, I'd come after you."

His rough-edged tone is delicious friction to my nerve endings. "No matter what you show me or what happens, I won't leave, Chris. If that's why *you* want to leave, it's the wrong reason, and the wrong thing for us."

He stares down at me, the seconds ticking by, his expression unreadable, before he steps up onto the sill and unties my wrists. Before I have time to lower my hands, he's stepped off the sill and is walking away to the other side of his canvas. He returns with a shirt in his hand.

"Put this on or we won't talk, and we need to." He holds it up so that I can slide my arms. Disappointingly, it smells of fabric softener, not Chris.

He leans on the wall and pulls me against him, his hands gliding up my back and molding me to him. "I don't want to leave."

"But you said—"

"I know what I said, and I meant it at the time. My first instinct when you were in danger was to get you the hell away from anything and everything that could steal you away from me."

"Including your past."

"No, Sara. When I brought you here, I was all in, and I still am. My need to do things at my own speed isn't about hesitation, it's about how I have to deal with certain events in my life. Wanting us to leave Paris was about keeping you safe. I don't like this Neuville and Ella situation."

"We need to stay and see through what we've started."

"I know. Believe me, I know. I've spent the past two hours battling my need to protect you, and the many reasons I wanted us here now. Next week . . ." He looks away, his jaw tensing, before he turns back to me. "Nothing is as important as your safety."

What happens next week? I open my mouth to ask, but his fingers snake into my hair, and his eyes glow with determination.

"I have people working on this Ella and Neuville situation, digging up information. If I find out anything that I think puts you in danger, we're leaving. Period."

"Chris—"

He kisses me, hard and fast. "Nonnegotiable. And if you take unnecessary risks, or try to play investigator yourself, I swear to

God, I'll drug you and put you on a plane, if that's what it takes to get you out of here."

Storm clouds lurk in his eyes, threatening to consume him again; something about next week has set him off again. So we'll deal with it next week. Right now I just want him to smile, so I smile and run my fingers over the newly forming stubble on his jaw. "Good thing you're so sexy when you act like a caveman."

He stares at me for a minute and then scoops me up and heads toward the door. "I'll show you caveman."

I bite my lip, pleased with his reaction. He's not smiling, but I'm pretty sure we both will be soon.

Eighteen

Chris and I spend the rest of Friday in various ways of being naked together, breaking only for food and conversation. Saturday starts just as wonderfully. Chris and I wake up together, eat together, laugh together. We dress casually and plan to hit some museums in the afternoon.

Midmorning, he heads to his studio to paint while I settle into my favorite chair in our bedroom, chatting with a worried Chantal while I watch the unending drizzle outside the window. Afterward, I have a chat with the business attorney about my venture. Though Chris set it up for me, he knows how important my own identity is to me, and that was the end of his involvement. I fall more in love with him every second.

When my call ends, I rush to Chris's gallery to share my excitement over how easy it will be to ramp up my new business. I'll need a name for it and already ideas are popping into my head.

I hear his murmured voice to the far right of the gallery and I follow the sound to a short, enclosed stairwell leading to another room. I head down and see Chris sitting behind a silver and gray desk. There's a massive mural of a dragon behind him on the wall, and I gape at the amazing work he's created. I can't believe I haven't asked to see the dragons he'd painted early in his career. He'd told me he keeps them here in Paris.

"I don't care how it happened, as long as she's not a suspect," Chris says into the phone, glancing up and motioning me forward. "Just get her passport reissued."

Chris falls into listening mode and I walk around the desk, leaning on the edge next to him as he says, "Of course, we'll go to the embassy for the paperwork. Just tell us when." He takes my hand and smiles up at me, and I smile back as I digest what I've just learned. I'm not a suspect in Rebecca's murder, and my passport situation seems to be in the process of being resolved. Add to that my business starting to take shape, and so far, today is a much better day than yesterday.

"I have another call coming in, Stephen," Chris announces. "Let me call you back—or better yet, call me back when you have Sara's paperwork in order."

He ends the call and glances at me. "Just one more minute. This will be fast." I nod and he hits the button on his phone to answer his incoming call. He immediately says, "I hear Garner Neuville has been making a showing there on the weekends."

I listen eagerly.

A female voice replies, "He might."

Something about the voice sends unease through me.

"That's a yes," Chris replies, sounding irritated.

"Not a yes, but a 'make it worth my while,'" the female replies, and my chest flutters with the suggestive comment.

Chris squeezes my hand, willing me to look at him. "I'm not in the mood for your games, Isabel." His tone is biting in a way I never hear from him. "Call me when he shows up. And don't tell him you did it." He kisses my hand.

"It's been weeks since he's been in, Chris." She sounds snappy now.

"Then he's due a visit," Chris replies, and hangs up. He reaches for me and pulls me in front of him. "She's just a contact to try to get to Neuville. I'm making sure Neuville doesn't get to screen me out. We have mutual acquaintances, and I'm putting them to use to get a one-on-one."

I nod and settle my hand on his jaw. "Yes. I know, and I appreciate all you're doing." I let my fingers trail downward, his one-day stubble rasping against the softness of my fingers.

His eyes narrow. "But?"

"I'm not jealous, if that's what you think. I just . . . I felt this pinch in my chest, hearing her taunt you like that. I'm not sure why."

His hand settles on my upper thigh. "You're in a strange country, and you've had a week of hell. I'd say that's a pretty good reason."

I lean in and kiss him, wondering why this is bothering me. "I love that I can say anything to you."

He tucks a lock of my hair behind my ear, warmth radiating in his voice when he says, "I love that you say what's on your mind, rather than get upset. How was your call?"

I ease back fully onto the desk. "It was good. Really good. I'll tell you about it, but is there any news on Ella at all?"

"Not yet. I'm working every angle I can. I have people looking into everything, from any changes to Neuville's financial portfolio to any trips out of the country. Speaking of which, your passport situation should be in order in the next few days. Stephen's been assured it was an administrative error."

"And yet the embassy questioned me and knew about Rebecca?"

"I said the same thing, but what matters is you're not a suspect, and they're clearing your passport." His hands settle on my hips. "Tell me about your call with the attorney." I relax and share all the details, and when I finish, he stands up and laces his fingers with mine. "I want to show you something."

Our destination turns out to be an empty room on the same floor as his gallery. "You can use this as an office."

"It's huge." The size of three corner offices, with its own archway window.

"You can use it to display the art you buy and haven't sold," he suggests.

The idea gets me excited all over again. "Only if you promise to paint me a dragon of my own. The one in your office is amazing. When do I get to see the collection you said you store here?"

He pulls me close. "Next weekend. I want us to go to the place my parents left me, right outside the city. That's where it's at."

I immediately think of how he'd started to say *next week* and stopped himself, when we'd been talking about his past.

This trip is about what he'd almost told me yesterday; I know it deep in my gut. There's something about this trip that will reveal one of his dreaded secrets.

I step close and wrap my arms around him. "Next weekend it is," I say, and I don't miss the shadows in his eyes before he kisses me.

It's near seven on Saturday evening when Chris and I finally break away from one of the staff members raving about his work at the Louvre. I tug my rain jacket closer and Chris tucks my hand in his as we step into the elevator leading to the parking garage.

"I still can't believe I saw the *Mona Lisa*," I say with a blissful sigh. "It's much smaller than I imagined it to be."

"It has a lot of hype," Chris comments, wrapping his arm around my shoulder and turning me toward him.

"It's the *Mona Lisa*."

"Yeah, yeah," he murmurs, acting as unimpressed as he had earlier. "Where do you want to go tomorrow?"

The elevator opens and our hands automatically meld together, as they have all day. "Back here," I say. "I love this place. There's so much I haven't seen yet, I could spend days here."

"It's a special place, and if you want to come back, then we'll come back."

I glance up at him, and my stomach flutters. The man has utterly charmed me today with his desire to be just another tourist, not the famous artist he is. Of course, it didn't work. People know him far too well in the Paris art community.

The Porsche 911 comes into view, and Chris has just clicked

the locks open when his cell phone rings. He stops and digs it from his pocket, glancing at the number, and tension rolls across his features.

He answers the call. "Is he there?" he asks without preamble, and listens before saying, "I'll be there in fifteen minutes. Make sure he doesn't leave." He grimaces at whatever is said to him, and adds, "You're resourceful. Figure it out." Hanging up, he stuffs his phone in his pocket.

"Neuville?" I ask immediately.

"Yes. Take the car home and I'll meet you in an hour." He tries to hand me the keys.

I refuse to take them. "I'm going with you."

"Forget it, Sara."

"I can't drive in Paris traffic. And even if I did, I can't sit around at home and wait for answers," I argue, pressing my hand to his chest. "I'll go insane. You know I will. Besides, I'll know things about Ella you won't. I'll catch lies you can't."

His lips thin. "Sara—"

"It's not like this will put me on his radar, Chris. I'm already on it. I'll be with you. I'll be safe."

He stares down at me for several intense seconds, his expression impassive while I hold my breath and wait for his reply. Finally he scrubs a hand down his face and studies the ceiling above me. "You do exactly what I say, when I say it. It won't be for no reason."

Relief washes over me. "Yes. I'll do whatever you say."

He studies me, his eyes glinting steel. "You never do whatever I say."

"I will this time." And I really try to mean it.

• • •

Not far from the Louvre, we pull up to a parking meter on a street that looks like any other side street I've seen in Paris. The same white, concrete, stucco-looking buildings lined up side by side. The same intimate sidewalks line narrow two-way roads paved with oversized bricks.

I don't see any retail shops or restaurants, but there seems to be a valet parking cars at a building across the street from us. "Where are we?"

"A private dinner club," he says. "We're avoiding the valet because we need to talk before we go inside."

My stomach flutters. "About what?"

"Isabel and I have a history."

Despite expecting it, the announcement still rattles me. "What does that mean?"

"It means she's good with a whip and at one point in my life I spent far too much time appreciating that skill." His tone is steady, unemotional.

I feel myself go pale. This is what I'd sensed when he'd been talking to her on the phone. It wasn't the existence of Isabel herself that had bothered me, but something in Chris's reaction to her. I desperately try to cut through the shadows, to read his expression, but fail. Finally, I say, "What does 'far too much time' mean?"

"It means it was an addiction and she was my drug dealer."

Acid burns in my throat and I remember him once telling me there had been a time when the beatings were all that got him from one day to the next day. "You say that so nonchalantly."

"Because it doesn't matter, Sara, and neither does she. She was just the person holding the whip."

"How often did you see her?" *How often had she beaten him?*

"It's the past."

But it's not the past or Dylan wouldn't have driven him to Mark's club to get whipped again. *"How often?"*

"Too often and for about five years. After that, I made the mistake of going back to her during my bad moments." He leans close to me and his expression softens, and his voice turns tender. "Sara." He runs a hand over my cheek and lets it fall away. "She didn't do anything to me I didn't ask her to do."

And yet he'd called her his drug dealer. I don't believe he'd call the random woman in Mark's club who'd used a whip on him the same thing.

"We have to go inside before Neuville leaves. Isabel will try to push your buttons. I need to know you won't let her."

"Why would she do that?"

"Because I had an affair with the whip, not her. When I didn't need it anymore, I didn't need her."

I try to control my reaction, afraid Chris will take it wrong. Afraid he will regret how he is sharing this part of himself with me, when he hasn't always, but anger burns through my body. This woman fed his need to be punished. This *bitch* used the one weakness Chris possesses, the heartache of loss, against him. "I can handle Isabel," I say, and somehow I keep my voice unaffected, though my fury is quickly eroding my calmness.

Chris doesn't look convinced by my façade, but he takes one glance at his watch and says, "We have to go in." He pulls me close, caressing my hair in that familiar, wonderful way he does. "Just remember. We're here for Ella. Isabel doesn't matter."

"I know." And I do. "I can do this."

And he's right. Isabel *doesn't* matter. Ella does, and he does.

The entryway to the dinner club is a small foyer with a coat closet and a big, burly doorman in a tuxedo.

He nods at Chris. "Mr. Merit." Then he looks at me with a Stallone-esque, heavy-lidded expression. "And a guest, I see." He gives my jeans a once-over and eyes Chris. "I see she's living by your dress code, not ours."

Chris shrugs out of his coat and sets it by an unattended coat check area, then reaches for mine. "Neither myself nor Ms. McMillan will be staying for dinner. Isabel is expecting us."

"Then by all means." He steps aside and motions us up a long flight of stairs too narrow for more than one person. Chris waves me forward first. Terrific. Into the wild world of Isabel without my own whip.

I'm almost at the top of the steps when I spot a woman I am certain is Isabel. She is gorgeous, with long, silky, dark brown hair and pale skin, and a short, fitted, silk emerald-green dress. There are no marks on her skin from a whip. No ink of a tattoo. There's an unworldly quality about her, and I guess her to be at least in her midthirties. Amber never had a chance against this woman and I'm willing to bet that Isabel was who came next. I am surprised to find I feel no inferiority to her, as I did Amber. Maybe it's due to my improved state of mind, or the growth Chris and I have managed in these short few days. Or maybe it's simply how much I instantly hate her for what she did to Chris.

I step onto the main dining room floor, directly in front of her.

"You must be Sara," she purrs in English, and her accent is positively sexy.

I don't ask how she knows who I am; I don't really care. "And you must be Isabel."

"I am," she confirms. "Welcome to my establishment."

She owns this place? I already felt like I was on enemy territory; now I feel like I'm in a minefield.

Chris steps to my side, his hand settling on my back, his hip pressed intimately against mine. It's a statement, and Isabel knows it. Her pale blue eyes sharpen, her red-painted lips pursing before her attention shifts to Chris.

Her irritation fades, replaced by unmistakable female admiration. She wants him, badly. "S'il vous plaît, Chris."

"Where is he?" Chris asks, seeming oblivious to her warm welcome. Chris is oblivious to nothing.

She purses her lips again. "Right to business. I see nothing has changed. This way."

Chris's fingers flex on my back, silently warning me to stay cool. I don't look at him, for fear he'll decide to usher me out of here. Which is probably smart, since I'm really pissed off.

We follow Isabel through an elegant dining room with white linen tablecloths, fancy red-cushioned chairs, and lots of art on the walls. I easily recognize several paintings as Chris's. The whip might have been what Chris had the affair with, but Isabel definitely wanted one with Chris.

Isabel halts at a staircase that snakes up to another level. "You'll find him in limited company."

While I understand that a cramped city of nearly twelve million has to be built in levels, I'd be a whole lot happier if Neuville had been on this one. I'm not looking forward to being the first to greet Neuville, especially considering my unfamiliar surroundings.

"Follow me," Chris orders, starting up the stairs first.

Isabel crosses her arms in front of her chest, her lips twitching like she knows something we don't. I frown and quickly follow Chris, afraid of what might await him upstairs.

He's already at the top and I hear him say, "Surprise—but then, imagine our surprise to be followed by someone who said they worked for you."

"*Our* surprise?" a deep male voice queries. "You and who else?"

I step up beside Chris, bringing a formal dining room into view. Another painting by a famous artist is on the wall, and the walnut table in the center of the room is large enough to fit a dozen people. There are only two. A twenty-something female with dirty blond hair, who would be quite beautiful if she weren't sitting next to the devastatingly handsome Garner Neuville.

He flicks me a look and then glances back at Chris, who says, "I'm sure you know Sara, since you had her followed."

Holding Chris's stare, Neuville doesn't react. He just sits there in his well-pressed, pale blue dress shirt, not a strand of his thick, slicked-back raven hair out of place. "Leave us, Stephanie," he finally says without looking at his companion.

She's walking toward me in a few seconds flat, and I can't help but wonder if Neuville is her Master. Are those the kinds of circles he and Chris run in together? They share a link to Isabel, after all.

"Would we like to sit down?" Chris asks, as if Neuville had offered. "Absolutely."

I fight a smirk as Chris's hand settles on my back, urging me to the table where he sits at the end, opposite Neuville. I sit at Chris's left.

Chris and Neuville lock eyes, and the air thickens as they prepare to match swords.

Nineteen

"Where's Ella?"

I blanch to find the piercing stare Neuville had been aiming at Chris suddenly directed at me.

"Why are you looking for her?" Chris asks before I can reply.

"Ella and I were"—he pauses for obvious effect—"involved. I moved too fast for her and she got spooked. She took off and I haven't seen her since."

The many ways I can read "involved" set my nerves further on edge. The idea of this man playing dominant to Ella is not a good one. "What does you 'moved too fast' mean?"

He arches a brow at me, looking rather smug. "Do you really want the gritty details?"

Yes! I scream in my head, and then amend my answer to No! I might come unglued if I heard details. "I just want to know where Ella is." I don't try to keep the bite from my voice.

"Then we have something in common, Ms. McMillan," he drawls.

"You've been quick with your answers," Chris comments. "Some might think you planned them in advance."

"Others might simply say I'm telling the truth," Neuville responds.

Chris doesn't miss a beat. "I guess it depends on how much that person knows about you."

Neuville arches his brow again, this time at Chris. "What exactly do you think you know about me?"

"More than who you like to fuck," Chris replies, and I barely hold back a gasp. "When did you last see Ella?"

"A week ago," Neuville says, as if Chris hadn't said anything unexpected at all. "I've been looking for her ever since, and, naturally, when I discovered her best friend was arriving in Paris, I assumed it was to be with her. I have yet to find that to be the case."

"Why not ask Sara through me, rather than have her followed?" Chris asks.

"I didn't know you were involved until I had her followed," is his rebuttal.

Chris doesn't look impressed by that answer. "And yet you didn't call me when you found out."

I want to ask about my stolen wallet and passport, but I hold back. It's not like the content is valid anymore, and Neuville is drumming his fingers on the table, irritation radiating off of him. "For the same reason you didn't just call me on the phone tonight. You didn't want me to escape before I heard you out. The same applies to me with Ella."

This answer has my attention. I do not like his use of the word *escape,* any more than I like remembering how enthralled Ella was by Rebecca's journals and the idea of a Master. If this man opened Ella up to one potential Master, could she be with another man now who might be dangerous?

I open my mouth to speak and Chris steals my question from my lips. "What happened to Ella's fiancé?"

Neuville snorts. "If you mean the idiot who'd upset her the night I met her, I have no clue."

"Where exactly did you meet Ella?" I quickly ask.

Neuville flicks me a look. "I was in her hotel on business."

Chris jumps on that. "What hotel?"

Again, no hesitation from Neuville as he replies, "Hôtel Lutetia."

Chris frowns. "Her doctor fiancé could afford Hôtel Lutetia?"

Neuville shrugs. "I have no intimate understanding of this man's wealth or lack thereof. I was in the lobby when Ella exited the elevator in tears and ran smack into me. She was upset, and I offered to buy her dinner at a nearby restaurant. When we returned to the hotel, her fiancé had checked out and left her with no money and no passport."

My jaw drops. "What? He took her passport?"

"He did," Neuville confirms. "As you can imagine, she was devastated about the entire situation. I offered to have her stay with me and she accepted."

This doesn't sound like the Ella I know—but then, the Ella I know would have called me weeks ago, too. "She just said 'yes' to staying with a stranger?"

"I don't believe she saw me as a stranger, Ms. McMillan." His lips twitch.

Something in his expression sets me off. I lean forward, one of my hands resting on the table, my blood pressure probably off the charts. "You're saying she slept with you when she thought David was waiting for her at the hotel?"

"I wasn't aware I said she slept with me," he replies. "Simply that we became fast friends."

"You implied more." My tone is biting.

"You assumed." His tone is crisp.

Chris takes control of the conversation again. "She was with you how long?"

"Three weeks," Neuville replies.

I narrow my eyes on this stranger who wants me to believe Ella to be someone I know her not to be. It doesn't sit well with me. He doesn't sit well with me. Why isn't he complaining about all of the questions? Maybe Chris is right. He practiced. He expected us. He was ready.

"I'll be able to find witnesses who saw her with you," Chris points out. "If there are none—"

"Dig around all you wish," Neuville interjects.

He's too confident. I don't know why I feel this, when honesty breeds confidence, but everything about this feels off. "Did Ella replace her passport?"

"Not while she was with me."

My brow furrows. "That makes no sense. She was due back to school."

He leans back in his chair, the long fingers of one hand resting on the table. "She wasn't in a hurry to return to the States."

Disappointment fills me as my hope of finding Ella through this man fades. "You really have no idea where she is?"

"Why else would I hire someone to look for her?"

"That's the question of the hour, isn't it?" Chris drawls softly, and Neuville's eyes narrow on him. The two men stare at each other, and I stare at Neuville, and several tense seconds pass before Chris says, "Sara, we need a few minutes alone. I'll meet you at the bar."

My gaze jerks to Chris's, but he's still in his stare-down with Neuville and I barely bite back an objection to leaving. I have to force myself to let go of my need to hear everything and try to control what I clearly cannot. I trust Chris. If he can get something out of Neuville by speaking to him alone, I want him to.

I stand up and walk away without another word. I'm pretty sure it's as surprising to Chris as it is to me.

At the bottom of the stairs is a waiter. I make a drinking motion with a pretend glass, and he points me in the direction of the bar, which is on a lower level. I discover the spacious basement level filled with a cluster of six tables and enough beautiful people standing and sitting around to need twice that, all wearing expensive dresses and tailored suits. Suddenly, my jeans feel out of place. No, not suddenly. The doorman started my walk down Awkward Lane and it simply continues.

I head to the U-shaped bar and flag the bartender for help with my escape. "Toilette?" I ask. I'm becoming quite a master at this one-word question.

The bartender points and I head behind him and down the

hall to his right. I'm gaining a powerful appreciation for the art of pointing and its ability to break the language barrier.

Inside the bathroom I find two large sinks to my left, and my nostrils flare from the scent of the cinnamon candle burning in the center of the marble counter. Three fancy wooden doors are farther inside the room and, after listening a moment, I determine the stalls are empty. Thankfully.

I lean on the sink and my image comes into view, then immediately fades as I replay everything Neuville has said to us, trying to figure out what bothered me most about him and the conversation. Three weeks, he'd said Ella had been with him. Three weeks. Hmmm. That feels off. Ella left San Francisco in late August. It's October. So Neuville's claim that he's been looking for her for a week might work, but it means that Ella and her fiancé broke up almost immediately after arriving in Paris. It also means that if Ella intended to come back to school for her October 1 schedule, she had waited until the last minute to have her passport reissued. But wouldn't Blake have discovered it had been reissued when he investigated her travel?

My thought process is waylaid as the bathroom door opens, and my skin prickles with warning even before I see Isabel in the mirror. Instantly stiffening, I turn to face her, readying myself for whatever comes next. And something is coming. It's in the crackle of the air.

She shuts the door and crosses her arms over her chest as she had when I'd headed up the stairs; she has another smug look on her face. I'm starting to think it's her permanent makeup. "You actually think he's yours, don't you?" she purrs, as if it amuses her.

"Talk about getting right down to business," I say. "At least we aren't going to play the fake-niceties game. He is mine."

She takes a step closer to me. And another. I curl my fingers into my palms but I don't move. She doesn't have a whip sharp enough to intimidate me. "Until he needs more," she promises. "The kind of 'more' only I can give him."

Anger lights me up like fire and my nails dig into the soft flesh of my palms. "If you mean until he needs pain, he won't."

She inches even closer, way beyond my personal space. We're toe-to-toe now and I can smell her floral perfume over the candle. It turns my stomach. "He will need pain," she promises. "He always has and he always will."

"You want him to think he does, because you think that means he needs you. Only he never needed you. It was the object you held in your hand. The whip anyone else can hold, if they're a big enough bitch to do it."

Her eyes light with fury and she snaps. One second I'm watching her livid expression turn her beautiful face ugly, the next she explodes at me, shoving me hard against the narrow wall behind me. I gasp with the impact, feeling sharp pain in my left shoulder. Her hands are still on me, pressing into me, holding me captive.

"You're the bitch," she hisses. "You're nothing, just one of his many attempts to deny what he really needs. He'll fail this time, like always. And when he comes back to me I'll fuck him extra hard, sweetheart, just for you. Maybe I'll add an extra few lashes with your name on them, too."

That's it. My shock at her attack morphs into anger and adrenaline rockets through me. Without a conscious thought to act, I shove her backward and keep moving until she slams against the wall. The air *woofs* out of her and I hold her by the shoulders like she had me. My arms shake with the force of white-hot anger.

"No," I grind out through my teeth, "he won't come back to you. You know why? Because I won't ever let him hurt that bad again, and I won't hurt him. And I damn sure won't let you hurt him."

The door opens abruptly and I don't have to look to know it's Chris. I keep my stare on Isabel, but I feel him. I always feel him.

"Problem?" he asks, sounding rather amused.

"No problem," I say coolly, still focused on the wicked witch of whips. She isn't looking at me or Chris. Her lashes have lowered, and I sense her anger has transformed into something else. I don't know what and I don't care, either. I just want her out of Chris's life.

I let go of her and turn to Chris. "Are we ready to go?"

He arches a brow, the amusement I'd heard in his voice lighting his eyes. "Are you ready to go?"

"I've done what I had to do here."

"Then by all means. Let's get out of here." He draws my hand in his and we head down the hallway together, leaving Isabel where she belongs: in Chris's past. I know Chris believes she's there already, but I'm going to make sure he knows how true that is.

We make our way through the bar and dining area and straight to the coat check. Once we step outside and start walking down the block toward the car, I ask the question burning in my mind. "What happened with Neuville?"

"We did the typical 'swordfight,' as you like to call it—and, as usual, it was highly unproductive. Rey is meeting us at the house to get an update so he and his brother can start following up on Neuville's claims. What happened with you and Isabel?"

"We did the typical 'catfight,' only ours was productive."

He arches a brow. "Was it, now?"

Maybe I'll add an extra few lashes with your name on them, too. I hear Isabel's words in my head and a whirlwind of emotions expand in my chest. I glance around, desperate for privacy, and I find the perfect place. I surprise Chris and shove him toward an alcove in front of a door where we're alone, behind a wall, the shadows engulfing us.

I look up at him, letting my eyes adjust to the shadows. "Do you remember when you shoved me into a corner like this one and warned me away from the gallery and from you?"

"I remember very well."

"You didn't scare me off then, and you won't scare me off now, or ever. But I lied to both of us when I said I'd watch your pain if that's what you needed. I won't watch. I won't let you be hurt again. I won't let you need that again. We need each other. We have each other. I love—"

He kisses me, a deep, heat-me-all-over, curl-my-toes, passionate kiss, and I melt into him. How had I ever doubted my decision to follow him to Paris? He is my home. He is my soul. "I love you, too," he says, his voice deep, thick with emotion. "And I've already told you. I only need you."

"No. You've never promised me you won't ever need that kind of escape again, Chris—but I'm not asking you to. I'm promising you that you won't. I will be here for you."

He stares down at me, and that edgy, mysterious Chris is clear and present. "I really have done a damn good job of corrupting you, haven't I? Straight to hell and the dark side, and asking for more."

"Yes." I wrap my arms around him. "Please take me home and corrupt me some more."

I expect him to argue, to warn me away, but he doesn't. His hand cups the back of my head and he brings my mouth to his. "I can't wait." Then he kisses me again.

Twenty

An hour later, Chris and I sit on the couch behind his desk in front of the dragon mural, and Rey is leaning on the desk facing us, giving us his perspective on Neuville.

"Finding out if anyone saw Ella with him isn't going to be a problem," he assures us, "but finding out details on Neuville's intimate personal and financial affairs is another story. His associations have long had him on law enforcement's radar, but no one has ever been able to connect him to anything illegal."

"What kind of associations?" I glance at Chris. "What haven't you told me?"

Chris sighs, casting Rey an irritated look. "Thank you, Rey."

Alarm bells are ringing. I should have asked why Chris didn't like Neuville. "Tell me what this is about." My voice wavers with a hint of demand and dread. I want to know, but already know I'm not going to like what I'm told.

Chris dodges giving me an answer. "Everything is speculation."

"Stop avoiding a proper answer," I warn. "Share the speculation." Chris's jaw tenses, and still he gives me no reply.

"He's long been suspected of a connection to the mob," Rey supplies.

"A mob connection!" I'm on my feet. "Ella was involved with someone in the mob?"

Chris reaches for my hand. "Sara, baby. Calm down."

"Calm *down*? Did you *really* just tell me to calm down? That's not a smart reply at this moment, Chris Merit. Why didn't you tell me this?"

"I think this is my cue to head out," Rey murmurs. "I'll call you, Chris."

"Coward," Chris grumbles. "You open your mouth and run away."

"I'm smart like that," Rey agrees, and his footsteps soon fade up the stairs.

"Why didn't you tell me?" I demand of Chris again, ignoring their exchange.

Chris stands up, towering over me, his hands coming down on my shoulders. "This is why. Your reaction is exactly what I expected."

"Don't not tell me something just because I might not like it. That's not how we do things. That's not what I expect of you."

He shuts his eyes for a moment and then opens them again. "It's not fact, and all it's doing is upsetting you." He leans me against the desk and I sit on the edge as he continues. "But this is why I wanted you out of Paris when his name came up. Once you insisted on staying, I decided to bring you with me today for two reasons. I wanted him to see that you're under my protection, and that you don't know where Ella is, either. So he'll lose interest in you now."

A million possibilities fly through my mind about what this means for Ella. "What if she's—"

"Don't do that to yourself," Chris warns. "Neuville doesn't think Ella's dead, or he wouldn't be looking for her. He has a lot of money and so do I. With both of us looking for Ella, the chances of finding her are high. This is good. Not bad."

My racing pulse slows slightly. "Why would he want to find a woman, one he just met a month ago, this badly?"

"Sara, a month after *we* met, I would have spent every dime I have to find you. We don't know what happened between them in those three weeks. We don't know if this is really anything more than a man infatuated with a woman."

A bit of hope blossoms inside me. "Maybe he really cares for her, and that's why he wants to find her?"

"We don't know," Chris says. "That's the point. If his story checks out and she lived with him even for a short time, it suggests a relationship. And if she was in that relationship up until a week ago, we have every reason to believe she's living a new life and simply left her past behind."

"She has to go back to America after ninety days from her arrival because of her passport, right? There's no exception to this."

"She has to return," he agrees. "And that's the way we'll find her if we don't catch up with her sooner."

The fight in me fades and my voice softens. "That's late next month." My gaze falls to his chest. "I don't know what to do about Ella."

His finger slides under my chin. "You've done everything you can—and Sara, she might be fine and you're worrying for nothing. It sounds like she is."

I glance up at him. "I know. I just . . . I have you, but not so long ago I was just like Rebecca. There was no one to look for me if I was lost."

"Mark would have looked for Rebecca if he'd known she was due back in San Francisco, Sara. He told me he thought she'd blown him off."

"You wouldn't have let me run like she did. You care about me. He let her. She was alone. Ella is alone, Chris. If she's blowing me off then fine. She's blowing me off, but I can't do that to her."

"We aren't blowing her off. We're trying to find her." His hands gently caress my hair. "I'm glad you know that I would come after you now. You didn't always." He settles his palms on either side of me on the desk and studies me a moment.

Thankful for what this beautiful man has added to my life, I reach out and play with a spiky lock of his blond hair. "I know now. That's what counts." I purse my lips at my momentary distraction. "I haven't forgotten what we're talking about. You aren't off the hook. You should have told me about the mob connection."

"If I tell you I was protecting you, you're going to come unglued, aren't you?"

My fingers fall from his hair. "Yes."

Obviously fighting a smile, he says, "Then I won't tell you. I think . . . hmmm, yes . . . this would be a good time for me to show you a way to escape."

My pulse is racing all over again. "Escape?" I ask for one of his "escapes" all of the time. He never gives them to me. He always says it's not the right time or I'm not ready. He never volunteers.

"I have something to show you," he adds, and there is a definitive, sensual gleam in his eyes. "Take your clothes off." He reaches for his shirt and pulls it over his head.

I'm used to Chris ordering me to take off my clothes but, for once, he's getting naked at the same time as I am rather than playing the power card of watching. And while I mean to join him in the process of undressing, his shirt comes off and my mouth goes dry. I think I'll take a moment and enjoy the view. I stall, hoping for more skin and a longer show. "We need to be naked for you to show me whatever you want to show me?"

"Yes." He sits down to take off his boots. "Get naked and I'll show you." He stands up, towering over me again. I forget how tall he is sometimes, but I never forget how deliciously male he is. He arches a blond brow. "Need help?"

My sex clenches and my nipples tighten. My entire body knows I'm about to delve into new territory. It's in the air. It's in the flecks of fire dancing in his eyes.

I pull my shirt over my head and toss it, revealing my black lace bra. He watches my face, and it's even more erotic than him looking at my almost-bare breasts.

He lifts my foot to his leg, barely glancing away from my face to tug off my shoe and sock, then repeats the process with the other foot. His hand on my denim-clad calf is incredibly arousing.

He lets go, taking several steps backward. "I'll let you do the rest."

He wants to watch me. It's all about time and anticipation with him, and it does what he intends. I'm wet. I'm ready. I *want* to know what he has to show me.

I unzip my jeans and shimmy them down my legs, kicking them away. My eyes meet his, and heat replaces the flutters in my belly. I reach for my black thong, shoving it down my legs. Still he holds my stare, and I unhook my bra and drop it. My breasts are heavy; my body is alive in ways only Chris can create.

Slowly, his gaze lowers to my breasts and my nipples tighten and throb. He doesn't touch me. I don't expect him to. This teasing is part of who he is, and he is what I want. Then his eyes lift, filled with male satisfaction and the knowledge of how easily he affects me; how easily he turns me into a wanton, eager player in his sensual games. And I'm fine with him knowing that. These games are sexy and they're no longer emotional tightropes.

Chris closes the distance between us and surprises me by touching me, his hands sliding to the side of my face. I think he likes to do what I won't expect, to keep me guessing and on edge.

He leans me against the desk, his body molding mine, and I love the way he is hard where I am soft. The way he absorbs everything that I am and somehow makes me more in the process. "Do you trust me, Sara?"

"Yes," I say, and my voice cracks with the ache I feel for

this man. "Like I've never trusted any other person in my life. Completely."

"Then trust me when I say what you witnessed that night at Mark's club was me going too far. What you and I do is not the same. When I tied you up, when I spanked you, that was mild BDSM. What you saw was extreme—*too* extreme. You and I decide what is right for us."

"Yes, I know. I like that."

He leans down and brushes his lips over mine. "I love you."

"I love you, too. And why does your saying that right now make me nervous?"

He rests his forehead against mine, trails his fingers down my arm. "Because you know I'm going to take you somewhere you've never been. That's part of the high, Sara. The adrenaline rushing through your body. The unknown soon to be discovered."

He straightens and then reaches over to open the center drawer of his desk. I watch as he removes a long velvet box and my stomach flip-flops at the sight. I've seen one of these boxes before. I know there's a toy inside.

I hold my breath as he holds it between us, and flips it open.

I stare down at a black flogger with eight ministraps dangling from the handle, and my heart jackhammers. All I can think of is my first night at the club, when I heard the painful cries of a woman being publicly flogged. "No . . . I . . . " I shake my head. "No."

"We define who we are and what we do," Chris reminds me.

"I know, but—"

He slides a hand back to my face and kisses me. *"Trust me."*

"I do, but—"

He presses the flogger into my palm. "It's silk," he says. "Feel it. It's soft. It won't hurt you. *I* won't ever hurt you. There are different kinds of material used to make these. Leather and rubber sting more. This won't. It's a good beginner's choice."

My fingers close around the eight strands dangling from the handle, and they're indeed soft to the touch. "It won't hurt?"

"I know what I'm doing. I know how to make it feel good."

And he does. I know he does. I close my eyes. "I . . ."

His mouth brushes over my mouth, and his tongue whispers past my lips. "Trust me, Sara," he murmurs again, teasing me with the possibility of another kiss. "Let me redefine what this is to you, and to us. Don't let what you saw in the club, or whatever Isabel said to you, do that for us."

I suddenly lean back to look at him. "You didn't even ask what she said to me."

"I don't care what she said. I care how you reacted. I care that whatever poison she tried to feed you didn't work. That says everything about where we are and what we can be."

My eyes burn with unshed tears. Do I dare believe that I've finally washed away his doubts? His *fears*? "It does?" I ask, needing confirmation.

"Yes. It does. Trust is everything, remember? That's what you gave me tonight. And I'm asking for it again. Will you give it to me?"

I cup his face. "I told you. You have it."

His eyes soften. "And I'll always deserve it—you have my

promise. But Sara, that doesn't mean you can't say no now. You can always say no."

"I know. I do." Chris makes me discover parts of me I never knew existed, parts that often work against how the past has conditioned me. But I feel safe enough with him to go to those places. I know I can be me, and he won't judge me or hurt me. Certainty fills me and I say, "I want to do this."

Twenty-one

This isn't something I'd ever have believed I'd agree to. But this is Chris, and we are everything I never knew I wanted, and everything I was once missing.

One of his long, talented fingers trails over my jaw, raising a shiver of erotic anticipation. "You're sure?"

"Yes, I'm sure, Chris. I want to try this."

His eyes fill with acceptance. "All right, then," he agrees, his voice low, seductive. "Flogging is similar to spanking. It will be delicious friction, nothing more. Not with this flogger, and not with me holding it."

He is what's delicious. He's what makes a spanking erotic. He, that makes me eager for what comes next.

"Hold out your hand. I want you to get used to how they feel on your skin."

I nod. I can't seem to find my voice, but I don't think he needs words. He's watching me, studying my every reaction.

He slowly drags the tails of the flogger over my arm, and then does it again. Anticipation builds in me, and I can feel my nerve endings coming alive.

He covers my arm with his hand for a moment, drawing my gaze to his. Heat simmers in the depths of his stare. He, too, is filled with anticipation, and it stirs confidence in me to know I can do that to him. That doing this with me excites him, not just me. His fingers drag seductively up and down my arm as he says, "Now I'm going to show you what an actual flogging motion is like."

He suddenly flicks his wrist, slapping the strands over my arm in kind of a circular motion, the slight sting just enough of a contrast to his soft touch to shock me. I jerk slightly but the next slap comes, and the next, and I become lost in the sensations that start to tingle on my skin. Incredibly, the small bites of silk become a warm sort of awareness that darts up my arm and over my chest to my nipples. They ache, and that ache radiates to my sex.

"You like it?" Chris asks, his voice deeper, warmer.

I glance up at him, meeting his stare, and whisper, "Yes."

Approval lights his eyes at my fast reply. "The longer I do this, the more your body should react."

I wet my lips. "Yes. Only . . ." I'm moved by the power radiating from his eyes, aroused by the raw sexuality so a part of who he is. "But I'm pretty sure I'm reacting to you, not the flogger."

His eyes darken, amber flecks of arousal simmering in their depths. "You're reacting to me using the flogger. And to the invisible 'more' you want and can't name."

Yes. I do want more. Please. Whatever it is, I want it.

As if hearing my silent plea, he sticks the flogger's handle in the top of his jeans. His hands go to my arms and he caresses a seductive path downward, pressing me backward at the same time. "Hands on the desk." He guides them there with his, covering mine on the glass behind me, his big body molding mine from the waist down. The position is intimate, arousing, the springy hair of his chest tickling the tips of my nipples, now thrust up between us.

Chris lowers his mouth to my ear, crushing my throbbing nipples against the hard wall of his chest. "I'm not going to tie you up." His breath is a warm wash over my ear and neck, promising I will soon be warm all over. His hand curves under my hair, possessive but gentle, and he leans back and looks down at me. "But we need to talk about rules."

My heart skips a beat and I instinctively try to move my hands. "Rules?"

"Relax," he purrs near my ear. "And don't move your hands."

I shut my eyes, forcing the muscles in my body to ease. "I am. I won't."

His hands leave mine and settle on my shoulders, and our eyes meet. "Only one simple rule. If you want to stop, just say no and I'll stop. Don't swipe at the tails or jerk away, or I could hurt you without meaning to. I need to have full control of the flogger."

Trepidation fills me. "Am I going to want to swipe at it?"

"No." He bends at the knees to bring us eye level and leans in and kisses me. "Just the opposite. You're going to like it. But knowledge is power. Knowing what to expect, and what to do, gives you control. Remember how I told you how many times I was going to spank you?"

"Yes. I liked knowing."

"Good. I won't ever surprise you, and the word *no* is always the ultimate power. You say it, I listen. Okay, baby?"

The endearment does more to calm my nerves than all the explanations in the world. "Okay."

He swipes away the hair that has fallen over my face, leaning in and kisses me, his tongue delving past my lips, one slow stroke followed by another. His hands settle on my waist and begin a sensual slide upward to caress my breasts and tease my nipples.

I moan and lift my hands from the desk to cover his.

He quickly captures them and presses them behind me onto the glass. "If I don't tie you up, I have to trust you to keep your hands there." He hardens his voice to a command. "Don't move them. Understand?"

"I won't move them."

He holds my stare, assessing my words, and then—seeming satisfied I mean them—his fingers leave my hands to trail up my arms over my shoulders. He surprises me yet again by squatting at my feet, his hands settling on my ankles. "I'm going to start flogging you here and then move higher." His hands caress over my calves, over my knees, to my thighs. "Then here." He presses them apart and slides the fingers of one hand into the V between my legs, exploring my sex.

"There? Won't that—"

He dips a finger inside me. "Feel good? Yes." The slow

stroke of him pulling out of me is sweet torture. He cups my sex and kisses my hip.

"Chris." It's a plea, wanting his mouth where his hand is, and he knows it. But he doesn't give it to me. I know he won't. Instead, he drags his lips over to my belly button, licking me, teasing me.

When he pushes to his feet, the male force of him overwhelms me. It's arousing. He's arousing. His hands glide from my waist to my breasts, and he teases my nipples, plucking at them. "And here, Sara. I'm going to flog your breasts." He plucks harder now, rougher, and I'm wet and aching, not thinking about the flogger. I'm thinking about him inside me.

"And finally," he murmurs, reaching around me to cup my backside hard against him. "Here. This is where I'll flog you right before I fuck you."

"Can we get right to that part?"

He smiles. "What fun would that be?"

"I think it would be lots of fun."

He kisses me. "The wait always makes it better."

"You always say that. It gets irritating."

He laughs and licks one of my nipples. "I'll work on that."

"No, you won't."

"No," he agrees. "I won't." His hands leave my body and he steps back from me. In a flash of movement he's shoved down his pants and boxers and kicks them aside. A second later he is gloriously naked, his body a work of art, his cock jutting forward, thick and pulsing.

My gaze shifts to his dragon tattoo and settles on the flogger in his hand. My heart seems to lodge in my throat, because I can't breathe. How had I forgotten this is really happening? He's going to *flog* me.

Chris steps close and leans in, pressing his hands on the desk next to mine without touching me, the dangling tails of the flogger teasing my arm. His cock between us taunts me, so very close to where I need it to be. Where I need *him* to be.

"Breathe, baby," he murmurs near my ear. "I'll take good care of you."

"I know," I whisper. "Just take good care of me quickly, before my heart explodes from my chest."

A low rumble of sexy laughter rumbles from the chest that I yearn to touch right now. "We wouldn't want that to happen, would we?"

I surprise myself by smiling. I'm about to be flogged, and I'm actually smiling. Chris and I really are nothing like how Rebecca described herself and Mark.

"Then let's get to it." He pushes off the desk. "I'm going to start now. Ready, Sara?"

"No. Yes." I take a deep breath. "Yes." He arches a brow and I say, "I'm ready."

"Close your eyes. You're making yourself crazy, staring at the flogger."

He's right, I am. I shut my eyes. Seconds tick by, and I'm just about to scream "Just do it! Just flog me!" when I feel the silk brush my calves. I jump a little. Not much. It doesn't hurt. The flogger lifts and hits me again. Then again.

The sound of the tails swiping at me becomes almost a song in my head, drugging, seductive, moving in the same rotation as it had on my arm. My skin starts to warm.

As if knowing when it does, Chris moves the tails up to my knees, and lingers there until the same warmth forms. Then he moves to my thighs, and I'm suddenly more than warm. I'm hot, and aroused, and arching my back. I know what comes next, yet when it does, I gasp.

The tails swipe my clit, the swooshing motions biting at the delicate skin and sending a burst of arousal through my entire body. I'm panting, nearly begging for more, not even knowing what I want more of. I just want it.

The tails move up my body, over my stomach and higher. Sizzling sensations roll through me and I tilt my head back, anticipating what comes next. When it does, I forget to breathe.

The silk slaps over my sensitized breasts and then bites at my nipples. For the first time, I feel pain. Another slap immediately follows, and another, and the pain spirals into pleasure. Suddenly I'm squeezing my thighs together, my sex clenching, so close to coming . . .

Chris's hands come down on my waist, his cock brushing my leg. "Oh, no you don't," he growls low in his throat. It's sexy. *He's* sexy. I want him. "Not yet."

"Yes!" I demand, but he turns me to face the desk, my hands on the glass.

"You come when I say you come. You know that rule."

I heat at the memory of him spanking me for coming too soon. *Please,* yes. Spank me. "And if I don't?" I taunt.

He nips my ear, and his cock presses against my backside. "Come *with* me, baby. We do things together, remember?"

I squeeze my eyes shut. "That is unfair. You know I can't say no to that."

LISA RENEE JONES

"Punish me later."

My eyes jerk open. "Chris—"

"I'm joking, Sara. But you punish me every time you put clothes on." As he starts to pull away, I reach behind me and grab him. He surprises me by dropping the flogger.

"Screw the flogging," he growls, lifting my hips as he presses the thick line of his shaft between my thighs. "You want me to fuck you now?"

"I wanted you to fuck me before you ever started flogging me."

He presses inside me. "You're too damn demanding to be submissive."

"You taught me what demanding is," I pant as he thrusts hard into me, and then curls his body around mine.

"You were like this the night I met you," he accuses, and suddenly his hands are under my knees and he's lifting me off the ground, leaning me back so that he's cradling me against his chest.

I gasp. "What are you doing?"

He sits on the couch with me on top of him, his face buried in my hair, his hands cupping my breasts. "Fucking you. Isn't that what you want?"

"Yes, I—" One of his hands presses on my stomach and his hips arch, his cock pumping into me. "I, ah . . ." My head turns, seeking his mouth, and somehow we manage a kiss, a caress of tongues.

With that the mood shifts, and the passion turns into something living and breathing, a part of us with demands of its own. Everything fades into the feel of his hands all over my body, the rhythms of our bodies moving together, the stroke of tongue against tongue. I escape.

And when we finally collapse together, lying side by side, he wraps around me from behind. I'm more at peace than I've ever been in my whole life. I'm no longer afraid of the parts of me I don't understand or know.

Chris understands. He knows me. And I understand him.

Still Saturday, July 14, 2012

I'm in San Francisco. He's not.

When I landed, I called his cell phone and he didn't answer. I rented a car and went to his house. He wasn't home. I took a taxi to the gallery and called him from outside. He didn't answer. I can't go inside the gallery, or even call there. Not until I decide if it's a part of my life again. If he is.

So against my better judgment, I drag my bags inside Cup O' Cafe next door and decide to wait here until the gallery closes. I don't like it here. She owns it. She, who was invited into our bed in the past, and hates me. I knew if she knew how to reach him, it meant that she was in his bed now. And she did know. He's on a plane to New York, on Riptide auction house business.

It's a blow to discover that he's gone. It's a bigger blow to discover he's still bringing her to his bed. I wonder if she's signed an agreement with him. I wonder if she is his, and I am . . . not.

No. It can't be. She'd have gloated, and he wouldn't have

asked me to come home, either. Is this home? I thought I had all the answers before I came here tonight. Now I'm about to head to a hotel alone.

I hate this feeling. I hate how she reminds me of what he can be and what he was with me. Am I fooling myself? Is our past a reflection of who we'll be in the future?

And if I'm evoking old pain this easily, do I really want to stay and find out?

Twenty-two

Tuesday morning starts with a workout and a long chat with Chris's godmother. By midmorning I've muddled through the language barrier of meeting the housekeeper, Sophie. Shortly after, Chris heads to his studio to paint and I find myself at the island in the kitchen with Chantal. Though the meeting with Sophie had motivated me for my morning lesson, after a rather terrible attempt at several "simple" French phrases—the simple part per Chantal (not me)—my brain is ready to explode. In need of an extra caffeine boost, I push off the stool to refill my mug and groan at the protest of my sex-sore body.

Chantal joins me at the coffeepot, looking adorable in a pair of distressed jeans and a pale blue tank. She seems to be relaxing into our friendship, rather than acting like she's headed to a corporate job every day. "This is enough for today. You don't seem to be processing another language this morning."

I feign shock. "No? I thought I was doing so well."

She grins. "Right. So very well. So, do you want me to help you call around about Ella again?"

I'd managed to keep the Rebecca story under wraps, telling her the investigation was related to my old boss, but she's been determined to help me find Ella. "I appreciate what you did yesterday, but Rey said we just called places he'd already called."

"Contacting the hospitals every day seems smart, though."

"Rey says he has that handled, too." I back down.

"Hello," a familiar female voice says from the stairs.

My surprised gaze narrows on Amber, whose long blond hair is a striking contrast to her black jeans and T-shirt. She holds up her hands in mock surrender as she joins us. "Before you get upset, I didn't let myself in. Chris took my key. He and Rey were outside talking when I got here and it's too cold to stand outside." She shivers. "I left my coat in my car and I really need coffee." She starts to move toward the pot, then catches herself. "*If* you don't mind?"

I'm shocked at her respecting how I might feel about her making herself at home. "Help yourself," I say, hoping her request is actual progress and not just a smoke screen.

She glances at Chantal first. "I'm Amber. An old friend of Chris's."

"Chantal," she replies, sounding less than friendly. "I'm a *new* friend of Sara's *and* Chris's."

"I'm not sure Sara thinks I'm a friend. We got off to a bumpy start." Amber looks at me cautiously. "I'm hoping we can change that." She heads over to the coffeepot without waiting for an answer, as if she knows I'll need to recover from her statement. She would be right.

She's being so nice, it makes me suspicious. I glance at Chantal, whose brow is furrowed, a question on her face. I tell her, "Amber and Chris have known each other since college."

"Yeah," Amber agrees, joining us at the island. "It's one of those 'if we both get to forty and we're unmarried, we'll probably end up together' kind of relationships."

I feel sucker-punched, and Chantal purses her lips disapprovingly.

"Well," she says curtly, "since Chris is going to marry Sara and make babies, I guess that won't happen."

I'm not sure if I'm more taken aback by Chantal's claws coming out, or the baby-making reference. Babies? Chris and I? He's good with them, but having our own? The idea of having a child terrifies me. A child I would love, who could be stolen away in a blink of an eye, like my mother was, like Dylan was from his family. I don't think I can do that.

Amber snorts. "Chris with kids? I can't imagine that one. Unless some drastic change has occurred, he's always said he doesn't want kids."

Chris picks that moment to walk into the kitchen, and the stormy look in his eyes tells me he heard the exchange. He stops beside me, his arm on the back of my stool, his body angled to mine, his attention on me and only me. And I see confirmation in his eyes. He, too, has lost too many people to risk loving and losing a child.

Chantal says something to Amber in French, and I'm pretty sure she's trying to give us a moment. I seize it.

I curl my fingers around Chris's smooth, freshly shaven jaw.

"I don't think I could bear the fear of losing a child, either." I say it as if he's already told me he feels this way.

His eyes soften, and relief floods his expression. "We never seem to have these conversations the right way or at the right time."

"There is no right way, remember? There's only our way."

I'm rewarded by a smile and a kiss on my temple, before he turns and sets an envelope onto the counter in front of Amber. "That should handle your situation." She reaches for it but he holds on to it, and her gaze lifts to his as he adds, "Make sure Tristan is okay with this."

"I'll deal with Tristan." She actually looks awkward, when I'm used to more of a gloat or a smirk from her, and I'm curious about what is in the envelope, almost certain it's money.

Chris releases it and she snatches it up. "I should go." Amber picks up her full coffee cup and puts it in the sink, then stops beside me on her way to the stairs. "Maybe we could do lunch one day soon." It's not a question but a statement.

I'm really not sure what to make of this change of attitude. I avoid meeting her eyes, knowing that's what Chris wants. "Once I get more settled, we can plan something."

"Sure," she says. "Right. When you get settled." Then she glances at Chris. "Thanks."

He gives her a nod and she takes off down the stairs. Chantal chases her progress with daggers flying from her eyes. and I warm inside at her protectiveness.

"She's your *friend*?" Chantal demands of Chris.

I fight a smile. While Chris's easy charm wins people over, most are too intimidated by that subtle crackle of power he oozes to challenge him. But not Chantal. She boldly goes where others don't dare. I learned that at the embassy.

Chris drapes a casual arm around my shoulders. "More like a troublesome sibling." He helps himself to my cup and takes a drink.

"She doesn't vibe like a sibling," Chantal replies.

"Vibe?" I ask, unable to hold back a grin at the odd choice of American slang as a description.

"Isn't that what you Americans say?" She frowns and says something to Chris in French.

"Yes," he agrees in English, sounding amused. "The word *vibe* would mean the same as what you said in French, but I'm not sure it's how I'd phrase it. It works, though."

She purses her lips. "Well then, like I said. She doesn't vibe like a sister. She said you two would end up married if you were forty and both alone."

Chris snorts. "Even *if* I were alone at forty"—he glances down at me—"and I won't be, I wouldn't be with Amber."

Despite his words, I don't like this conversation, so I say, "Speaking of Amber, she said Rey was here. Did he have any news on Ella?"

"Good news, I hope," Chantal adds.

"At least four people around Neuville's home turf knew Ella by sight when shown a photo, and they'd seen her as recently as a week ago."

Chantal looks happy. "That's positive, right? That means she's okay?"

"Yes," I agree. And it *is* positive.

Chris continues, "Rey's still digging around about when

she left and why, to figure out if anyone saw anything strange. So far, nothing. The witnesses said Ella was very pleasant and seemed happy. They also all seemed to think Neuville was quite taken with her, which stood out because it's not the norm for him with a woman."

More good news. But the fact that Ella hasn't contacted me, and didn't show up to work or call the school, still isn't normal.

"On another subject," Chris says, turning to me, "you remember that I have the boys' camp at the Louvre Friday night, right? I asked Rey if he could stay with you that night."

I frown. "Why would Rey stay with me?"

"I'd just rather know you're safe." His avoidance is done with an oh-so-casual tone.

I narrow my eyes. "What don't I know that I should, Chris?"

"Neuville breeds caution in me."

"But you said—"

He kisses me. "Humor me. I'll worry if you're alone."

"You're going to make me paranoid," I argue. "We talked about this before."

"I can come stay over, too," Chantal offers. "We can have a girls' night."

I perk up. "That's a great idea!" Then I turn to Chris. "That way you'll know I'm not alone, and I won't be tortured by Rey's hovering."

"Hmmm," Chantal says. "I wouldn't mind him hovering."

I glower at her. "You aren't helping my cause here."

"Oh, right." She eyes Chris. "I'll protect her. I'm pretty tough."

That draws a chuckle from both of us. "That I don't doubt, Chantal," he says, and I am in full agreement.

When her phone chimes she glances at an incoming text and sighs. "I have to go cover the shop. My mom is with my grandmother again. So am I staying over?"

I give Chris a pleading look. "This is a good compromise, and we have a state-of-the-art security system. And I'll have you and Rey on auto-dial."

He sighs and says, "I want Rey to come by and check on you. And before you argue, that's also a compromise."

I smile. "I can live with that."

Chantal grabs her purse. "I'm off." She points at me. "Try to practice. You're really not giving your French much effort. You're going to force me to only speak French to you." She rushes off down the stairs.

"Hey," Chris says, pulling me around to face him. "You okay?"

I touch his face. "I'm always okay when I'm with you." My brow furrows. "What was all that about with Amber?"

"She has some money issues at the Script."

"So you gave her money, and Tristan won't be happy about it?"

"No. The two of them have had a turbulent relationship. He's not happy about me being in her life."

I can understand how he feels. "How much did you give her?" I dare to ask.

"Ten thousand euros."

I gape. "That's a lot of money."

"You should see the check I agreed to write to the museum."

"So you did agree to a donation?"

"As long as my financial guy sits on the board. I have too many commitments with my charity this year to do it myself. I'll never get time to paint." He turns the topic back to Amber. "You know I have to help her, right?"

I nod. "Yes, I do. I don't fully understand why, but I do." It's an opening for more explanation, but he simply kisses me and pulls me to my feet, tugging me toward the stairs.

A few minutes later I'm in his studio with him, watching him paint, and I shove away thoughts of Amber. I simply have to trust that our trip out of town this weekend will deliver answers. Even if I have to push Chris to talk.

Friday afternoon, Chris and I are in the elevator headed to the attorney's office to discuss some of my last-minute business questions when he announces, "Amber's stopping by in about an hour to meet with the attorney, as well."

I blink. "What? Why?"

"About her business struggles."

"Oh. Okay."

He wraps me in his arms. "Sara—"

I kiss him. "It's okay. Really."

The elevator dings but he doesn't move. "It doesn't seem okay."

"It is." But I feel uneasy about Amber. I always feel uneasy about Amber. I drag his hand into mine as the door opens. "Let's go get my business started."

A few minutes later, Chris and I settle into a chair inside the attorney's office and my excitement washes everything else away. We quickly go through my concerns, and it seems my business is ready to launch.

Once Chris and I finish up, I leave Chris to discuss some details about his donation to the museum and head to the lobby, seeking the "toilette," only to find Amber has arrived. My unease is officially back.

She stands up, looking as professional in her black pin-striped skirt and red blouse as I do in my black, slim-cut dress, with a matching jacket and high-heeled boots. "Is it my turn?" she asks, actually looking nervous.

"Not yet," I tell her. "Chris has some things to finish up, but he should be fast. We need to head out."

"He has that charity event tonight, right?"

"Yes." How did she know?

"I get the Louvre newsletters," she replies, clearly reading my expression. She shrugs. "I used to follow the art world pretty closely. It was never really me, but I tried because of Chris."

I suddenly want to be away from her. "I need to freshen up before we leave." I start to move on, and she steps in front of me.

"Thanks for letting him do this for me."

She seems sincere, but there's something beneath the surface. I still think she hates me, but there's pain, too. Heartache. Loneliness. She's such a confusing person. Or maybe I'm just confused.

I must be, because suddenly I don't want her to hate me. I don't want to cause her more pain. "You don't have to thank me. Chris cares about you." I hesitate and softly add, "He's not going to shut you out, Amber. And neither am I."

Surprise flickers on her face. "Thank you." She hesitates, and then reaches for her purse. "We should exchange numbers. I really want to do that lunch."

I hesitate. "Okay." She pulls out her phone and I do the same, and in the process her sleeve rises and I see fresh lash marks. When we finish inputting our numbers, I gently touch her shoulder. "If you need to talk, now you know how to reach me."

She tilts her head and gives me the oddest look before she says, "Thank you, Sara."

There's nothing wrong with this reply, and yet something about it is very wrong. Fifteen minutes later, when Chris and I head to the car, I'm still thinking about it.

Near six that evening I sit at my new mahogany desk, which was delivered today along with chairs and a bookshelf. I'm writing out the goals for my business in a red leather journal; it's my link to Rebecca. It's hard to let her go. I still can't believe she's dead. And really, no body has been found. Maybe . . . no. It's a crazy thought. A ridiculous thought. She's not alive.

"Paperwork has arrived," Chris announces, sauntering into the room, wearing a Superman shirt he says is to motivate the kids to be their own superheroes. "Your official business documents." He sets a large yellow envelope in front of me and lounges in my new guest chair.

"Already?" I ask, eagerly reaching for the documents. "We just met with the attorney a few hours ago."

"I made sure he hurried things along."

My hero. "I don't suppose you did the same on my passport?"

266

"Stephen said there's red tape, but it will be clear soon."

"That's the same answer he keeps giving us."

He lifts his chin toward the envelope. "Open it and make sure everything is in order."

My excitement overpowers my worry over the passport, and I remove the forms and start scanning. Chris grabs one of the documents and laughs. "I can't believe you stuck with 'SM Consulting' for a name."

I glower at him. "Yes, I did. And don't even start with S&M jokes again. It stands for my first and last name, and it's good luck." The *M* would still be accurate if I marry Chris, but I don't say that. We both know. It's in the air every time we talk about this.

"I'll be your S&M lucky charm any day, baby," he teases. "Unfortunately, not tonight." He runs his hands over his jean-clad legs and stands. "Tonight I'll be playing with the boys. When is Chantal getting here?"

"She has to close up the family shop again for her mom. Her grandmother is having issues again."

Now Chris glowers. "I knew I should have had Rey come over."

"You already have him checking in on me later." I push to my stocking feet and go to him, wrapping my arms around him. "I don't need a babysitter. Chantal will be here, and I'm sure you will text me and call me like some crazy stalker man."

"Crazy stalker man?"

I grin. "You can be my crazy stalker man any day, baby."

He doesn't laugh. "Sara—"

I rise up on my toes and kiss him. "Go play with the boys. Then come home tomorrow and play with me."

"You do remember there's a price for making me worry, don't you?"

"And you do know that Chantal's conflict isn't my fault? Besides, that doesn't work as a threat anymore, right? I like the price way too much."

He gives me a scorching three-second look before he picks me up and sets me on the desk, shoving my dress up my legs. "I don't have to leave yet, and you need a taste of that 'price' right now." He goes down on his knees and spreads my legs. "Or maybe I'm the one who needs a taste."

And all I can think as he shoves my panties aside and his mouth closes down on me is, Punish me, baby.

Twenty-three

By ten o'clock I'm curled up on the bed in shorts and a tank, once again on the phone with Chantal. She has called me almost as many times as Chris and Rey combined. "I'm so sorry, Sara," Chantal says for the second time in two minutes. "My grandmother is not good, and my mother is a mess."

I toss the TV remote control on the bed, having muted the movie I've been watching. Thankfully, Chris has English satellite channels on the monstrous television that lowers from the ceiling, and an old movie has been keeping me company. "Stay with your family," I reassure her. "We can do a girls' night another time. I'm perfectly fine. Rey dropped by a few minutes ago, and Chris has been calling and texting with me all evening." Somehow, I'd finally convinced Rey to keep a meeting with his brother who had some ideas to toss around on Ella's case. I didn't want to blow a chance to find Ella over Rey babysitting me.

Chantal sighs heavily. "I really was looking forward to tonight."

We chat a few more minutes before hanging up, and Chris messages me right as I do. I glance down at a photo of a row of kids in sleeping bags and smile. He doesn't need to have kids. He's adopting them everywhere he goes.

I flip the TV sound back, snuggle under the covers, and find an old *Seinfeld* episode. A good laugh will keep my restless mind busy.

Sometime later my phone beeps with a message and I jump, surprised to realize I've dozed off. I glance at the time and see that I slept for an hour, but I smile as I scan several pictures of kids sitting in a circle. The message from Chris reads, Scary story time, with me as the storyteller.

A sad memory of Dylan's face as he begged Chris to tell him a scary story makes my chest tighten. I text Chris, worried about how this might be affecting him, checking his mood.

Did you find the boogie man?

Yes, he replies. His name is Leonardo. He disguises himself as an artist.

Relieved at this humor, I laugh and type, I love you, Chris.

I love you too, Sara.

I'm going to take a bath and then head to bed.

I wish I was there for both.

I sigh and type, Me too.

A few minutes later I'm sitting on the edge of the tub when my phone rings, and expecting Chris, I answer without looking. "Sara," a female voice half shouts over loud music, and my stomach knots with dread.

"Amber?"

"Yes, Sara, I need help." She sounds upset, maybe crying. "I know Chris is . . . he's at the charity thing. I . . ." She sobs.

I stand up. "What's wrong?"

"Tristan and I . . . we had a fight. I've been drinking, and he won't let the coat people give me my keys and purse. I need a ride. Please." She pauses and I can tell she is walking since the music fades a bit. "My head is spinning and I can't think . . . I just . . . need to get out of here. Tristan found out I borrowed money from Chris. He's my Master. You must know what that means. I broke our rules. He's going to punish me. Please, Sara. Come quickly."

All kinds of warning bells go off in my head for her, and for myself. This feels like a setup, but what if it isn't? I've seen the marks on her arms. "Text me your address."

"I will. Thank you, Sara. Thank you so much. I'll text now."

I end the call and sink back down on the edge of the tub with my mind ticking through all my options. I can't call Chris. He'll freak out and leave the museum. If I call Rey, he'll call Chris and Chris will freak out and leave the museum. He'll also abandon his meeting with his brother over Ella. I'm not jeopardizing finding Ella over Amber. Besides, Amber's in an abusive relationship with a man, and I don't even know if she likes or trusts Rey. And what if Rey finds something out about Chris that Chris doesn't want him to find out? Chris is too private a person to risk that. No. As much as I want Rey to be an option, he isn't.

My phone beeps with the address. I inhale and stare at it, considering a moment before I text back, I'm sending a cab to get you.

I wait for a reply. And wait.

I text again. Amber, please confirm you're okay.

No reply.

Damn. Damn. Damn.

I dial her number. It rings and rings with no answer.

I hold the phone to my forehead. Chris is going to be furious if I do this. And it really feels like a setup. Guilt twists inside me for thinking that, and for just sitting here if she really needs help. I have to do what's right, even if she isn't.

I go to my closet and put on a black knee-length skirt, a long-sleeved lilac lace top, and my knee-high boots with four-inch heels. I know I'm going to a club, and if it's a place where Chris has intimate connections, I'm not showing up in ratty jeans and a T-shirt.

I rush to the sink and grab my purse, planning to fix my face in the back of the taxi, the taxi that I should have already called for. I can't drive; I don't know where I'm going. I'll pay the taxi driver to wait while I go inside and get Amber.

I call a taxi, then I try Amber again. No answer. When I think of the marks on her arms, I can't help but worry she's being punished.

I head for the door, but pause. I don't like to do stupid things, and I fear that's exactly what I'm about to do. I have to add a little smart to the mix.

I go to the nightstand where I've left the journal I started, and scribble a note. *Gone to pick up Amber at some club. She was crying and scared. I took a taxi.* I add the address and leave it on the pillow.

There's no reason why anyone should see this. Rey isn't

going to call or come by again. Chris is putting the kids to bed and staying at the museum. I'll be home long before he'd see the note.

Acid burns in my throat the instant the cab pulls up to the address Amber gave me. It's next door to Isabel's restaurant. This is just too coincidental to sit well, and I know there's a connection. Whatever this club is, Isabel is a part of it, maybe even owns it.

I pay the taxi driver, and offer him a hefty tip for waiting for me to return. Before getting out, though, I try to dial Amber again.

She doesn't answer.

I text, I'm outside in a taxi. Please come out.

I wait. No reply.

I picture Chris being beaten in Mark's club, and remember the pain I've seen in Amber's eyes. If Tristan is like Isabel, Amber needs saving.

Decision made, I slide my purse cross-body and shove open the door. I am going to keep on this path, even though it's probably foolish.

I head toward the large steel double gates marked with the address I seek. Cold air lifts my long hair, and I wish I'd brought my coat. Even more, I wish I were back in the taxi.

Passing the gates, I find a long walkway to another white stone building and see another couple walking in the same direction as I am. I let them move ahead of me, and I study them, hoping that doing so might tell me about where I am headed. The man is in jeans. The woman is in a leather skirt. This tells me very little, but I guess I should be happy they aren't in head-to-toe leather and chains. I cling to whatever I can find in the hope that I'm not about to go into the unfamiliar land of full-on BDSM action without Chris by my side.

With a lot of trepidation, I follow the couple to the large wooden door and wait as the woman hits a buzzer. The door opens and a man in a suit waves the couple inside.

I step forward, intending to follow the couple inside, but the man holds up a hand and says something in French.

"English?" I ask hopefully.

"Couple only," he replies.

Couples only? That's strange. "I'm here to pick up Amber."

Someone says something to the man from behind. The doorman glances at me and waves me forward. "Welcome, mademoiselle."

I draw a breath and walk past him into the small, dimly lit room, much like the one at Isabel's restaurant. Too much like it for comfort. It feels like this is her doing, and I wonder about the absence of the loud music I'd heard on the phone with Amber.

A coat check area is to my right, and the lady who manages it steps in front of me and points at my purse. "You must leave it here," she says in heavily accented English.

"No." I cling to my purse. "No, I—"

"It's the rules," she says sharply.

I reach for my phone to take it with me and she shakes her head. "No phones. They have cameras."

My heart sinks and I hesitate, thinking of Amber and hearing her sobs on the phone in my head. I stuff my phone in my purse and give both up. The woman rewards me with a ticket stub that I stuff in my boot.

I walk down a long, narrow hall, and the hazy bedroom lighting is really creeping me out. I'm about to reach what looks like a much larger room when Amber rounds the corner, dressed in a tank top and a red leather skirt that barely clears her hips. With her arms exposed, I see the fresh welts on them.

"Sara." She rushes toward me, and I gape at the low neckline of her dress, which leaves all but her nipples exposed, before she hugs me. "Thank you for trying to help me." She steps back. "I convinced Tristan we're entertaining you, so he won't take me to the chamber. He told the doorman not to let me leave. We have to sneak out."

I shake my head. "Let's just walk out right now."

The sound of several people behind me makes me turn, and I find a couple staring at me with such lusty expressions, I feel like a starving man's dinner. I can't let them by without body contact, and I quickly turn to Amber, who grabs my hand and tugs me forward. This is so not going well.

She leads me down a set of stairs and pushes through a door, where music blasts around us. I blink into the smoky room to find a bar to my left and a dance floor beyond it, with a lot of skin in every direction I look. This place is crawling with skimpily clad women, with men and women draped all over them. Against walls, by the bar, on the dance floor, and in seats around it. But no sex. Just lots of wishing for sex, I think.

Amber pulls me to a spot by the bar and I turn to her, settling my back against the leather rail behind me. I have no intention of staying.

Amber flags down the bartender. "Two shots of tequila."

"No," I say. "I have a taxi outside waiting."

"I can't hear you," she complains as she leans in close to me, her hand reaching over my chest, arm pressing on my breasts to hold the bar at my opposite shoulder. I stiffen, aware of how intimate and unnecessary the move is as she repeats, "What did you say?"

I fight the urge to push her away, afraid it will turn into more touching. "I have a taxi waiting for us."

"A new doorman comes on in thirty minutes. He likes me. He'll let us pass." She leans back and looks at me, then strokes the hair from my eyes. "You really are very pretty."

My breath hitches. What is happening? What is she doing? "Amber—"

"You're never going to stop making him pay, are you?"

At the sound of Tristan's voice, Amber turns to him, her arm thankfully dropping from my chest. I blink Tristan into view, his long dark hair framing crystal-blue eyes. He's staring at me, his expression hard, unreadable.

Amber touches my hair and I instinctively pull back, but she's focused on Tristan. "I need this. It's your duty to fulfill my needs."

Tristan stares at her, several intense moments ticking by before he pulls her to him, his hand on the back of her head. "It's time to let him go. It's past time, Amber." His gaze slides to mine and there is something unidentifiable in his stare. Then he is kissing her, his hand sliding over her breast and yanking down her top, exposing her nipple right there.

I can't breathe, but the look Tristan gave me . . . I don't

know why, but I think he's giving me an escape, and I need it. I sidestep away from them and dash for the hallway, then stop abruptly. There's a woman with her shirt pulled down to her waist, with a man sucking her nipples right in front of the exit. I turn away, looking for any direction but back toward Tristan and Amber, and calling myself every kind of fool.

I dart to my left and down a hallway, hoping for a bathroom. There's only a doorway that seems to lead to a room. I turn to find Tristan and Amber headed toward me, and I rush forward . . . and straight into hell.

I stop dead just inside a dark room filled with bodies. Naked bodies huddled together. I can't believe what I'm seeing. There is a woman with a man behind her, rubbing her breasts, while another woman is between her thighs, licking her. Beside them, a man is masturbating while watching. Behind him is a threesome of some sort. And it goes on and on. All around me, people are all over each other.

"This is what he wants," Amber says, wrapping herself around me.

I don't even fight her. My body is frozen, my heart ice. "No," I whisper. "It's not."

"Yes," she promises, turning me to face her, her hands on my shoulders. "You will be one of those people, with him right there with you."

No. Chris doesn't share.

Tristan steps beside Amber and pulls her into his arms, and I blink as they begin to passionately kiss and touch each other.

No. No. *No.* This is not what Chris wants us to be.

And still I stand there, watching them peel away each other's clothes. I wonder at why I didn't dart past the naked bodies at the exit? Maybe some part of me had to know what was in this club. What Chris was being accused of being a part of.

A stranger comes up behind me and touches me, and reality slaps me in the face. I shove the man away and rush for the door and down the hall. Somehow I find the bathroom I'd missed before, and I go inside and lock the door. I lean against the hard surface and wonder if there are peepholes for people to watch me. My stomach churns at the idea. This can't be what Chris wants. It can't. He doesn't share. I know he doesn't.

But what are these secrets he doesn't want to tell me? What could be so bad after all I've seen but this? I'm lost. I don't believe this is Chris, but Amber and Isabel and even Tristan are all parts of his life. And his desperateness to keep me away from them is pretty damning. Maybe this is his past, not his present. Except the Chris I know wouldn't have a past like this, any more than a present. What if, like Ella, I don't really know Chris at all? I'm confused. I hurt. I hurt badly. I'm not crying, but I will. There's a storm coming and I don't want it to happen here.

Ready to be out of here now, I unlock the bathroom door and make my way toward the exit, but I can't help but stop and glance at the bar. Suddenly, I think I need that drink I'd been offered early in the night, or the storm I know is coming might just erupt before I get home. I know this place isn't Chris's present life, but I am terrified this will be like the beatings he'd said he'd never need again and did. Tonight has dug up all of my hot buttons and insecurities I'd thought I'd buried. I wasn't enough for Chris when Dylan died. When will I live that hell again? The idea is almost too much to bear and I want out of my own head. The more I think, the more the hole in my heart bleeds.

Rushing forward, I wave at the bartender, who happily supplies me with a shot of tequila. I choke it down and ask for another. I am not myself. I do not even know who I am right now. I don't know who Chris is. I don't know who Ella is or was. I know. . . . nothing.

Amber is suddenly by my side, wrapping her arm around my shoulders. "If you love him, you'll get used to it. I promise. I did."

Her voice and her touch are making me hurt more. I down my second shot and ask for another. My head starts to spin. Amber drags me to the dance floor and I welcome the American music playing. I need something that feels familiar, something to put a floor beneath the ground I feel has fallen from beneath my feet. I know the words and I sing to them, blocking out the bad things trying to speak in my mind. Only I can't stand the way Amber keeps trying to touch me, how several strangers paw at me, and I shove away from the crowd.

All I want is . . . Chris. I want these people to go away. I want to call him and I want him to be the Chris I know, not the Chris Amber knows. I stop dancing. He is. He is that Chris. *My Chris.* These people do not know him. *Amber* does not know him. I want out of here, but now I've made a mistake. I've let the tequila go to my head and I don't think I can get home. Not without Chris.

My gaze goes to an empty pedestal and I climb on top. I am alone. So alone, and I shut my eyes, try to block out everything but the music and the dancing. I don't want to think. I don't want to feel anything.

Until his hand touches my leg, and I hear his voice calling my name, permeating the loud beat in my head. I look down to find Chris standing there.

Twenty-four

I stare down at Chris and blink, not sure if he's real. He's supposed to be at the museum. He can't know I'm here. And why does he look angry? I'm the one—

"Come down!" he shouts at me over the loud music.

Swaying slightly, I swallow hard. He's really here. Chris is here, and I'm not ready to hear what he's going to say.

I shake my head, and the room spins.

Chris reaches up and grabs my legs. I sway again. He shackles my wrist and tugs. I tumble forward with a yelp, only to find myself down on the dance floor, lying against Chris's hard body, his arms wrapped around me.

"What the fuck are you doing here, Sara? And dressed like you want to be here."

Tequila, anger, and hurt collide and ignite my tongue. I push against his chest and reel back, and all but snarl, "Why the fuck do *you* want me here? Because you do, right? This is one of your many secrets, right? You wanted me to join you in fucking half of Paris."

His expression is searing anger, his voice a growl permeating the music. "This is not my secret, Sara. *Secret,* singular. There's only one thing I haven't told you."

"That's news. Even how many secrets you have seems to be a secret."

His eyes flash. "I don't want you here in this place now or ever. We're leaving." He turns me toward the exit, fitting me under his arm, at his hip, and it's a good thing. The tequila has my feet not listening to my brain, and I stagger, then stumble.

I grab Chris's Superman shirt for balance, and he tightens his hold on me. Our eyes collide and for a moment we stand still, lost in an intense clash of sexual heat and anger. He is warm and strong and sexy, and I just want to wrap my arms around him and hold him. I can barely remember why I can't, or shouldn't, until someone bumps into us and the spell is broken, and reality zooms back into place.

Chris sets us in motion again, and not even the tequila can block out the bodies pressed to bodies, or the scent of sex in the air. I fight the urge to scream, or run, or . . . I just need out of this place. Now.

Chris pulls me to the stairs leading to the small walkway to exit the club. Thankfully, this time they're free of the naked bodies that blocked the way during my earlier attempt to leave. The instant we're on the stairwell, out of sight of prying eyes, I twist around and confront him, needing to know just how well connected he is to this place. "How did you know I was here?"

He gives me a hard look. "Why didn't I know you *were* here, is more important. Why didn't you call me?"

"Answer the question, Chris. How did you know I was here?"

"Tristan had a moment of conscience."

"Tristan?"

"Yes, Tristan. Why didn't you call me?"

"You were helping kids."

He's looking at me with such accusation that I feel like I'm the one who should feel guilty, and I'm confused. I do feel guilty.

"Amber told me Tristan was going to beat her. I've seen the welts on her arms." My head spins and I have to lean on the wall. "I tried to call her a cab, and she stopped answering her phone. I thought I could just grab her and get out of here."

His gaze slides up and down my body, before he presses a hand above my head and leans closer. His wonderful earthy scent calls to me, even as his accusations push me away. "Why did picking up Amber require 'come fuck me' clothing?"

I flinch as if I've been slapped. "Because I feel as if I'm being judged by a past I don't even understand." My eyes burn and I turn away from him, wobbling down the stairs. He follows. Despite the wicked mix of emotions inside me, I'm acutely aware of how he's stopped touching me, and how much I want him to touch me, and how, considering the implications of this place, I shouldn't. But then, I'm brilliant at being stupid tonight, both with and without the help of tequila.

We stop at the coat check and I dig for my ticket in my boot, but can't seem to make my hands work. "I can't get it," I say helplessly, frustrated at myself for drinking. I hate being like this, and what good did it do me?

Chris squats down and unzips my boot. The memory of him just like this, seducing me into the flogging, sends a rush of heat up my thighs. He glances up at me, holding the ticket, and I see the mix of anger and desire in his face. He's thinking about the same thing I am, and he isn't any happier about it than I am. He's pissed at me, and I don't know if that's good or bad. I guess it depends on why, and what this place really is to him.

He stands up and presents the lady with my ticket, and she hands him my things. Chris takes it upon himself to slide my purse cross-body over my head and I hate that he thinks I'm too drunk to manage it myself. I hate that I might be. I don't meet his eyes. I can't meet his eyes. I wait, and when the strap settles into place and he steps aside, I rush for the door and I don't stop. I push past it, stepping outside and inhaling the cold air, trying to sober my mind and body. I walk as fast as I can away from this place; I'd run if I weren't afraid of falling.

"Sara," Chris calls, then he grabs my arm and turns me to him.

I explode on him. "Is this what you want from me, Chris? Because it's not me. I can't and won't be part of what I saw in there. I *won't*."

"Does anything about this place scream 'me' to you?"

"No. But I know Isabel is connected to this place, and you're connected to her, and Tristan and Amber. And"—my voice hitches—"I didn't think Ava was a murderer, or that Ella would blow me off like I was nothing, either. I thought I knew her. I thought I knew me, through you. And if I don't know you . . . I don't know what I know."

He pulls me against him, his hard, warm body absorbing mine. "You know me, Sara. And I know you. *We* are not that place."

"I want to believe that, but you don't even know me well enough to believe I can handle whatever you haven't told me. You keep putting it off. You dread it that much—and then you wonder how I can think this place might be the secret? If you know me, what else could you think would make me react like this?"

"Nothing. There is nothing."

He stares down at me, his eyes hard, his jaw tense. "I'll tell you. In the car." He draws my hand into his and starts walking, pulling me toward the street.

I'm stunned. He's finally going to tell me?

I'm suddenly not sure I should have pushed him. He said next week. He said that was important to him. Why did I push? Why did I come to this damnable place? Why why why?

Chris turns us to the left and stops by a black sedan a block down, opening the back door. "Where's the 911?"

"There was car service at the museum. It was faster than getting my car from the garage."

He was that anxious to get to me, that upset I was here. I step toward the door and stumble. Once again, Chris catches me, his strong hands steadying me. The world spins around me and I squeeze my eyes shut. Damn tequila. Damn bad decisions.

With Chris's help, I slide into the sedan. He follows me

inside, says something to the driver in French, and the driver gets out of the car.

Then we're alone. And silent. We sit in the darkness, each by a door, and the space between us feels miles wide.

Chris finally turns to look at me and says, "Not even in my younger, experimental days would I have been drawn to that place, Sara. Amber knows that. She was trying to hurt me through you."

I whirl on him again, ignoring the protest of my head and stomach. "Then why do you let her in your life? She's not a nice person, Chris. She plotted and schemed to get my sympathy tonight, to get me here. She'll tear us apart if you let her, and I know you know that—yet she's still in our life. If you think that didn't affect how I responded to everything that happened tonight, from me thinking she was worth trying to save, to hearing her lies, you're wrong."

He cuts his gaze away, his elbows settle on his knees, and his head drops between his shoulders. His hands tunnel roughly into his hair and stay there, like he's trying to relieve pressure. He can barely force himself to say whatever he has to say—and I can barely breathe, waiting for him to tell me.

Scrubbing his jaw, he sits up, still staring ahead and seeming to struggle before he speaks, his voice a soft, raspy, emotion-laden confession. "Next week . . ." He hesitates. "Next week is the anniversary of my mother's death."

My shoulders slump and I feel as if I've been punched. His words replay in my head. *There is a right place and a right time. You'll understand what I mean, soon, I promise. I'm asking you to trust me on this.* I shouldn't have pushed him. I should have waited. "Oh God. Oh Chris. I—"

He turns to face me. "Ten years ago, during the week of the anniversary of her death, I took Amber and her parents out to dinner. We were walking to the car when we were mugged by two armed men in ski masks."

"Oh," I breathe out. "No. Tell me no."

"I took one of the attackers' guns and he ran off, but the other one . . ." He looks at the ceiling a long moment before his eyes meet mine again. "I saw his eyes and I knew he was going to pull the trigger on his weapon. I shot him, but not before he shot Amber's parents. He died, and so did they." His lips tighten. "He turned out to be a sixteen-year-old kid."

My hand presses to my stomach. I think I'm going to be sick. "Chris, I—"

"I don't feel guilty for killing him, Sara. I saw his eyes. I saw how coldhearted he was. What eats me alive is not killing him before he killed them."

I'm across the seat and flinging my arms around him before he finishes, tears streaming down my cheeks. "I'm so sorry I did this to you. I'm so sorry. Chris, I—"

He kisses me. "Don't. Don't say you're sorry. I should have just told you. I should—"

I kiss him, tasting the salty tang of my tears on both our lips, and I can't stop touching him. His face. His hair. Our foreheads come together and I press my hand to his cheek. "I love you. I love you so much. How could you think I would judge you for this?"

"I killed a sixteen-year-old and I don't feel guilty, Sara."

I lean back to look at him. "You put it in a box, Chris, and it's locked away. You only have so much capacity. It's your mind's way of surviving what you can't control. You saved Amber's life and your own. You're a hero. You're a hero in so many ways and you never see it. But I do. I see it for both of us."

I have to swallow against the churn of my stomach. "And I hate that I drank tonight, when I promised you I wouldn't get drunk again. I hate that I still can't shake it, and think of all the right things to say to fix everything I did wrong tonight."

He frames my face with his hands and stares down at me. "You did nothing wrong tonight. You tried to help Amber and she played a game with you and us. And I let that happen by staying silent too long."

"I did *many* things wrong tonight, Chris, but more than anything, I should have let you tell me everything next week when you were ready. I know this wasn't about secrets, now. It was about how you deal with things, about you limiting the temptation of the whip by choosing how, when, and where you told me everything. I don't know how to make this up to you. I don't know how I ever can."

"Tell me you can live with what I can't some days. Tell me you know me and you won't doubt me anymore."

"I can't live without you, Chris, and no more doubt. Not ever again."

He studies me a moment and then leans back against the seat, and pulls me close. I rest my head on his chest, listening to his heartbeat, sensing he has more to say, this time waiting until he is ready.

"I wasn't in love with Amber before the mugging," he says softly after a few moments. "I knew we didn't have a future, but after that night I couldn't leave her. She resented me, though, and between her resentment and my guilt, I got pretty fucked up. That's when things got extreme for me and when Isabel came into the picture. I wanted pain and Isabel gave it to me."

I lean up to look at him. "While you were with Amber?"

"No sex. Just pain. And Amber knew. She also resented the fact that I didn't trust her with a whip in her hand. She hated me. That's not someone you want punishing you."

"She loves you."

"Ah, yes. A fine line, isn't it? She's very confused, Sara. And Tristan loves the hell out of her."

"He whips her horribly. That isn't love."

"Isabel whips her. Tristan refuses to do it."

"Isabel?"

"Yes. Isabel. When I wouldn't stop seeing her, Amber decided she'd escape reality the same way I did."

"With the whip."

"Yes. Just another reason for me to feel guilty. She's followed me down the wrong path."

Chris did this to me. Now I know what Amber had meant that day in The Script.

"That's when I knew we were destroying each other," Chris continues. "I broke things off with Amber, told her we'd always be friends. But not before I helped her self-destruct, just like Mark did Rebecca."

"You didn't," I say quickly. "She made her choices. We all do."

"She's not as strong as you, Sara. I influenced Amber in ways

I can't undo. But when Tristan came into the picture a few years ago, I was hopeful that maybe Amber was finally moving on. It didn't happen, and Tristan says that's my fault. He says Amber will never be able to move on until I do.

"He doesn't understand why I can't just cut the ties. He doesn't understand the guilt, shame, and responsibility I feel over everything to do with how Amber's life has turned out." He runs a rough hand through his hair. "And maybe I should. I just don't know."

I want to tell him all the reasons he shouldn't hurt like he does, but my gut tells me that isn't what he wants to hear right now. So instead, I say, "I don't know either, but we'll figure it out. Together, Chris. Together we'll find the answer."

His arm wraps around my waist. "This is why I didn't want you around Tristan. I didn't know what he'd tell you, and I wasn't sure he wouldn't use you to hurt me, like Amber tried to tonight."

"But he called you to come and get me."

"Yes, and I was sure he was setting me up and I'd find you in some compromising position sure to rip my heart out."

"You doubted me, then, too."

"I didn't know what they'd told you or made you believe about me, Sara. I didn't know if Amber told you about her parents. Or if she convinced people to lie and say I frequented that place. Believe me—my imagination went wild on the drive over here."

I hug him. "No more secrets. No more doubt."

He strokes hair from my face, and softly repeats, "No more secrets. No more doubt."

Still in the coffee shop . . .

There's a convention in town and I can't get a cab. So although I can't believe it, I'm going to let Ava drive me to a hotel. I can only hope tomorrow will be better. Maybe I'll call "him" after all. Maybe I won't. Maybe I'll just wait until he comes back. Or maybe I'll let tomorrow decide for me. Maybe then I'll even feel 100 percent like the old Rebecca Mason. Tonight . . . I'm almost home.

Twenty-five

I blink awake the next morning, inhale the scent of Chris clinging to the sheets, and almost forget he'd returned to the museum for the night. I run my hand over his empty place beside me, wishing he were here. Wishing I wasn't alone, he wasn't alone in his battle against the old demons I'd awakened last night. *Alone.* I'd fallen asleep hating that word, wearing one of Chris's shirts, and missing him horribly.

The sound of water running confuses me and I sit up, then realize it's the shower. It takes me a moment to process that Chris is home, and he didn't awaken me. I glance at the clock and it's already ten.

I know he's eager to get on the road today, and I throw off the blankets and head toward the bathroom. Fighting nausea from the tequila, I lean on the door frame to steady myself. His head is dropped forward under the water, his broad shoulders and back angled toward me. Wondering how he's feeling after last night's confession, I tug off my shirt, then cross to the shower door.

When I open it Chris's gaze shifts to me, and he pulls me to him under the spray of water and wraps his arms around me.

"I missed you," I say, touching his face.

He lowers his head to mine. "I missed you, too."

We just stand there a few moments, and the sense that he's struggling is strong. "Are you okay?"

"It's always a rough few days."

This is about his parents, and years of punishing himself for what he couldn't prevent. But knowing about Amber's parents now, I can see why he can't let go of the pain. "When is the actual day?" I ask.

"Tomorrow."

I wonder how many times he's taken a beating to get through this anniversary—but this year, he's spending it with me. The significance washes over me with the water, a flood of understanding. He's letting me be there for him. This amazing, wonderful, flawed man is giving himself completely to me, instead of shutting me out, as he had with Dylan.

I hug him tightly, silently telling him that I'm there for him. And when I raise my head and he kisses me, and passion claims us, I hope that I'm helping him escape his past, as he's helped with mine.

And I vow he will never need a whip again.

The drive to Fontainebleau, a commune on the outskirts of Paris, begins with a call from our attorney about my passport. I listen closely as Chris talks to Stephen, trying to decipher what's being said.

Chris's sigh when he hangs up isn't encouraging. "There's no movement on the passport yet. Without a body, they can't build a case against Ava they can be certain will stick. That means they have to charge her with attempted murder to ensure a conviction."

"Of me," I supply.

"Yes. Stephen thinks they're holding your passport hostage to get you to agree to come back and testify for the grand jury."

"Can they do that?"

"No, but they aren't admitting they're doing it, either." He glances at me. "They can't get an indictment without you, Sara."

"So we have to go back."

"It would be the right thing to do. We're done here after this weekend. We can head to San Francisco and stay a few months."

"What about your charity events?"

"I want to be here for tomorrow's event, but then I don't have to be back until late November. This will give us a chance to clear your passport for a longer stay in France anyway." He gives me a small smile. "You can learn French before we return."

I give a short laugh. "Don't count on that one." I open my mouth to express my concern that this is a ploy by the police to get me back and investigate me for Rebecca's death, but stop myself. This weekend is about Chris. Only Chris. "We would make Katie happy."

He cuts me a sideways look. "That we would. In fact, she

called to check on me today. I can't talk to her." His lips tighten. "Maybe you could call? Tell her traffic is bad and I can't talk?"

"Of course." I dial Katie, and her warm greeting is welcome right now. We chat a few minutes, and when she asks to speak to Chris and I give my prepared excuse, she says, "Tell him it's okay. He doesn't have to talk. I know he has you, and you'll take good care of him."

"I will," I promise. "I absolutely will."

"I know, honey. We love you for loving him the way you do. Call me when you can, and let me know how he is."

I promise and we hang up. I stare out of the window, fighting the tears I don't want Chris to see, determined to be strong for him.

"She didn't believe the traffic thing," Chris says.

I shake my head. "Not for a second." To get his mind off the bad stuff, I start asking questions about our trip. We spend the rest of the hour drive talking about the amazing forest surrounding Fontainebleau, which, with its towering trees, is nature's artwork, and about the château his parents bought as a vacation home when he was a small child, even before he moved to Paris with his father. But no matter how I try to keep him talking, the closer we get to our destination, the quieter Chris becomes.

When finally we pull up to the secluded, several-acre property, I'm blown away by what looks like a medieval castle. It's more the size of a hotel than a house, with steepled points to its rooftops and towering white stone walls, set in the middle of short, sloping hilltops.

"It's amazing, Chris," I say, turning to find him staring at it as if he's never seen it before.

"I don't get out here much, so I have a lady and her young daughter, who live in the property behind the house, look after it for me." He glances at me. "Grab your jacket. I want to show you something before we go inside."

I slide my coat on and Chris walks around the 911 to open my door. He helps me out and slides his arm around my shoulders, his big body sheltering me from the cool day. I think he has something in his other hand, held down by his side, but I can't tell what. I'm about to ask what it is but he points to a hill under a massive, leafless tree with huge draping branches, which I'm sure is gorgeous in full bloom. As we get closer, my stomach clenches as I discover we're about to visit not one, but two graves.

I don't say anything. I'm not sure what *to* say, and if I talk too much, Chris won't have a chance to say what he needs to say. Today is about listening, or just being silent by his side, if that's what he needs.

Under the tree by the graves, Chris sets down the item in his hands—a bottle of wine and a corkscrew. He is one big, dark storm cloud ready to burst, and I prepare myself for the downpour, complete with plenty of lightning and thunder.

After shrugging out of his coat, he spreads it out on the ground and motions for me to sit. Glad I have on my favorite worn, faded jeans, I scoot over to allow him to share my seat.

Chris opens the wine, sits on the cold ground beside me, and then gulps a big swig of wine right from the bottle. "Have some," he says, offering it to me. "It's one of my father's prized ten-thousand-dollar bottles. Good stuff. Don't waste it."

Knowing this is significant for him, I accept the bottle and chug some wine. The light, sweet flavor explodes on my tongue, and it would be delicious if it weren't laced with the bitterness of his father drinking himself to death, after years of shutting his son out of his life.

Chris takes another long drink and offers me one, as well. I hold up my hand. "No, thanks." I just can't stomach it.

"There's something else I haven't told you," he says.

In his eyes, I read that the "something else" is big. I grab the bottle and tip it back, then hand it back to him.

"The accident that killed my mother happened a few miles from here." He slugs more wine, then lies back on the ground, the bottle in one hand, his other arm over his eyes. "And I was in the car."

My breath lodges in my throat. He'd been a small child. Much too small to have to watch his mother die. I'd barely handled the loss of mine as an adult.

"A truck hit us," he continues. "The man driving had a diabetic attack and blacked out. He crossed the lane and hit us head-on. Metal rammed through the windshield." He pauses, his breathing ragged. "I was in the backseat in a seat belt, and both myself and my father were remarkably unharmed—but I remember the glass and the blood. I should have been too young to remember, but I do. In bloody, vivid, fucking color, I remember my mother bleeding, and my father screaming and crying and begging her to breathe."

Tears streak my cheeks and I wipe them away. As the

seconds tick by, Chris doesn't move. He lies there, his hand over his face, that bottle of wine in his hand. And I know that there is no right thing to say—there is only what I *do*.

I push to my feet and take his hand. "Get up, and come with me."

His hand drops from his face and I can see the redness in his eyes, the tears he's hidden from me. I don't want him to hide anything from me. "Where are we going?" he asks.

"We're going inside." I tug his hand. "I have something to show you."

"Inside?" He doesn't move. "Where you have never been before."

"That's right. Come on."

"All right," he agrees, and, thankfully, he hefts himself up to his feet, takes a swig of the wine, and throws the bottle away across the open hilltop. "Show me what you want to show me." There is curiosity in his eyes.

Curious is good. It's far better than pain. This is working.

We cross the hilly lawn and head to the door. Chris's big body is tense as he unlocks the door and waves me forward.

The spacious entry is paved with stone, and my gaze sweeps the stairwell to the left. A wooden balcony wraps around an upper level that spans the entire room, and I admire the incredible chandelier suspended from the center of the vaulted ceiling.

When Chris shuts the door, I step directly in front of him. "Undress," I command.

A shocked look slides over his face. "What?"

I barely contain my smile. "Now you sound like me." I cross

my arms over my chest and try to seem as authoritative as he always does. "You heard me. Take off your clothes."

His expression starts to soften, a hint of amusement lighting his troubled eyes. "Let me get this straight." He points a finger between us. "*You* are ordering *me* to take my clothes off."

"That's right."

He stares at me for several beats and then laughs. Hugging me close, he murmurs near my ear, "After you, baby. That's how this works. You should know this by now."

"Hmmm," I reply, and he eases back to look at me.

"Hmmm?"

I play with a spiky strand of his blond hair by his collar. "Hmmm," I repeat. "I don't seem to comprehend this rule. I'm afraid you might have to spank me to get your point across."

His eyes heat and, with a low growl, he picks me up and starts carrying me to what I assume is our new bedroom. And that's where we are going to ride out this storm.

I wake the next morning, immediately aware of the delicious ache in my body from the prior afternoon and evening with Chris. I smile and reach for him, only to find him missing. Remembering what today is jerks me to a sitting position, and I glance around the fancy bedroom with elegant, mahogany-trimmed walls and expensive mahogany furniture and confirm he's not here. I reach for my cell phone by the bed and glance at the time—eight o'clock. I wonder if he slept at all.

Then I see a piece of paper on the pillow next to me: a hand-drawn map, for finding Chris in this gigantic maze of a castle. I rush to the bathroom to brush my teeth and wash my face, admiring the magnificent vintage claw-foot tub that sits smack in the center of the bathroom. Not because it's gorgeous, which it is, but because Chris and I spent some interesting time in that tub last night.

I hurry and make myself presentable, dig slippers and a robe from my suitcase, and snatch my map. Not surprisingly, the two stone corridors, and several doorways and passages I travel, end at a long stairwell. I might not be in the city anymore, but Parisians seem to love building things in levels. I don't mind. It seems everything Parisian is growing on me.

Hugging myself against the chill in the house, I head down the fifteen or so stairs to a dimly lit, dungeon-like room, and gasp. Chris is standing at a wall, working on a dragon mural like the one in his office, and all around him, more paintings of dragons sit on easels. As my gaze eagerly travels over the paintings, I can see the progression of the young artist who became the master he is today. These are the works in which he's placed a piece of himself; pieces he doesn't want to share, or he'd have auctioned them off years ago for charity. But he's shared them with me.

Chris sets his brush on a stand by the wall he's painting and turns to face me. I walk to him and wrap my arms around his waist. "You have no idea what it means to me, to get to see this part of you."

"You have no idea how much it means to me, to have you here." He tilts his head toward the mural. "I came here alone last year and started this. It's how I got through the day. But it didn't work. This place, and the history it comes with, still brought me to my knees."

"But you didn't need Isabel," I point out.

"No. I didn't need Isabel. I will never need her again. Do you know how I know that? I know because I lay in bed and watched you sleep last night, and I felt at peace like I never have before. I decided then that *you* are what's going to bring me to my knees, Sara. You're what's going to change what this day means to me."

"What does that mean?" I ask softly. "I don't understand."

He goes down on one knee. "Marry me, baby. Be my wife, and spend the rest of your life painting dragons with me. I know a jeweler in San Francisco. We'll have an amazing ring custom-made, and—"

I pull him up and kiss him. "I don't care about a ring. I just want you. Yes, I'll marry you."

He's on his feet in an instant, wrapping me in his arms and kissing me. And I finally dare to believe that nothing can ever tear us apart.

Epilogue

Somewhere in Italy . . .

Racing through the dark street, I search desperately for a phone. I have to let someone know that I'm Ella Ferguson, not the person my passport says I am. I can't call Sara without putting her in danger, which means I have to call "him." I don't want to call him but I have no other choice.

My gaze catches on a store window with the lights on, and I rush toward it. Bursting through the door of the small wine shop, my chest heaving, I search the rows of bottles for some form of life. An elderly man appears from the back and I rush toward him. "Phone. Please. Can I use a phone? It's an emergency."

He says something in Italian I don't understand, and desperation rises in me. "Telephone?" I say, and hold my hand to my ear, and his eyes go wide.

Relief washes over me as he motions me to the back room, where I'll be out of sight from the window. He hands me a phone and I punch in the operator code. "Yes. Hello. I need to make a collect call. It's international."

"No! No!" the man exclaims, evidently knowing at least one word in English. I try to move out of his reach but he grabs my arm and snatches the one chance I have of calling for help away from me.

"Wait," I plea. "It's collect—free. It's no cost to you."

He shakes his head. "No international call."

The bells to the shop jangle and my heart jackhammers. I glance around wildly and search for an escape. Spotting a back door, I dash for it, push it open, and burst into a dark alley between buildings, cold air smacking me in the face. I take off running, far more afraid of what will happen if they catch me than I am of what might await me in the darkness.

Then the door behind me creaks open and slams against the wall.

I run faster. I have to get away.

Something hard like a brick slams into my back and I gasp, stumbling and flying forward. As the ground rises up to meet me I try to catch myself with my hands, but another thud hits my back, and I slam into the concrete. My head smacks the pavement, and spots fill my vision. *No!* I fight the fog overcoming me . . . but it's too powerful.

Everything goes dark.